CLOUDLESS RAIN

Book One in the *Stellar Eclipse* Series

Written by Avalon Roselin

Roselin Productions

Roselin Productions
California
www.roselinproductions.com

This is a work of fiction. Names, characters, places, and incidents are a product of the author's imagination. Locales and public names are sometimes used for atmospheric purposes. Any resemblance to actual people, living or dead, or to businesses, companies, events, institutions, or locales is completely coincidental.

Book Layout © 2014 BookDesignTemplates.com
Cover edited by M. Carr

Edited by J. Smith and J. Rudolph

Stellar Eclipse: Cloudless Rain/ Avalon Roselin. -- 1st ed.
ISBN 978-0-9976479-4-5

Visit us at www.roselinproductions.com

With thanks to my wonderful team, who helped me bring my vision to life in the best way possible;

And with special thanks to M. Boucher and A. Pear, whose support has been invaluable throughout this process.

I couldn't have done it without you!

Act One

GATHERING CLOUDS

I

Looking back, everything took a sharp turn for the worse the day Baltan's roommate brought home a dead body.

The late autumn storm that rolled in a few days before was winding down, despite the remaining cloud coverage. Soon the last traces of the humid summer would give way to the bitter cold of Capricorn and lead to more days where all Baltan wanted to do was stay in bed.

The taste of stale gin made his mouth dry and wouldn't let him stay in the warmth and safety of his blankets any longer, and he struggled to untangle himself. The day had to be faced, however late.

For a moment Baltan thought that he must have slept in until after dusk. The sky was nearly black, and his room wasn't much better. The living room downstairs was worse, having hardly any natural lighting even in the summer. Baltan tried to flick on the lamp at the foot of the stairs as he passed, but nothing happened. He toed his way around the clutter of the living room and managed to make it to the kitchen without tripping over a stack of books or empty soda bottles.

The near silence unnerved Baltan more than the darkness. The house was never without a steady pulse of noise when Eureka was there; either the radio was on, he was humming an old folk song to himself, or he was clanging around in the kitchen while he crafted his latest culinary masterpiece, if not all three. Quiet meant the house was empty, and when the weather was this horrendous there were only a few possible reasons why.

Judging from the dishes still in the sink from dinner the day before and the lack of breakfast leftovers in the refrigerator, Eureka had left in a hurry that morning. Probably during the brief lull when the rain and wind roaring through the city would have eased up. The rain was coming down in a steady torrent again, so he must have stayed out longer than he intended.

There was no note saying where he had gone, what he was doing, or when he'd be back, which was almost as good as a signed admission of guilt. There was only one logical conclusion.

Baltan would soon be up to his waist in stray cats.

With a sigh, he reached into the refrigerator and grabbed a bottle of grapefruit soda from among the rows and rows of different flavors on the bottom shelf.

He didn't mind at all that Eureka liked to take care of the strays in the area. At least he was *doing* something, which was a lot more than Baltan could say for himself.

What Baltan *did* mind was Eureka's numerous attempts to bring the cats home and hide them in the pantry, his closet, his oversized trench coat, or anywhere else in the house where they might fit. He knew that there were no areas where they might fit because—as Baltan had pointed out several times—they lived in the Grid, the slums of Marina Delta. There was hardly enough room for the two of them, let alone Eureka's army of felines.

However, Eureka would usually respond that their living conditions were entirely by choice, and they could afford a bigger house if they wanted.

Baltan wasn't convinced. An early retirement, even one taken with more money saved than either of them could practically spend, had to be planned out carefully. Buying a borderline claustrophobic house in the southeast side of Marina Delta, where the streets were numbered instead of named, was one of the ways to make sure the money lasted comfortably through their lives. It was what they had decided on when they'd left their work for the Investigative Department.

Baltan was more at ease living among the Azures in the poorer neighborhoods. Moving to a nicer part of the city meant dealing with the prying eyes and upturned noses of other Easterners. He might look like them, but he refused to *be* like them.

He popped the cap off the soda bottle and took a drink on his way to the frumpy old couch. The moment he sat down, the lamp finally flickered on as power returned to the block. The living room was a mess, but Baltan could navigate it blindfolded if he had to. His computer desk and the radio sat in one corner across from the couch and the small coffee table, and nearly all the space between was filled in with cookbooks, mystery novels, and newspapers. Paths were cleared over time between the front door, the kitchen, the couch, and the radio.

The walls were almost bare, save for a few framed newspaper articles from the times that Baltan and Eureka had managed to make the front page. Among some of the headlines were, 'Kidnapped Heiress Found, Returned Safely' and, 'Marina Omega Massacre, Culprit Apprehended, Justice for 33 Victims.' One of them—'Wonder Investigators Leaving Force'—was only hung up due to Eureka's insistence that it was a, "heartfelt send-off."

That week's newspaper sat purposefully on the table. There wasn't much left besides the featured articles and the funnies. Eureka must have gutted it, the rest probably lining shelter boxes by now, but one segment was carefully folded and placed on top of the stack.

The precariously flickering light of the lamp revealed an article circled by an orange highlighter.

Woman Murdered, Azure Suspect

Between the lines of media bias, political waffling, and cautionary reminders, Baltan was able to gather at least a few concrete statements.

When the storm was at its worst, a middle-aged woman named Evanne was murdered in her beachfront home. Autopsy revealed the cause of death to be a bullet from a common model pistol through the back of her head. One of the neighbors found the body while checking to see if she was alright after the heavy rain and thunder, living as close to the unsettled ocean as she did, but they reported no signs of forced entry. That much was confirmed by investigators. Photographs found in the home revealed that Evanne had a young male Azure living with her, who was not found at the scene of the crime. Neighbors testified that they had never seen the boy before, nor heard Evanne mention having a child in her care.

Homeless Azures were known to frequent the area, though they usually stayed closer to the docks to look for work on fishing boats. Still, the young male Azure was deemed the prime suspect for the murder and the Investigative Department of Marina Delta was offering its usual ransom to anyone able to secure him or turn over good leads, despite the fact that Azure blood had also been found at the scene of the crime. An unnamed private party, presumably related to Evanne, was also offering an undisclosed sum of money to anyone with information on the murder.

"Crap." Baltan threw the paper onto the other side of the couch and guzzled down soda to calm his nerves. *Thirty cats was been better than this.*

It wasn't as if he didn't find anything odd about the case. An Azure's claws and fangs were deadly enough on their own, so why would the suspect need a gun to kill someone? And the article said Evanne had been shot from behind, so why would there be Azure blood at the scene, assuming she had no chance to fight back? Not that Azures didn't bleed easily, but the article was trying to spin a story where Evanne was taken by complete surprise and killed without any reasonable motive.

And if the Azure was one of the homeless vagrants, as insinuated, why hadn't the neighbors seen him before and why did Evanne have photographs of him in her home? It was true that she could have been feeding him and thus taking pictures every so often to track his progress, but that would remove all motivation to kill her—and despite how deranged and delusional some of the killers Baltan had encountered were, they all believed they had a good motive when they committed their crimes. He couldn't find that important piece of information anywhere in the article.

Something was definitely not right. Baltan couldn't blame Eureka for wanting to look into it, but there were much better and less actively-involved ways to do it.

He headed over to the computer desk and booted up the old system. It seemed to be in good working order despite a prominent layer of dust and a distinct humming from the motor that was a little louder than he remembered. Once the screen loaded he clicked on the icon for the Investigative Department's public records and was met with several warnings about loose criminals. The murder case he'd read about was surprisingly high considering the smugglers and serial killers that usually occupied the priority warnings. Another oddity to be explored.

He typed in the code that made up the letters of Evanne's name and address. Moments later he was met with strings of numbers and letters that he decoded into very little information. Only her name, age, sex, and current residence were listed. There was nothing about her family, occupation, or schooling; none of the data could be used to trace her identity back anywhere other than her current address. Even if she'd been an anonymous orphan whose birth constellation and place of birth were unknown, her record should have shown the name of her primary caretaker and the institution she'd been housed in.

Obviously the file was tampered with. Of course it would have been updated with her death, but it was wiped as clean as it could be, just short of deletion. *Short* records usually took him a solid evening to get through.

This keeps getting weirder, Baltan thought, his mind abuzz with all the questions it could hold. He was certain most of the information in the news article was false. So little of it added up. Had no one at the Investigative Department noticed, or were they purposefully misleading the journalists they'd spoken to in order to keep certain facts obscure? Unfortunately, it was too easy for Baltan to believe the former. There weren't many detectives of the same caliber as when he and Eureka were a part of the force. If he went out to the scene of the crime and got a good look around, coupled with what information he could get from the article and Evanne's record, he'd come up with a much more likely lead than some injured Azure kid.

A loud knock rattled him out of his thoughts. Baltan muttered a curse under his breath as he turned off the computer and moved to answer the door. Although he knew exactly what he'd find on the other side, he silently hoped his suspicion was wrong and his roommate had gone out to do some emergency grocery shopping or had brought back a box full of kittens to warm by the stove.

Baltan took a deep breath and opened the door. Standing there was the massive form of his ex-partner, outlined by a downpour of rain as heavy as a waterfall and as black as ink. Curled in his arms, and even tinier by comparison, was the limp body of a young boy. The coat he was wrapped in kept Baltan from getting a good look, but he could *smell* him just fine, and he winced at the stench of blood and brine.

It was clear the boy was dead, at least temporarily.

"Absolutely not," Baltan said flatly, and slammed the door shut.

"Baltan!" There was a note of desperation in Eureka's voice. He'd gone through a lot to get that body there and Baltan knew it, but he didn't want to face it yet. Letting it into the house would make it somehow more real than seeing it. It could still go away if he didn't let it in.

"Hiding kittens in the house is one thing, but this is where I draw the line! Take him to the Investigative Department and let them handle it," Baltan shouted back.

"You know I can't do that," Eureka responded, raising his voice only enough to be heard. "Please, at least hear me out."

Baltan willed himself to not give in, just this once. This wasn't a stray cat spending the night or trying a new dish that he wasn't sure he was going to like. This was getting involved with a serious crime.

Exactly the sort of crime they'd become well known for bringing to justice while they were still investigators. He had to admit getting to the bottom of a mystery this strange did tempt him, but he reminded himself that they'd given it up for a reason. Too much risk, too much danger, too many trips to the hospital.

But they were good. The best. There were plenty more articles about their exploits than what Eureka had put up on the wall.

Fear and anxiety gripped him when he looked back on those years, but he could still remember the rush of tracking down a dangerous criminal with Eureka at his side, the triumph of seeing their quarry behind bars. His strongest memories were of the people they had helped. He never forgot the relief on the faces of the victims' families and friends, and when he closed his eyes he saw them prominently for the first time in years.

There's a killer on the loose. What are you doing about it? What use are you being to anybody? To Eureka?

He shook his head at himself for being so stupid and opened the door. He had one last chance to salvage his resolve and stick to the status quo.

"I thought you agreed we would go into early retirement and enjoy our lives in psychopath-free bliss before we're too old. We don't have to get too involved. We can tell them what we've observed, point them in the right direction, and then let them take over from there. It would be easy."

The words were spoken, but neither really heard them. After seeing the suspect, Baltan was more intrigued by the case. A little kid shooting his caretaker in the head for no reason? He didn't think it was impossible, but he had serious doubts there wasn't more to the story than that. If the Azure blood at the scene had come from him, which was most likely the case given his condition, Baltan doubted he'd have had the energy to shoot Evanne with such accuracy. The article had also indicated that the shot was dead center, not from an angle.

The wheels and cogs in Baltan's head were turning fast, but the last thing he wanted was to do field work over this. The multiple scars Eureka had acquired over the years burned a permanent map in his brain. They had quit for a *reason.*

Investigative work always held risks, but they were different for Azures like Eureka.

They were thought of as dangerous animals to the supposedly civilized and normal population of Easterners, and looking at Eureka, it was easy to see why. They were bigger, stronger, and had faster reflexes. Their teeth were sharply pointed fangs, and they had claws as strong as bone instead of puny, easily-broken nails. Eureka himself stood at almost exactly two and a half meters tall, and his shoulders were so wide that even without his height, he had trouble fitting through most doors. Size wasn't all that made them stand out; all of their pigmentation was an unnatural blue—blue skin, blue hair, blue eyes, blue blood—and some even had animalistic ears and tails.

If all that didn't make Azures intimidating enough, they also had the ability to heal quickly from injury, even from the brink of death. It wasn't perfect or guaranteed, but most adult Azures could recover from a fatal injury, sometimes *after* being pronounced dead. Eastern scientists still hadn't figured out how, but they did find a few weaknesses. While Azures might be able to reanimate and heal quickly, their thinner skin meant they were hurt and killed more easily, and they could never recover from being burned. Silver made the healing process slow down, and people had taken to using bullets and knives made with silver because of it.

Azures were nothing at all like the more 'reasonably' sized, blonde, gray-eyed Easterners, who lacked any natural weapons, tails, or pointed ears; whose skin was a perfectly normal tan and who never had miraculous recoveries from fatal injuries without the intervention of a top-notch doctor.

Baltan had seen Eureka get hurt and 'die' more than a few times during their career, and it was something he had absolutely no desire to see again. Agreeing to shelter a young boy who would likely be delirious and potentially violent when he woke up, *if* he woke up, was not the best way to avoid that.

"Just follow me," Eureka said after the long pause.

As if Baltan was going to go back to the couch and finish reading the paper with a murder suspect in the house. If he couldn't convince Eureka to abandon this insanity, and he knew he couldn't, then the only thing left to do was join him in it.

II

Eureka set the boy in the tub and went straight to washing off some of the blood with lukewarm water. His coat and the tattered remains of the boy's shirt sat on the floor in a soggy heap.

"Look here," Eureka said, pointing with one claw at the gash across the boy's chest—a circular cut with three linear slashes running through it, spread out from a point near the bottom of the circle. "Ignoring that Evanne was supposedly killed by a gunshot wound to the back of the head and wouldn't have a chance to retaliate, could someone fighting for their life make precise cuts like that?"

Baltan knelt by his side to get a closer look. "They look clean, too. I don't even think a surgeon could have done that if the kid was alive and kicking." He had grown a thick skin when it came to blood and flayed-open flesh, but something about the marking made his skin crawl and his chest tighten. There was a familiarity to the shape, a circle with three lines of varying lengths connected in the center. He noticed Eureka wasn't looking straight at it, either.

"As gruesome as this is, it wouldn't be enough to leave him in this condition. The cuts are already starting to heal. They'll need treatment, leave some nasty scars, sure. And getting these would have hurt. But this isn't what killed him, although this death is temporary. Which raises the question: why *not* kill him permanently? Why cut him up like this, kill him in some other way, and then leave him to recover? The assailant would have had plenty of time to cut open the major veins and make sure that he bled out beyond the point of return."

"So they meant for him to get blamed for the murder. Seems like a pretty solid scapegoat, as long as no one actually does any actual investigating. Who else are they going to blame?" Baltan said, less as a response and more to himself as he tried to puzzle it out.

"That's why we can't take him to the Investigative Department. He'd never have a chance at a fair trial. The court won't wait for him to give his side of the story before sentencing him. Zero-tolerance laws, you remember. The fact that he ran off would be evidence enough without a good defender, and no one is going to volunteer for that."

Baltan could already see where this was going and it chilled something inside him. Too many of his mystery novels featured old detectives days away from retirement dying on their last cases. Eureka might already be retired, but Baltan wasn't sure that would save him.

He swallowed. That superstition was far too silly to sway Eureka.

"I'm not going to tell you he can stay." Like it mattered what Baltan said when it came to protecting the small and meek. "But I'll admit it's an odd case, and the kid is our best bet of finding out who really did it before this can happen again. Someone has to bring the real killer to justice while the investigators are occupied chasing a red herring." He rolled his eyes. "We *could* still slip them clues, but they'd spend more time trying to figure out the identity of their anonymous tip than actually using anything we gave them."

"So, you're on board?" Eureka asked, eyes bright. That was the finishing blow; one look at Eureka's seafoam-green eyes, and Baltan couldn't say no.

Baltan groaned, "Yeah, I'm in. But this is the *last* case that we are *ever* solving, *ever*. I mean it. You will owe me a vacation."

"I knew you'd come around. I'd give you a hug, but…" Eureka glanced down, addressing the saltwater and blood dripping from his sweater.

"I haven't 'come around.' I just think it'd be a waste if you died now after everything you've managed to live through—thanks to *me*," Baltan replied, suppressing a nervous laugh.

"Well, there's no need to put yourself in harm's way for my sake. That's my job."

It was meant as a joke, but Baltan didn't need the reminder that most of Eureka's scars had come from attacks meant for him. "That smell is making me nauseous. Hurry and get those cuts stitched up before I'm sick."

"Sorry. You don't have to stay, I only wanted to show you what I saw," Eureka replied. He picked up a loofah and ran it under the water spout, then set to work on the blood crusted onto the boy's skin. When it was chipped away, fresh blood ran into the water and the smell of it soon overpowered the soap. The more noticeable rising and falling of the boy's chest prompted Eureka to work a little faster.

"Sure I don't. And when he wakes up and tries to murder you..."

"That's not a nice thing to say. He's a kid."

"He's a kid with sharp claws and teeth and no idea where he is or who you are. If you woke up in that kind of situation, wouldn't you try to fight your way free?" Baltan covered his nose as the combined smell of saltwater and blood struck it again. "Where'd you find him, anyway?"

"On the beach, half-drowned. It was a good thing I got to him when I did; the tide was coming in. He was sort of wandering around in a daze. I think he saw me, but he collapsed before I could get close. And to put your fears to rest, look..." Eureka lifted one of the boy's hands out of the blue-dyed water. "See that? His claws have been cut and filed down. He couldn't scratch me if he wanted to."

"If someone was trying to frame him for the murder, cutting his claws would give him a motive to use the gun," Baltan pointed out. "Though it's a stretch. Seems like a lot more work than it's worth."

"I don't think the killer did it. They look like they've been that way for a while." With the blood now cleaned off, Eureka ran shampoo through the boy's hair and rinsed it out, making sure to get the white, cat-like ears that poked out from either side of his head. More blood dripped down. Eureka unplugged the drain and started running the faucet again to freshen the bathwater, not bothered at all.

"Wouldn't it hurt? I mean, aren't there more nerve endings or something?" Baltan had heard that somewhere, maybe from Eureka, maybe from someone else. He never thought it would be important.

"Yes. It would be like having the tips of your fingers amputated."

"You think Evanne...?"

"According to the article, no one else seemed to be aware of his existence before the murder. It took me almost all day to track down where he could have gone to hide, and I found him more through luck than anything. I can't imagine anyone else could have done this to him."

"That's abuse. It would give him a motive to kill her," Baltan added. "And if she did that, she could have cut his chest, too. Maybe that pushed him over the edge." He still didn't believe it, but they couldn't debunk the theory until they talked about it.

"Like I said, no one else seemed to be aware of his existence before the murder. I'm sure that's the *least* of the abuse that went on. Even if he was home schooled, someone from the school district would have been stopping by to check on him. *No one* knew about him. Evanne was probably keeping him locked up inside all the time. He wouldn't have known any different."

Eureka carefully checked the cuts to see how much they were still bleeding. Blood stained the water blue as it trickled down the boy's chest, but it wasn't as dark as before. Eureka brushed some of the hair out of his face, giving Baltan his first clear look at the suspect.

He was maybe eleven or twelve if Baltan had to guess, which made Eureka's assumption of his innocence more credible. They had encountered a few teens who made bad decisions due to harsh conditions or severe mental illness, but none quite that young.

Eureka cradled the boy's face in one hand. "The way he was looking at the ocean, the sand, everything—like it was the first time he'd ever been outside. Even when he looked at me, it was like he'd never seen another human being. I don't think he would kill her if she was all he knew, no matter how horrible she was to him." His shoulders sagged as he sighed and let his hand slip away. "Could you grab the medical kit for me?"

Baltan wasted no time retrieving the small box from beneath the sink and handing it to Eureka. He examined the gashes on the boy's chest with the eye of a practiced doctor before threading a needle. "It looks like it will heal completely by the end of the week, but he's feverish. Being on his own out there hasn't done him any favors."

Baltan looked away as Eureka swabbed the cuts with iodine solution from the kit and readied the needle's sharp point at one end of the cuts.

Eureka was too focused on the task at hand to say more, so Baltan stood there, staring hard into the mirror. He tried to imagine that the pointed face, curved nose, and gray eyes belonged to the murderer.

If he was a killer, what would the point of all this be? What message would he be trying to get across? The markings were significant, obviously, but what were they and why kill this boy and his caretaker, specifically?

The boy did have *white* ears, and white spots on an Azure meant only one thing. One of his parents was Eastern. Something about the mix of Eastern and Azure genes occasionally resulted in spots of white pigmentation on their children—something the article left out, he noted. That could be a motive all on its own for the real killer, but that didn't explain the symbol, or why it made them so uncomfortable.

The sharp *twing!* of Eureka cutting the thread between his teeth signaled that he was done stitching their suspect up. "Would you mind getting one of my old sweaters?"

"No problem," Baltan answered. He was rather impressed with himself for not making a run for it sooner. He didn't bother looking for an old sweater from Eureka's wardrobe, instead grabbing the first one within his reach.

When he returned Eureka was pressing a dry towel to the boy's hair. He was almost, but not completely, limp; he would probably wake up before dawn came. Once he was dry, Eureka wrapped the fresh stitches with a protective layer of bandages.

Baltan helped him dress the boy, holding his arms up so Eureka could more easily guide them through the sleeves. His hand accidentally brushed against the kid's side when he let go and he felt each rib distinctly—further evidence of abuse.

The sweater hung off of him like a nightgown, but that was its intended purpose.

"Evanne lived on one of the beachfront properties. The storm must have been deafening that close to the ocean wall," Baltan remarked.

"I wouldn't doubt it. The gunshot would have been almost completely inaudible between the waves and the thunder," Eureka answered, carefully lifting the boy into his arms and carrying him out of the bathroom. "I would've liked to check out the house itself and see if there were any clues the investigators may have missed, but it wasn't worth the risk of being caught snooping around."

"Where are you taking him now?" Baltan asked sharply when he saw that Eureka wasn't headed for the stairs.

"He needs to rest," Eureka answered with a half-shrug.

"Not in *my* bed!"

"We need to keep him in one room until he's calmed down," Eureka reasoned. "You were right about not being able to predict how he'll react when he wakes up. I'd like to keep him in a smaller space while he adjusts."

"And what's wrong with *your* room?" Baltan protested. "You're the one who brought him here in the first place!"

"My room connects directly the bathroom, which also connects to the hall. It would be too easy for him to get out. We can prop a chair against your door's handle to lock him in until he's well." Eureka shifted his shoulders, "And, well, I don't like the idea of not having a bathroom to use while we're keeping him in there."

"But—"

"If it helps, I'll sleep on the couch and you can have my bed."

The boy stirred with a small whine. He hadn't regained consciousness, but he was getting closer. Baltan wasn't sure if the pain was waking him, or if it was keeping him unconscious. He had no envy for the boy either way.

"There's no time to argue. I'll make it up to you, Baltan—I'm sorry."

"No, you're not," Baltan sighed, but he'd already forgiven him, and he knew Eureka knew it, which made it almost unbearable.

Baltan went downstairs as Eureka secured the bedroom, finishing off his grapefruit soda and opening a lemon-lime flavored one. He sat back down on the couch and took the newspaper into his hands once again, snatching up the comics this time. It did no good; he was completely unable to focus on any of the colorful caricatures. With a low growl from his stomach he became acutely aware that he hadn't eaten all that day, and Eureka probably wasn't in the mood for cooking.

He would just have to go hungry. After eating Eureka's cooking, he couldn't go back to instant meals, and he'd never bothered learning how to cook anything more complex than that.

He heard the water running upstairs again. The boy must still be asleep if Eureka was chancing a shower.

Good, he needs one, Baltan thought.

He couldn't say he was surprised by how things had turned out. There was no stopping Eureka when he found something he wanted to take care of. Countless kittens, puppies, and even an old, flightless parrot had all found temporary homes in Baltan's bedroom because it was smaller, or it had a nice view from the window, or because Baltan didn't spend as many nights in his own bed.

It wasn't as if Eureka was being intentionally selfish by using Baltan's bedroom. He always offered to sleep on the couch. But they both knew that in these kinds of situations, they'd always end up next to each other in Eureka's oversized bed.

Baltan would never admit it, but he didn't mind sharing with him when it was cold out. His own body temperature had a tendency to drop quickly and at least Eureka's bulk would keep them both warm.

He was almost done with the bottle of soda by the time Eureka came down to the living room.

"He's still out," Eureka reported, settling onto the couch. "I did what I could for his fever, but without him being able to take medicine, it wasn't much."

"Good."

"Are you mad?"

"No."

"I would understand if you were. I'm asking a lot of you," Eureka said, and Baltan spared him a glance.

He knew what was coming. This wasn't the first time they'd had this talk, but it never got easier. Not really. He let Eureka keep talking; he'd already said everything he'd ever have to say about it.

"I'm sorry if I've made you uncomfortable. I know things between us aren't what you'd like them to be, but I still care about you." *Here it comes.* "You're my best friend. I don't want to hurt you, but I know that, well, sometimes..."

Baltan wanted to finish his sentence with, *you can't help it.* There was no avoiding those brief flashes of foolish hope with someone as affectionate and open as Eureka. That was part of what had gotten Baltan into this mess in the first place.

"Noted," Baltan said, trying not to sound like he blamed Eureka for this, because it wasn't his fault. "Is there anything else on your mind?"

"There's something off about this murder and I don't like it. Those cuts were placed where they were deliberately, I'm sure of it. They looked almost... familiar." He shook his head. "Who could *do* that to a kid?"

"I can think of a few people," Baltan replied with a gesture to the collage of newspaper clippings detailing some of their cases.

"I can, too. One in particular. I'm starting to think that Evanne wasn't the intended target after all," Eureka added quietly.

Baltan didn't want to stay on the topic anymore. He could all too easily see where it was going, and he would do anything to avoid talking about their first case.

"I wonder what the kid's name is. It's not listed in the paper and he's not registered under Evanne's family in public records. As a matter of fact, she has hardly any information at all. Most of the standard stuff is missing. I can understand removing some of it or changing it around a little bit since she's dead, but I've *never* seen something like that unless someone was trying to cover something up." Baltan tried to keep the worry out of his voice, tried not to make it obvious that he was derailing, but he knew Eureka would know. If he was lucky, maybe Eureka would play along for a while.

"I can't understand why anyone would want to kill them." Eureka stared at the rain-streaked glass door to their tiny yard. "They seemed quiet, kept to themselves, but I don't believe this is a random act of violence with precise knife work like that."

"Maybe that's just what's being covered up here," Baltan suggested.

Silence followed, heavy with unspoken thoughts.

Neither could bear to let it last, but Eureka was the one to break it, picking up a different conversation Baltan had laid the groundwork for. "We'll have to call him something. We won't get far with 'hey, kid' and 'you.'"

"He can probably write it down for us, assuming he hasn't gone completely insane after all this. I hope it isn't some crazy Azure name."

"Azure names are beautiful!" Eureka replied, feigning offense.

"Didn't say they aren't. But how many people mispronounce your name?" Baltan smirked, ready to indulge in the distraction for as long as he possibly could. "Remember the first time the newspaper ran a photo of you? You had people trying to say about twenty different names every time they saw you."

"'Eh-yoo-reh-kuh.' It's not *that* hard. All you have to do is fully pronounce each syllable, which is how it should be." Eureka rolled his eyes. "Eastern is much more difficult, all those unspoken letters. Why are they there, if they aren't supposed to produce a sound?"

"Mine's easy," Baltan pointed out, keeping it going with a knowing smirk. Teasing each other about their names was at least relatively normal.

"That's because everyone has it! If my name were as common, no one would have trouble pronouncing it, either."

Baltan was pleased to see a warm smile on Eureka's face again.

This was good. This was normal. He could handle this as long as he pretended the lead in to this conversation had been anything else.

Then Eureka's smile faded and he shook his head.

"We're letting ourselves get sidetracked. Back to the matter at hand—since we've got no other motive and he seems to have been a predetermined victim in our theory, let's go with prejudice as a motive. Someone radically anti-Azure finds out that Evanne is sheltering a half-Azure. That makes him the primary target, and the killer goes after Evanne to get rid of a witness."

"That's still a pretty long list of potential killers," Baltan said with a hint of resentment.

"It's a start," Eureka replied, picking up the newspaper article and scanning it for the address. "If we can get the names of the neighbors, you can look them up in public records and find out who's got a history of involvement with violent crimes against Azures. There's no way that the killer traveled very far from home in that storm. Definitely not at night. And who knows? They could be lying about not knowing him to cover up the fact that they were condoning child abuse."

"One of the neighbors found the body. It wouldn't be too hard to find out which one."

"We'll also ask if anything unusual was going on, or if anyone had been hanging around the house before the murder." Eureka folded his arms in thought. "Then again, he wasn't *permanently* killed. If it were a hate crime, I doubt he'd have been left alive, unless the killer wanted to torture him, and if *that* were true, he or she could have abducted him without any problem."

A rumble from Baltan's stomach interrupted their brainstorming.

Eureka's face fell. "Have you eaten anything?"

"No."

"You weren't in bed *all day* again, were you?"

Baltan tried to find something to look at other than Eureka's face.

"Baltan…"

Why did he have to say it like that? Baltan would have preferred Eureka getting mad and saying he was irresponsible and needed to do better. But all that came out was his name, quiet and concerned and too caring for what they had.

"I'll fix us something to eat."

A bright flash of lightning illuminated the room. Eureka lifted a brow as the lamp flickered.

"I'll fix us something to eat, *quickly*."

Baltan nodded and took Eureka's seat on the couch as soon as he stood up. His stomach hurt more than he realized, and it occurred to him that some of his nausea was probably due to the hunger, too.

It definitely wasn't because he finally remembered where he'd seen the symbol on the boy's chest.

It's not him, Baltan thought. It did nothing against the sinking feeling that dragged his heart into his stomach. *It couldn't possibly be him.*

III

It was cold.

He hadn't expected otherwise. No matter how many blankets he hid under, he was always cold when he woke up. Evanne told him it was because they lived by the sea. The air that blew over the waves would come in through the windows and walls during the night.

Usually he managed to protect a little bit of warmth by curling up, but he hadn't been curled up like normal. Instead he found himself lying on his back with a thin blanket draped over him. It was green, not white like he was used to.

He lifted an arm to feel the fabric and winced. That was all it took for the pain to seep back into his senses, the stabbing feeling coming from all over his body, but especially his chest and collarbone. Despite the burning in his limbs, he touched the spot on his chest that hurt most and felt string against his skin.

His heart jolted.

Why?

He plucked at the string, trying to get it off.

The pain was worse than stubbing his toe or having his ears pulled or Evanne cutting his nails. It was worse than the time Evanne had slammed a door on him to keep him from going outside—for his own good, of course, she said. The world wouldn't tolerate a freak like him walking around, even at night when the dark would hide him from the few people who were out.

Am I dying?

He didn't know much about death or dying. It was supposed to be very painful and frightening, and he was experiencing both of those things more than he ever had.

He wanted to call out to Evanne, but he couldn't find his voice. That much was normal, at least. He wondered where he would find it this time, if he could find it at all.

He tried to get up once the pain died down enough for him to move again. If he could get up, he couldn't be dying.

Tiny rasping sounds escaped his mouth as he struggled to his feet, and when he tried to take a step he faltered and fell to his knees. The pain in his chest made his stomach hurt worse than it already did, and for a moment he worried that he might be sick. Evanne wouldn't like that.

There was a flash of light and then a very loud crashing sound from the sky. Normally he knew these were lightning and thunder and they could not harm him, but that night they seemed incredibly dangerous and menacing, and the light practically stabbed his eyes. He cowered there on the floor, eyes closed tight and ears flat to his head as his body began to tremble.

Tears built up in his eyes and spilled over, and that scared him most of all because Evanne hated nothing more than crying. If she came into the room now and saw him like this she would yell, and he hated that, but he couldn't stop himself. He tried to wipe his eyes, but to wipe them he had to sit up and move his arms and fingers, which made his chest and stomach and head hurt, which made him cry more.

After a moment he forced himself upright and slowly turned his head to look around.

The first thing he noticed was that he was not in his room, nor any other he had ever seen in Evanne's house. His room was much smaller, with only enough space for the bed and a trunk. All his possessions—a blanket, some clothes, and a few music books, which weren't *really* his anyway—had to fit in there, or they were thrown away. Most importantly, his room didn't have any windows, and all the windows in Evanne's house were always covered.

This room not only had a window, but one he could see through if he tried hard enough. There was also a closet, an overflowing bookshelf, and a bed stand with a few bottles on it. He turned his head to try to get a better look at the window, pausing when his shoulder nearly slipped out of the collar. He couldn't be wearing one of his own sweaters; it was far too big for him or Evanne to own, and it didn't smell familiar.

Another flash had him pulling his sore body as quickly as he could onto the bed and under the blanket to hide. He coughed against the dryness of his throat and mouth. His ears had flicked upward on instinct, but they were once again flat against his head.

He was too afraid to get up and try the door. It was probably locked anyway.

Had he been kidnapped? Evanne had told him about kidnappers, one of the many types of Bad people in the world. They took smaller people like him away and locked them up and then killed them if their parents didn't give them money, which he was pretty sure Evanne wouldn't do.

Something about the situation struck him as deeper than that, though. Something had happened to him, and Evanne, too. He wished he could remember what, but his head was throbbing too painfully for him to try and think too hard.

He tried to make himself smaller but he knew there was no escape for the time being. When his kidnappers opened the door to kill him he would run as fast as he could and go home. Of course, he'd never left his home so he didn't know if it was far away from where he was now, but Evanne told him they lived by the sea, so he would start there. He had always wanted to see it himself.

Have I seen it?

He could imagine it easily enough, big and dark and moving like a living thing. Then a sound, deep like the thunder and the ocean waves together, rolling over each other, but calm...

He would need all of his strength to escape, so he tried as hard as he could to go to sleep.

He must have been a lot more tired than he thought, because after a few moments of being still he began to drift off.

When he opened his eyes again he expected to be in his own bed, surrounded by the familiar sights, smells, and sounds of his home, but nothing changed by the time morning came. He stayed under the blanket and shut his eyes to try to deny it, but he could smell citrus from the bottles on the nightstand. The sour smell made him nauseous.

Even worse, now he could hear the kidnappers downstairs. Papers rustled and the voice that sounded like thunder and ocean waves said, "Do you think the horoscopes survived? Ah, here they are... Sky-Aquarius, today's energy is ideal for beginnings! If there is something you've been meaning to do, today is the day to start."

"There's one of those every constellation," a voice more like the whistle of wind responded.

"Well, then—Sun-Pisces, you are exceptionally grumpy and probably woke up on the wrong side of the bed..."

"Because I wasn't sleeping in *my* bed!"

That's right, he thought. *This isn't my bed, which means it's someone else's.* And that someone else had to be one of his kidnappers. Would he be angry? He sounded like he was, at least a little bit.

He had come to know every different type of anger well in his time with Evanne. The kidnapper didn't sound mad enough to strike him, but he wasn't talking *to* him at the moment.

The humorous tone left the oceanic voice, but its deep rumble brought the boy more peace and assurance than fear. "I may need your help once he's awake. We still don't have a full grasp of what happened and I'll need to do a medical exam to see how he's healing."

"I'll do what I can." The words were sharp, but the tone was dulled with admiration and a touch of nervousness.

He recognized the creak of weight on old stairs. Could he get down a flight of stairs without falling when he made a run for it?

"Are you really sure you should check on him now, though?" the windy voice said, concern masked by annoyance. He didn't understand why this one pretended to have different feelings, but it was probably some adult thing he wasn't old enough to know about yet.

"It's been a long night for him, too."

"*If* he even woke up completely. But more to the point, neither of us have eaten since yesterday. We'll need our strength to handle him if he's disoriented."

A pause, followed by, "Fine, but nothing complicated this morning."

The voices grew softer once again. "Let him settle himself in for a while…"

He didn't have very long to plan an escape, and his body was still weak. When he tried to get up his head swam and his heart started pounding. He fell back to the mattress and covered his eyes.

Soon the smell of food filled the air, and his stomach began to ache worse. How long had it been since he had eaten anything? It seemed from the conversation that he'd been there one night, maybe two, but he couldn't be certain.

So, maybe three or four days since he'd eaten in total, though he wasn't sure his stomach was hurting from hunger. The idea of eating made him nervous.

I did eat something, he thought. *Something bad. It tasted awful and hurt my stomach.*

He vaguely recalled there was something important about that, but trying to remember made his head pound harder. He would have to delve into that when he felt a little better.

The aroma wafting up from the kitchen was more and more appealing the longer he lay there. Perhaps that was one more way his kidnappers meant to torture him—let him smell their delicious food and not let him have any, or give it to him while he was too sick to eat it. Not that he needed to eat when they were going to kill him. But if they *were* going to then he would prefer it not be by starvation. He hoped for something quick, clean, painless, and not like the tortures Evanne often described to him before bed.

Of course, he couldn't tell them. He couldn't say he was hungry or sick or awake or plead for them to not kill him and take him home. His voice wasn't there.

They were still talking, but they were being much quieter now and he couldn't hear them over the sizzle of whatever was cooking. No matter how he tried to refocus, all of his senses were trained on breakfast.

He was probably starting to starve. He was all too familiar with the feeling. Maybe if he could get to the kitchen, he could grab something before he tried to make a dash back home—assuming he could run at all.

He managed his way out of bed, but the pain was still too great for him to stand up on his own. He crawled to the door as fast as his body would allow and tried to lean up against the frame. He was too weak to pull himself up and laid there on the floor, frustrated and ready to cry, but he quieted the urge. He couldn't risk getting any more dehydrated.

Creaking alerted him to movement on the stairs again. Moments later a lock clicked and the door eased open. Now was his chance to run, and he couldn't even get to his feet, not that it much mattered. The kidnapper standing in the doorframe was both as tall and wide as the entrance. There was no room around him, and those long legs would catch up in a heartbeat no matter how quick he normally was.

Any thought of escape vanished when he saw that the man's skin and hair were *blue*.

Like me, he thought, looking at his own pale blue hands. *But he's still one of the Bad people.* He only considered it for a moment, his attention focused on the kidnapper in front of him. And, more importantly, the plate of food and glass of water in his hands.

The man stepped into the room, closed the door, and set the food and water on the stand. Then he leaned down— even then he still towered over him—and extended a hand toward him. "Hey, there. How are you feeling today?"

This is the one that sounds like the ocean. So where's the windy one? Maybe getting the murder weapon ready!

He drew back as far as he could and curled his lips to reveal sharp teeth, but the man didn't hesitate to place his hand on his head. Even from such a soft gesture he could feel how strong the kidnapper was and how easily he could kill him. Maybe he would snap his neck after all. Quick and painless.

He didn't.

Instead, the man stroked his hair and spoke in that soothing rumble, and he even leaned into the touch when he did the same with his ears, at least until he caught himself and pulled back again.

"Your fever's broken. That's a good sign." At this the man offered him the water and plate of food: eggs, sausage, and fruit cut into shapes. He sniffed at it but turned away, pretending to be uninterested. His stomach betrayed him with a growl louder than any his voice could muster.

"Go on," the man said, holding up a forkful of scrambled egg. "You must be hungry, and you'll need your strength to recover."

He leaned in. It smelled good. *So* good. Evanne never cooked for him like this.

He opened his mouth, and then closed it again. This man was a kidnapper, one of the Bad people he'd been warned about! He couldn't eat his food! Besides, his stomach was clenching up again.

"What's the matter?" the kidnapper asked. The boy hissed at him in an attempt to scare him off, but the man didn't notice his silent threat. He took the bite of egg into his own mouth and chewed on it briefly before swallowing. "There. It's fine, see? No poison or razor blades. I promise."

He gave him a long look, trying to figure out whether or not he was lying, but it seemed pretty reasonable that if he'd eaten it, it was probably safe. He shifted forward and prodded the sausage and fruit with his nose since it was easier than lifting his arm, gesturing to the man to take a bite out of that too, and he did. Everything was safe.

He drained the water, relieved when his stomach hurt a little less once there was something in it. Then he gobbled down every morsel despite the man gently warning him not to eat too fast or he'd make himself sick. He didn't really mean to, but how could he not? His stomach already hurt, he was hungry, and each bite was bliss. It was easily the best food he'd ever had in all his life. He even licked the plate when he was done, and received another welcome rub around the ears. It was getting hard to believe the man meant him any harm.

However, once the food was gone, he pulled back again. Good food, a soothing voice, and a calming touch were nice, but the man was a stranger, a Bad person. Evanne said everyone outside, except a very select few, were Bad people. But this man didn't seem capable of being Bad. He might be one of the safe, good ones—or very skilled at hiding his true intentions. It could all be a trick.

"How are you feeling?"

Everything still hurt. A lot. But his voice wasn't back, so he couldn't say so.

"I'm sorry. I got you home as quickly as I could to fix you up, but who knows how long you were wandering around out there like that."

He tilted his head curiously toward the kidnapper. Out *where*? He'd gone to sleep and woken up there. He hadn't even left the house. Had he? Another sharp pain shot across his chest and up to his head. He couldn't think about it without hurting worse.

"Do you remember anything that happened yesterday?"

He shook his head slowly. What did the kidnapper know and how could he ask?

He must have looked troubled because the man started petting his ears again. He flicked them and nipped his hand gently, not really biting so much as holding it in his teeth. He wasn't sure how the kidnapper would react. Usually Evanne smacked him on the nose if he showed his teeth, but his arms were dead weights attached to his torso, so there was nothing else he could do.

"Sorry," he repeated and moved his hand away.

He looked up at the man, trying to find the hidden meanings in his facial expressions the way he did with Evanne. He wasn't sure it would work with a stranger, but it would help if he could figure out when the man was lying.

His eyes were full of sincere concern, and something about their color struck a chord in his head that broke through the pain for a moment.

Blue-green. Sea green. Like the ocean.

The ocean, so angry, so loud...

"You want to go see the ocean, don't you, little one?"

He remembered everything.

IV

"Sit still," Evanne scolded, even though he was sitting as perfectly still as he could while she raked the comb through his uneven hair. "We are having an important guest today. A *very* important guest."

Any guest was important really, because they never had any. Ever. Whenever Evanne saw people, she went outside the house to do it. No one from outside was supposed to see him because they were all Bad people, and Evanne was convinced he could turn Bad at any moment.

"It's in your blood," she would say whenever he questioned her about what he'd done to be Bad. "See how you're blue? That's a sign that one of your parents was evil, but you might be saved yet." On the day the important guest was arrived, she said, "It looks like you'll finally have your chance to become good like me."

He wasn't sure he wanted to be good like Evanne. He didn't want to go around yelling at people (he was pretty sure he couldn't, or his voice would run away), and he didn't want to hit anyone or pull on their ears or make them sit alone in the dark instead of eating supper. While he'd never said it out loud, he was fairly certain Evanne's behavior was purely Bad, but maybe she was allowed to do such things on account of being so good.

Or maybe the people outside were even worse.

"You see," she said one day after pulling him away from the windows, "The world itself is a Bad place, and that's why it's full of Bad people. If you go out there, you will either be killed or become Bad. That's why you have to stay inside with me."

Not that it ever stopped him from wanting to go out, but he supposed that was the Badness in him.

Evanne was never in a better mood than she was on the day the important visitor was coming. After she was done making him presentable she made herself up with lipstick and eye shadow and nice clothes, and put on a pot of her best tea that she'd been saving for ages in case a special occasion arose.

"Don't speak unless you're spoken to," she reminded him. "The Prophet is incredibly powerful and wise, so you be on your best behavior and show him how good you can be. I can't believe, after all these years... I'll be promoted, made one of his closest confidants, maybe even his left hand! After all, he did choose *me* to be in charge of such a vital mission." She actually smiled at him. "Remember when I told you that the world is a terrible, awful, Bad place? It still is, but soon that's going to change. You're going to help the Prophet make the world much better and get rid of all the Bad people, so do whatever he tells you. Don't ask any questions."

He wanted to ask a *dozen* questions about what all of that meant, but she wasn't *really* speaking to him, so he didn't. That would be breaking two rules, and important guest or not, she would still probably strike him for it. She always hit where his clothes would cover it up, anyway. She hated looking at his bruises, and he usually had one or two.

Despite all the primping and preening she'd put him through, Evanne shoved him away into his room when the knock on the door signified that the important guest, the Prophet, was finally there.

Evanne and the Prophet spoke in hushed tones for a long time, and then there was a frail knock on his door. He opened it carefully, and there stood a blue man. He supposed that should have made him feel more at ease, knowing the Prophet had some sort of evilness in him too, but it didn't. This man's evilness was right under the surface and ready to come up at any moment, like a breaching whale from one of Evanne's pictures.

He didn't look strong. In fact, he looked somewhat weak. He was taller than Evanne but also thinner, and he swayed a little when he stood, as if he might fall over. He must have been aware of it because he was leaning against the doorframe to hold himself up properly. The heavy smell of his cologne was sickening.

The vile nature he sensed probably came from the fact that one of the Prophet's eyes was stitched open, wide and bloodshot and always staring because it couldn't blink. It was hard to look directly at it.

"Hello," the Prophet said, and his voice was so foreign to his ears that at first he thought he might be speaking a different language. "I think we should talk privately for a moment."

He nodded, not sure how to respond with words, and the man ducked under the doorframe and sat on the floor next to his bed. "Rather small in here, isn't it?" The Prophet smiled, but it was forced, as if something was pulling at the corners of his mouth.

He nodded again and didn't say anything. His eyes kept slipping away from the stitched eye by themselves, so he tried to focus on the other one. It was nicer, with little bits of light in it that made him feel safe.

"You are a quiet child, I see," the Prophet continued. "Do not be afraid. I know I must seem odd to you, after you've been kept inside so long, but it was all necessary." The man studied his face and made that slightly strained smile appear on his face again. This time only half of it was forced, and the other half looked genuine. The fearful look in the unstitched eye subsided a little. "You have such lovely eyes, child. Usually people like us have all blue features, but your eyes have a little green in them. They call that color sea green, because it looks like the ocean. Yes, lovely eyes..."

He really didn't like the man talking about his eyes, because he thought becoming a good person might involve having one of his own stitched open like that, and it looked painful and horrible and he might rather be Bad after all.

The Prophet spoke again, and he decided he'd better pay attention if he wanted to keep his eyes as they were. "I knew a man with eyes like that, once. A good man. In fact," at this he lowered his voice, "I think it would be an exceedingly good thing if you were to find this man."

He wanted to say, "But I can't go outside," but his voice decided against it. The Prophet's presence was too intimidating to allow disagreement. Besides, didn't Evanne say he was supposed to do what this man told him to? To make the world better.

Am I really going to help change the world? he wondered. He didn't see how he could.

Even without words, the Prophet seemed to understand exactly what he wanted to say. "You are far more special than you've been led to think. I intend to have a little discussion with Evanne about that later, when we're done speaking. I'm here for you, after all, not her." He glanced toward the door with his unstitched eye. "You want to go see the ocean, don't you, little one?"

His ears flattened to the sides of his head. How did he know that?

He calmed himself as best he could. Evanne probably told him about all the Bad things he'd done, like trying to get out of the house. The Prophet couldn't know that, despite never having seen it, he dreamed of the ocean—the waves, the sandy beach, the stars shining bright overhead, the whispering of words from the great, ancient things that lived under the water's surface...

"Now is your chance. Evanne's role in your life is over. She won't be keeping you locked up in here any longer."

His ears flicked up in curiosity. Did that mean he was moving away from the house? Not with the Prophet, he hoped. He might prefer Evanne over this stranger.

I hope he can't read minds because that was a little rude, he thought.

"I have a job for you to do," the Prophet said. "You'll get to go outside and, I suppose, have something like a grand adventure out there. However, opportunities like that require a little sacrifice. Do you understand the concept of sacrifice, child?"

"Sacrifice?" he asked, the first word he'd spoken in days.

"Yes. Sacrifice means you have to give something away to get something you want. Sometimes you have to experience a little suffering before you can have happiness. The sacrifice I ask of you isn't much—in fact, you won't be awake for most of it. And once you've gone through that little suffering, you can go outside and find the man whose eyes are like the ocean. It won't be too difficult. I'll arrange things so he'll be nearby. I have lots of friends, and having lots of friends means I can sometimes make things happen that other people wouldn't be able to. So, what do you think? Are you willing to make a small sacrifice so you can go outside and see the world?"

He took a moment to think about it. He didn't like being hurt, but if Evanne had taught him anything, it was that people who intended to hurt others were going to hurt them no matter what. Getting something out of it was better than being hurt and left with nothing at all. And a chance to go outside, see the ocean that was always out of reach and out of sight, was tempting. When he was younger and his voice a little more bold, he'd begged and pleaded with Evanne until they were both exhausted to let him go see the ocean. He'd tried to glimpse it through windows, but the ones that faced the sea were boarded up.

Hurt a little, find the man with eyes like the sea—eyes like his own—and get to see the ocean and feel the sunlight and be out there with everyone else, good and Bad... how could he turn that chance down? He nodded, and the Prophet grinned at him.

"Good child." He produced a small vial filled with dark berries from his pocket and dumped a few onto his palm. "This is a strong sleeping medicine. It will make you feel sick, but you'll be asleep soon. When you wake up, you won't be here anymore, and you may forget a few things, so I want to make certain you are clear on this: *find the man with sea green eyes, like the ocean.* Understood?"

He nodded. This didn't sound too difficult, especially since the Prophet had already said he'd make sure the man was close by. He wasn't sure why he needed him to find the man at all, if he could do it himself, but he wasn't going to argue and ruin his chance of getting to go outside and see the ocean.

The Prophet handed him the medicine. "It's a little sweet, but I would still advise swallowing quickly."

Without another moment's hesitation, thinking dreamily of the ocean and what it might be like in person, he downed the medicine. The taste lingered on his tongue even though it was only in his mouth for a moment or two.

This isn't so bad.

He knew the moment it reached his stomach because he felt like he'd swallowed a huge chunk of ice. His insides were frozen, but he was sweating, and his skin felt hot.

True to the Prophet's word, it lasted only a moment before he lost consciousness, but the pain was still there when he woke up. He could hear the ocean, but everything was dark and blurry.

Go to the ocean, he thought. There was something important he was supposed to find there. *Sea green.* But the ocean wasn't blue or green or anything between, it was black, like the sky. In his dreams, there were always stars. Where were the stars?

Cold water lapped at his feet and shins, surging around him and pulling. He nearly fell, and the next wave toppled him over and dragged him toward that angry, churning foam…

He thought he might have heard something whispering as the water washed over his ears.

"Hold on, I'm coming! Hold on!"

The kidnapper was holding him and rubbing his back in soothing circles when he returned to the present. His shoulders were shaking from his sobs, and the man was whispering, "There, there, now. You poor thing... it's okay, shh. You're safe. No one is going to hurt you."

He was warm, and everywhere the man touched a little bit of that warmth seeped into his cold, tired body and made it feel better. It was almost enough to make him lean into it, close his eyes, and sleep for a while. Even if the Prophet was strange and frightening, he was right; this man had to be good.

In a way, this was how he had always thought the ocean would feel, warm and inviting, ready to gently carry him away to some place better where he could see the world lit up by the sun and breathe fresh air. Now he was disappointed that the ocean was really a cruel, frothy beast, ready to drag him down and drown him if no one was there to save him from its pull. His dreams were only dreams after all.

I found him, he thought. *I found the good man with the sea-colored eyes, but what am I supposed to do now? And when is it going to stop hurting?*

Was this the sacrifice the Prophet meant?

The pain he could handle, but the fear might be too much.

It wasn't his stomach that hurt the worst anymore, though, but his chest. He pushed his way out of the man's arms and touched the places that hurt the most. The texture of gauze bandages met his fingers. Despite being able to see and blink fine, he checked his eyes to make sure nothing awful had happened to them. He couldn't feel any stitches.

The man stood. "I'm sorry, I should probably give you a little more space. It can't be easy to wake up in an unfamiliar place like this, and I know I'm not too reassuring a sight. I just..." he sighed, "Well, that doesn't matter."

He looked at the man again, this time not focusing on the color of his eyes or his skin. He was horribly scarred, one jagged line splitting his face diagonally from his right eyebrow to his left jaw. There was another scar on the right side of his jaw, and a bit of that ear was missing.

"You've been through a lot," he continued, carefully placing him back on the bed. "You're better than you were when I found you, but you still need to recover. I'll bring you some more water."

The man started for the door. He wanted to ask him to stay—he was already starting to miss the warmth of his arms—but he couldn't manage it. He was more relieved than he should have been when the man stopped himself just as he was clearing the doorframe, but then he asked, "What's your name? Can you tell me that?"

Name—that was an almost foreign concept. Evanne was Evanne, and he was whatever she decided to call him that day. What could he answer with? Idiot, child, moron, you, brat? He didn't want the man to think he was insulting him or talking back.

He shook his head. Those words were insults, which he knew because Evanne had given him a sound beating when he'd referred to her using them once. They weren't names.

"Can you write it?"

He shook his head again. He didn't know how to read or write. He could recognize a book because Evanne had a few, but he wasn't ever supposed to look in them, and she'd never made any attempts to teach him what the squiggles on the paper meant.

"Do you..." He paused as if the question was too ridiculous, but he asked it anyway, "Do you have a name?"

He shook his head.

"I see." The man looked disappointed, and his gut twisted, feeling as if he'd failed something important. "My name is Eureka, and my partner is named Baltan. Get some rest. I'll be back with water and then lunch soon. And if you need anything before then, call for one of us. We want to help you, so please ask us for anything you need."

One of us—so the other might come, too. He didn't know if he liked that idea. He wasn't sure yet about this man, even though he was pretty certain he could trust him. In all honesty, he didn't have much choice unless the Prophet showed up again. He wasn't sure he liked that idea, either.

Eureka squeezed through the doorway and closed it behind him. This time he didn't hear it lock, so he assumed it was open in case he wanted to go downstairs, but he still doubted he could manage the walk. Instead he settled into the blankets and tried to focus on preserving some of Eureka's warmth. Without even realizing it, he slipped into another soothing dream about the ocean where he floated away from Evanne's house on soft waves. The stars were still gone, but there was a bright blue sky overhead.

You're safe now, the water murmured in Eureka's voice. He believed it.

V

"Did he hide from you?" Baltan asked, but his eyes were already scanning Eureka's exposed skin for scratches or bites in case the encounter had gone worse than that. Although he hadn't called for assistance, their ideas of 'going well' sometimes differed.

"No. He was cooperative enough, given the circumstances," Eureka said, sitting down on the couch with a somber expression. "Cried a bit. He must be terrified, the poor thing. I think he understands we won't hurt him, but it's going to take time to build trust. We'll both need to work on that." He took a deep breath and forced his shoulders to relax. He didn't look any less tense. "He doesn't have a name."

Baltan blinked, taking the information in and letting it go just as quickly. They already knew his caretaker mistreated him, and while not having a name was more extreme than Baltan expected, there was nothing he could do about it.

Still, it might become a problem if they didn't have anything to call him. They could always—

"No," Baltan said, sensing where that was going. "No, no. You aren't naming him."

"He needs a name," Eureka replied. "Even if it doesn't stick permanently, even if he's not here permanently, he deserves a proper name."

Baltan didn't believe that for a moment. Bringing the child into their home was already a step too far. Naming him was almost certain to cement whatever attachment Eureka had formed.

"I don't disagree with that, but I thoroughly object to *you* naming him," Baltan said, arms folding firmly across his chest. "What did you call the last cat you found? Yellowy or something, right? What kind of name is that? If you're allowed to name the poor kid, he'll be more traumatized."

"It wasn't *Yellowy*, it was Yellow."

"And the others?"

Eureka counted them off on his fingers. "Tux, Grey, Stripes, Fussy, and Fire for the little orange tabby."

"Point proven," Baltan said, but it wasn't as if he'd spent any time coming up with names for the kid. He hadn't thought it would be necessary. He didn't want it to go so far so fast, but he took a deep breath and tried to be open to the idea, for Eureka's sake if nothing else. "Run them by me first. What's your first suggestion?"

"Azurite," Eureka said.

"Because of the rock? Or because he's an Azure?" Baltan asked.

"Both?"

Baltan shook his head. He should have guessed, since azurite was blue. "What else do you have?"

"Uh…" Eureka looked down at the stained carpet, "You know, there's nothing wrong with simple, descriptive names. That's how they are in the tribe. Take my name, for example. It means 'horse,' because my parents hoped I'd be as strong and healthy as a horse. Nothing wrong with that."

"So what name did you want to give him, if not Azurite?" Baltan asked.

"Seasires."

"Which means?"

"… 'Blue.'"

Baltan turned away and went to the refrigerator to grab a soda, rolling his eyes. How had he come to respect and admire this man so much when he thought naming everything after what color it happened to be was a good idea? "Your lack of taste in names matches your lack of taste in fashion. Fine. Azurite it is, if the kid doesn't decide he wants to be called something else. Which he probably will, because Azurite is an awful name."

"It's not so bad," Eureka protested. "And we could call him 'Azzie' for short. It's cute."

It sounds too cute, Baltan thought, but he decided to let Eureka have his moment. He had made his distaste known already, and Eureka was disheartened enough by how the child—Azzie—had been treated. Anything that put a smile back on his face was worth the embarrassment, and it wasn't like Baltan had to live with it anyway.

As much as he hated to break the teasing atmosphere, he felt the need to come out with his thoughts directly.

"We can't keep him, Eureka. He isn't ours. Getting attached is going to make it harder to let him go when this is all over."

"I know that," Eureka said, a flash of fierceness in his eyes that reminded Baltan he was not city-born and *not* used to kowtowing to Easterners. It was a warning, however brief, that one did not come between an Azure and his child and walk away without having plenty to remember it by.

"You've never gotten this emotional over one of our cases before," Baltan said.

Eureka's gaze filled with sorrow. "I did once."

Baltan knew they would have this conversation eventually. He'd known the moment Eureka brought the boy home, maybe even when he'd read that ludicrous news article. "We don't know that it's him. It could be a copycat, or—"

"Don't try to fool yourself," Eureka said, rubbing the scar that ringed his left arm, just above the elbow. Baltan paled thinking about that particular incident. "You're worried about me getting hurt for a reason, and you saw that mark as clearly as I did. It's him, Baltan."

The details of the case surfaced in Baltan's mind like the flashes of lighting the day before.

His first case, a chance to prove himself as the prodigy he knew he was.

His annoyance at being paired with an equally inexperienced Azure who had just joined the Investigative Department after working in a *morgue*, of all places.

Over thirty children dead. Beheaded.

All of them marked the same way as the boy upstairs in his room. Some not much younger than Baltan was then.

He felt a hand rise to his throat protectively.

The feeling that he was always being watched, phone calls before dawn with no one on the other end. If he strained his ears, he could hear soft laughter before the call dropped.

Fear that only subsided when Eureka was with him, working on the case. He couldn't begin to imagine the devastation Eureka must have felt. His paternal instincts were apparent even after only a few days of knowing him.

His certainty that he'd found the killer's hideout, only for it to be abandoned and rigged with traps that had nearly cost Eureka his arm, and would have cost Baltan his life otherwise.

Over thirty children dead, always watched, always afraid...

They'd never had trouble working one of the high-bounty cases after that. Nothing compared to the terror or the pain that psycho could cause. Nothing compared to looking at thirty headless children in a morgue and talking to countless grieving family members. It had taken an entire constellation's time for the Investigative Department to interview them all.

Baltan took a breath after a moment of unintentionally holding it. "No. He should be dead. Fifteen years in prison is a life sentence for an Azure, he'd have died in captivity." The silver-infused bars of a prison cell could kill an Azure at peak health in about three years, and their killer hadn't been at peak *anything* when he'd gone in. "It's one of his followers, maybe. Someone not quite skilled enough to pull off what he did.

That explains the kid surviving. It has to be a copycat. It *has* to be."

"Why don't you do some research on it, then?" Eureka offered. "Find out when he died, if he's dead, and who might want to try and take his place as leader of that cult."

Baltan thought of Evanne's file in the public record and how it had been wiped of any pertinent information. Somehow he doubted it would be easy to get his hands on that death date or any of the cult members' current activity, but having something to focus on, something to *do*, would probably help. And once he found the death date, he could put to rest any fears of having another encounter with the child-killing monster that had haunted his nightmares in all the years since.

And replace him with a new child-killing monster, he thought bitterly.

"Alright, I'll do it, but only if you remember not to get too attached. Even if, Heavens forbid, it *is* him, we still can't keep the kid."

He had to find a way to nip that in the bud somehow, no matter how low he felt for it. Eureka was getting on in years, pushing forty now, and still had no girlfriend and certainly no children of his own. All he had was Baltan.

Eureka was quiet, and the long pause let the guilt sink in. Even if Baltan phrased it as if it ought to be common sense, it wasn't an easy compromise for Eureka to make. This could be his one chance at having a family, and his closest friend was asking him to give it up before he could even enjoy a moment of hope.

It's for his own good in the long run, Baltan thought as he sat down at the computer. "I'm going to get to work. I'll let you know what I find."

"Baltan," Eureka said, and paused again as he tried to transform his thoughts into words. Once he settled on his phrasing he spoke firmly. "I want to protect Azzie. I want to make sure what happened to those other children doesn't happen to him, and he doesn't end up on the street when this is all over. But that doesn't mean I've forgotten anything about our work, or how dangerous it can be. I won't put you in danger for the sake of my feelings."

Baltan snorted as the computer booted up, groaning in protest over all the activity in the past day. "I'm not worried about *me*, you idiot."

"Then don't be worried," Eureka answered and headed to the kitchen.

"He's not one of them," Baltan murmured. "Saving him doesn't change what happened to the others, no matter how much we might want it to."

The computer screen lit up. Things got quiet again as the desktop loaded and Baltan kept his attention there instead of looking over. He didn't want to see how badly he'd hurt Eureka, even if it was for the best.

Eureka cleared his throat. "I feel like baking something. What do you think? Garlic braid good for investigative research?"

Baltan closed his eyes and ignored the obvious change of topic. "Yes, please."

"Could you take some to Azzie when you're done? I've still got cleaning up to do, and I think it would do you both some good to get acquainted, even if it's, well, temporary. And please don't scare him with any gory details."

"Don't you think that—"

"It's important he learns to trust *both* of us." Baltan must not have looked entirely convinced because he added, "Do it and I'll make cake for dessert, too."

"Okay, fine. But I'm not calling him 'Azzie' until he's had a proper chance to suggest something else."

Baltan took his time getting to the public records file. He perused local news for a moment, looking for cases similar to the boy's to see if the killer had struck anywhere else. He checked Evanne's file again to see if anything had changed. He even read the *full* daily horoscope for any good or bad omens, just in case. He wasn't one to put stock into superstition, but Eureka might want to know if there was anything ironic listed under their signs.

Try as he might, he couldn't put it off forever. There was only one way to confirm or dismiss Eureka's suspicions. *Let him be wrong for once*, Baltan hoped.

He was glad Eureka was busying himself with lunch in the kitchen and couldn't see him muffle a cry of alarm behind the back of his hand.

Selkess
Azure, Illdresil Gera
193 centimeters, slim
Born first week of Aries, 39 BCY
Current resident status unknown

Applied for marriage registration Libra, 16 BCY.
Registration Status: EXPIRED

Criminal record:
33 Charges   Intentional Murder (Azure Minor)
**   GUILTY**
2 Charges   Intentional Murder (Azure Adult)
**   GUILTY**
2 Charges   Armed Assault of ID Member
**   GUILTY**
1 Charge   Illegal Religious Activity
**   GUILTY**
**   Sentenced to 15 years of incarceration in MD High Security Correctional Facility, to begin Sagittarius, 15 BCY; No less than one year in isolated confinement.**
**   Released from incarceration in Sagittarius, CY**

It's not possible.
Baltan's chest tightened. It was hard to breathe as memories assaulted his mind.
Released from incarceration?!
He grabbed the phone from the desk, and in his haste he knocked the receiver onto the floor. Eureka's sharp ears picked that up. "Everything okay?" he asked.

"I'm going to find out," Baltan answered, punching in the number for the head office of the Investigative Department. The phone rang briefly before the receptionist picked up, and immediately patched him through to the Captain. He was glad his name still held a little clout around the office. Hopefully enough to get the information he needed.

"You thinking of re-enlisting, brat?" came the growl that Baltan had learned to tolerate years ago, but the Captain sounded older now. There was a suppressed cough behind his words.

Failing health, Captain Stotsan? Baltan wondered. *How long before you retire?* And who would be Captain after him? Baltan hadn't ever given it any thought. The Captain had always seemed more stone than man, ageless and rough.

"Doing some research for a pet project," Baltan parried. "It's on a case that was near and dear to me, for obvious reasons. I wanted to get a status update on Selkess. Cozy in his cell, I presume?"

Baltan swore he could have heard a pen drop in the Captain's office from across the city.

"We didn't have a choice," Stotsan said finally, cutting right to Baltan's real question.

No. It had to be a joke. Just Stotsan's rotten sense of humor.

Baltan started to feel dizzy when Stotsan didn't make some smug remark about gullibility.

"You really did it? You let him *out*?" Baltan exclaimed. There was no hiding that from Eureka, who was at his side in the blink of an eye. "How could you ever think that was a good idea? This monster killed over thirty kids and you let him *walk*?"

"His sentence was up," Stotsan responded.

"He was an obvious danger—"

"He completed his mental rehabilitation courses and evaluations with no complaint, had excellent behavior with the guards and other inmates... we had no reason to keep him locked up once he'd served his time." The Captain let out a deep sigh and a few coughs. "Look, Baltan. The fact is, he hasn't caused anyone any trouble in years. After the health examination he was free to go."

"To do it all again! You know some offenders immediately go back to the way they were before when they're let out, even with the mental evaluations in place."

"We can't dog him based on that alone, and we couldn't spare the staff even if we wanted to." A coughing fit interrupted him, but he managed to add, "And I expect you to keep your nose out of it and not harass our latest batch of witnesses, unless you're thinking of joining up again."

"I'd rather gouge my own eyes out!" Baltan snarled, slamming the phone down before the Captain could respond. He wasn't a part of the department anymore; he didn't have to act with respect or wait for permission to end the conversation. And he wasn't going to tell any task force a thing about finding the child that had somehow climbed so high up their list of wanted suspects. Not if their immediate reaction to such an odd incident—child missing, caretaker dead, no motive—wasn't checking into the child killer they'd just released.

Current resident status unknown. They didn't even know where he was!

Maybe the Captain was past due for retirement.

Baltan ran his fingers through his hair, tugging in frustration. He took a deep breath and let it all out at once.

He felt Eureka's hands on his shoulders, then a soft squeeze. "I'm sorry, Baltan. I didn't want it to be true any more than you did."

"But it is," Baltan said. "Selkess is at large again, and no doubt gathering his followers. He might have a substantial number of them already regrouped—I'm sure they didn't stay too far away from him. Never saw a more loyal batch of nut-jobs."

What did that make the kid, then? A message? A warning?

The first casualty of another massacre?

"Evanne must have been a part of the cult." He removed his fingers from his hair and took another deep breath. There wasn't any time to get anxious or feel sorry for himself. If Selkess was planning to murder more children, they didn't have a moment to waste, and they couldn't rely on the Investigative Department for backup.

They're too scared of him, Baltan realized, and while it still made his blood boil he couldn't blame them for that. It wasn't that they didn't have the staff, it was that none of them were willing to go after him. *Except me and Eureka.* No wonder Captain Stotsan had sounded as close as he ever came to desperate for them to enlist in the force again. Baltan knew that door was open to them whenever they needed it, but his pride wouldn't allow him to go back after he'd announced his retirement and washed his hands of that life.

Maybe they hadn't come as clean as he'd thought.

Eureka started to say something comforting, but the shrill screech of the oven's timer cut him off. He returned from the kitchen moments later with infinitely more comforting garlic braids on two plates.

"Are you sure you're up to this?" Eureka asked, offering the plates. "I can go with you, since Azzie knows me already."

Baltan accepted them, inhaling the mouthwatering smells of garlic, butter, and fresh-baked bread to clear his head. He was home, with Eureka, and there was nowhere safer in the world. Selkess might be out there somewhere, plotting his next move, but he wasn't *here*.

"I've handled a lot more dangerous missions than this alone. Besides, we won't all fit in the room."

VI

He was chasing a seashell along the beach. It flipped and twirled across the sand like a living thing and he was determined to catch it. Maybe he could find more than one and make a wind chime that would work without a breeze.

Behind him, following but not crowding, was Eureka. Each step he took made the waves flow and ebb, ever present, gentle, and calm. The ocean was whispering again, but he couldn't quite hear what it said. He wasn't paying too much attention, as the voices from the sea were too quiet and peaceful to have anything urgent to tell him.

A noisy seagull dove out of the sky and stole the shell, but he was happy to watch the bird fly. He'd never told Evanne, but once he had seen a gull through a crack in the window—a real one, not a picture—and he was certain it was a magical animal. How else could it move through the sky when everything else was stuck on land? He tried it, but he always came right back down after he jumped, even if he tried leaping from furniture.

The gull gave a shrill caw and woke him to something better than the dream.

He'd eaten plenty earlier, but his stomach growled again at the delicious aroma of bread, garlic, and butter. Did he get to have some of that, too?

He was happy to find that he was actually hungry instead of his stomach hurting for some other reason. He took deeper breaths as he tried to work himself up to calling for Eureka.

He should probably try to actually say something. He wasn't sure he could get his tongue around Eureka's name, but a simple, 'hello,' followed by, 'thank you,' or, 'where am I?' shouldn't be so hard to muster.

A knock on the door beat him to it.

"I'm coming in now, okay?"

The other voice. He pulled up his blanket, tightening it around himself. He didn't know anything about Baltan but his name. If Eureka trusted him, he might be alright, but that wasn't sure.

The door opened. The man standing on the other side was much smaller than Eureka, and looked much more like Evanne. His throat tightened.

Baltan sat down on the edge of the bed and placed a plate of food in front of him, but he was still anxious. He wouldn't be saying anything for a while.

"Hey," Baltan said. "I brought lunch. It's a garlic braid, good stuff. Eureka made it. So eat, alright?" He took a bite of his own food. "There, no poison, see?"

Baltan didn't look directly at him when he spoke, and he kept his speech limited to short, choppy sentences. Telltale signs of nervousness.

What does he have to be nervous about? He knows where he is. He had to ponder that for a moment. *Is he nervous about me? Is it because he knows I shouldn't be outside?*

"Look—you're here, I'm here, and it's going to have to be that way for a while. So let's work together, alright?"

He flicked his ears. Everything about Baltan was sharp, from his nose to his eyes to his voice, but that meant he got right to the point. It was a different kind of honesty than Eureka's, but it was one he could trust. He nodded.

"Great," Baltan leaned away from him. "Eureka tells me you don't have a name. Is that true?"

He nodded, wishing he could come up with something, but he wouldn't be able to tell Baltan if he did.

"That's what I was afraid of, because Eureka's decided to give you a name. As great as Eureka is at some things—" they both took a bite of their garlic braids "—there are some things he's absolutely terrible at, like dressing himself and naming things."

He tilted his head. Where was Baltan going with this? There could be no name worse than 'Idiot' or 'Leech.' Was Eureka naming him one of those things?

"He wants to call you 'Azurite'—'Azzie' for short. It's a type of blue crystal. Unfortunately that's one of the better names that he's ever come up with, so unless you have any other ideas I'd suggest going with it."

He blinked. He was going to be named after a crystal? Weren't they beautiful things? He didn't understand how that could be as bad as Baltan made it seem.

Azurite. Azzie. A name of his own, shared by a pretty blue crystal, given to him by a good person.

It sounded familiar. Was that what the ocean had been whispering to him?

He took another bite of the garlic braid, his mouth working its way into a little smile. Maybe this was all for the best, just a part of the plan. After all, if he was supposed to make the world a better place, it would help to know what the end goal was supposed to be. Delicious food, warm touches that didn't make him flinch, honest and genuine care; those were the things he would fill the world with when he changed it alongside the Prophet. Perhaps they weren't going to get rid of the Bad people. They were going to show them how nice being good was instead.

Azzie was certain he was good now. He'd made his sacrifice, he'd done what was asked of him, and now he was being rewarded for not being Bad anymore. His world was in harmony, and he wanted to share that with everyone else. It probably wouldn't take too long. How many people could there be in the world? As many as five tens? A hundred, maybe? He couldn't count higher than that.

"You aren't cringing, so I guess you like the name," the not-kidnapper added with a shrug. "My name's Baltan, by the way. It's not that impressive either, if it makes you feel better."

Azzie already knew what his name was, but it was nice to be introduced anyway. He hoped his voice would come back soon. He wanted to tell the two he appreciated the food and kind treatment and that soon the whole world would be that way for everyone.

He communicated the idea as well as he could, making eye contact with Baltan for a brief moment. The gray of his eyes reminded him of the storm outside, tumultuous and as full of unspoken thoughts as the clouds were unshed rain. It was clear Baltan's mind was elsewhere. Azzie wondered where exactly, and what was there that made him so jumpy.

Once they had eaten the garlic braids—and it didn't take long—Azzie shuffled out of the blanket and flipped a corner of it over to Baltan. He was pleased that he didn't hurt as much anymore. The food must have helped heal him.

Baltan looked at the blanket, which landed a few centimeters off from his thigh. He gave Azzie a hard look.

"I'm not supposed to scare you," Baltan said, almost to himself. "But I think you deserve to know the truth, or at least as much as we know. If I were in your situation I'd want to know what was going on."

Azzie nodded. He wasn't sure what Baltan was going to say or why it would scare him, but answers were exactly what he wanted. He knew Eureka and Baltan's names, and that they were good and wanted to help him, but not much else. Nothing about why he was with them, aside from the Prophet wanting him to find Eureka.

"Was Evanne your mother?"

Azzie shook his head. Evanne had been very adamant that he never refer to her as his mother. His mother had given him to her.

"I hope that makes this easier for you," Baltan said, but it seemed that it made things harder for him. He kept rubbing the back of his neck and tapping his foot. He did not look at Azzie once while he spoke. "Evanne was murdered, and you're a suspect. That means people think you might have killed her. Eureka and I don't believe that. We're going to do all we can to make sure the real killer gets punished and you stay safe. We need your help. It may be hard, but we need you to tell us as much as you can about that night so we can stop the killer from hurting anyone else."

Azzie's stomach clenched. He wasn't scared, but he felt awful. Even more horrible than when the Prophet had given him the strange medicine.

Evanne was dead?

He was keenly aware of what death was. Evanne herself had very efficiently explained it to him. 'Dead' was gone, permanently, forever. He would never see Evanne again.

The worst feeling of all was that, after the shock wore off, he didn't feel as bad as he thought he should. He rarely thought of Evanne's death, but he had always been a lot sadder when he thought about it than now, when it actually happened.

Baltan carefully nudged the blanket back toward Azzie. "I'm sorry. I know this can't be easy for you."

The Prophet's words about sacrifice swam through Azzie's head—that Evanne's role in his life was over. That she had made him feel less important than he really was and fulfilling his purpose went directly against the strict rules she raised him with. And if he wanted the things Evanne had always denied him, then he needed to make a sacrifice.

Maybe the medicine wasn't the real sacrifice. Maybe Evanne's life was.

"I did it," he said, his voice quiet and cracking. He doubted it would stay long. "It's my fault."

He thought Baltan would stand and get away from him, or go downstairs to tell Eureka that there was a killer in the house, or strike him. Instead sympathy softened his sharp gaze. "Did you shoot her? Did you pull the trigger? Think hard, back to that night. Did you actually shoot and kill her?"

Pull the trigger? Azzie shook his head. He didn't understand what those words even meant.

"Then you didn't do it, and it isn't your fault," Baltan replied. "You didn't even know she was dead until I told you. You can't have killed her."

His words made sense, but Azzie still felt guilty. He couldn't help thinking that if he'd done something differently, she wouldn't be dead. He could have refused the Prophet's offer and stuck to her rules. What if it was a test, and if he chose wrong Evanne died and he was forced out into the harsh, unforgiving world she'd always told him about?

But it's not harsh and unforgiving so far, he thought, and he felt even guiltier that he wanted to trust Eureka and Baltan far more than he wanted to be afraid of them. They hadn't done anything to make him afraid, and nothing about their body language led him to think they were lying to him. No matter how good Evanne claimed to be, actions would always matter more to Azzie than words. From the moment he had woken up, Eureka and Baltan had tried their hardest to make him feel safe and welcome in their home. Evanne had made him feel like a burden and a prisoner. He couldn't be blamed for preferring them already, could he?

Baltan didn't come any closer or offer an arm or shoulder for him to cling to until he felt better. He was still too fidgety, probably about finding out who Evanne's killer really was.

So they were *definitely* good people, and Azzie could feel a little less awful about trusting them.

He let the blanket fall away and tried to leave the bed, partially to get to Eureka, partially to see if Baltan would stop him and confine him to the room, and partially to see if he could stand up and walk on his own. His footing was unsteady and he swayed a little. Baltan neither stopped him nor extended a hand to help him, though he did stay within arm's reach as Azzie teetered his way toward the door and down the stairs.

"We've got company," Baltan called to Eureka, who was busy examining a collection of papers on a small table. From the smell of things, something sweet was baking in the oven.

The living room was messy, in an oddly neat sort of way. There were heaps of books and bottles lying around everywhere, but the piles seemed purposefully arranged to be that way. It wasn't like Evanne's home, which was usually messy unless she got into one of her cleaning moods. There was a purpose to Eureka and Baltan's mess, even if Azzie was pretty sure they *also* didn't care much for tidying up.

Azzie clambered over the clutter and climbed onto the couch with Eureka. He gripped his arm as tightly as possible and buried his face in the scratchy knit of his sweater.

He felt Eureka's massive palm rest on his head, patting him a few times before he asked Baltan, "What did you tell him?"

"The truth."

VII

Selkess. The name itself was like poison dripping off a knife.

Baltan accessed the Encyclopedia of Public Records and began digging through information about Selkess's cult. In truth, it wasn't *his* cult. The banned church had been around centuries before their leader, but he had been the one to organize it into something more than a scary story to tell naughty children. How, Baltan didn't know. Maybe the craziest nutcase in the batch got to be in charge.

Searching for information on the cult directly turned up nothing more than a vague notice.

The Cult of Kreor was officially outlawed by the Emperor three hundred and twenty five years before the current year. Information about its practices is strictly limited to a select few scholars and advisors within His Imperial Majes-

ty's legal court. The restriction of public knowledge about this banned cult is called for due to the extremely violent nature through which worship of Kreor is carried out, so as not to encourage any deranged individuals from attempting to practice such rituals.

Good job of that, Baltan thought. Selkess had gotten ahold of that information somehow and revived the cult fifteen years ago, if not earlier.

'Deranged individuals,' sounded like the perfect description for Kreor's followers. Maybe Selkess didn't need the real texts to lead them. Most of the cult members apprehended alongside him had been so unhinged that one wrong look or word could drive them to murder.

Unfortunately, the ban did mean a law-abiding citizen like Baltan had almost no chance of actually viewing any of the cult's practices or beliefs to figure out what they were up to.

So go by memory, he grimaced. He'd spent a lot of time trying to repress everything about that case.

More children's bodies than would fit in a standard school bus, cut up with the same markings Eureka had pointed out on Azzie. That had to be a part of some ritual or another.

But what *for?*

Baltan keyed in the code for a marginally better topic: Eastern religion. If Kreor was a god, there might be a few offhand mentions about what exactly its duties were in other myths. He accessed a family tree to see if he could get any bearings on where Kreor might fit in with the greater mythology of the East. He was immediately sent swimming through a spider-web graph with so many lines that in places it looked solid.

He rolled his eyes. The East had a deity for *everything.*

Start with the bad stuff, he told himself. Any god demanding a sacrifice of children's lives had to fall on the evil side of the pantheon. He pulled up the search tool and started entering all the names he could remember, one by one.

Hizth, god of death, no connections. Of course. A god of death wouldn't have any familial ties to any other deity, being completely lifeless. Next.

Zatiln, the god of chains. This one Baltan almost felt guilty searching with Eureka in the room. 'Chains,' to Easterners meant, 'slaves,' which meant Azures forced to perform hard labor that weaker Eastern bodies couldn't manage. The practice was outlawed in the West due to a peace treaty with the tribes, but it was still legal—if not sleazy—in the East. No connections to Kreor there, either.

On a whim, Baltan searched Khalpi, the four-headed god of law and justice. The god that was supposed to be *his* god, but Baltan hadn't been willing to sell his soul to a cult. Even at thirteen, he couldn't pretend he believed in deities or great dragons shaping the world. By then he'd seen too much senseless suffering and pain to believe there was any benevolent force running things behind the scenes, no matter what his Uncle told him.

No connections to Kreor. Not even delivering a divine sentence to punish the vile demon.

Great, Baltan inwardly groaned. He'd have to start all the way at the top with Ahezia, the god of the royal family and ruler of all other deities. No records of Ahezia's worship existed outside of the royal family, and that was passed from generation to generation by word rather than writing. But there were a few stories.

A match. Baltan's eyes widened briefly.

There was only one mention of Kreor, but it was enough.

"Ahezia, the All Wise and All Powerful, did make one known mistake in His ruling. It was tedious and beneath a god of such regality and importance to observe the passing of each moment in time, and He had so many various duties to attend and so many gods to oversee that He thought He could entrust the simple task of timekeeping to one of His lesser children.

While the rest of the world kept track of the passing time with the constellations that would appear and signal the change of the seasons, when to plant and harvest, when game would migrate, and so on, this lone godling kept track in much more minute detail. Each and every passing moment was recorded meticulously, regardless of importance.

Eager to please his Father and claim full godhood, the godling worked his job too well. He grew two more heads to help him with the work, so that he had a head for the time past, the time currently passing, and the time that would soon pass. Each head shared the first's eagerness and attention to detail.

Not long after this began, the head of the past began to obsess over long-forgotten exchanges and actions that could no longer be changed and was filled with regret. The head of the future began to obsess over the coming possibilities, seeing all the futures that may or may not be, and was filled with paranoia and fear over choosing the right path.

The head of the present, the original godling, was broken and betrayed by his own powers.

Soon he could take no more and let out a declaration that shook the world to its very core. 'It must all be destroyed.'

Ahezia took notice and came to stop the destruction, but the heads of the past and future, not recognizing Him as their Father, turned on Him, but Ahezia defeated them easily and spoke:

'You have become a mad creature. I apologize for the hand I had to play in this. The passing of time is not so important that it should cause such insanity and suffering. You are relieved of your duty and will be cared for until you are well again.'

The godling was enraged by this. In his twisted view, Ahezia was standing against his destiny rather than extending mercy and healing, and he spat His blessing back at Him.

'This world will come to ashes, and we will count down all the time it has left!' all the heads howled together.

Regretfully, Ahezia saw that He had no choice. He sealed the creature away into the stars, creating the constellation that we call the Dread Serpent, which appears during the first night of Capricorn, the day before Fallen Day. Under

Ahezia's seal, the deranged demon could no longer threaten His creation, but unfortunately it also prevented the godling from being reached by Ahezia's healing energy.

The original name of the deity is unknown, but it is now called Kreor, the Mad God, whose domains are time and insanity."

An old fairytale, Baltan thought with a scoff. Still, if the cult *believed* this...

He changed tactics, looking up the legal rationale for banning the cult in the East.

He was not disappointed.

Besides being an unpopular god simply due to its nature, worship of Kreor was permanently banned in the East when a cult member impersonated a royal guardsman and slaughtered a sizeable chunk of the royal family on the first night of Capricorn.

It was late Sagittarius now. Baltan tried to remember how long it would be until Capricorn began. Before the storm had blotted out the stars, they were positioned... thirteen days out?

Which meant there were only ten days left until the first day of Capricorn. Ten days to find out if Selkess was planning another mass-murder, which was nearly a guarantee. Ten days to get to the bottom of where, when, and how, *and* stop it before more children were slaughtered.

Evanne's murder and Azzie's cuts were a warning, an invitation to play the game again. Selkess was sure to have much bigger plans than a single child and his caretaker. How many vulnerable children lived in Marina Delta now? Hundreds, at least. Maybe thousands.

Could Selkess convince streetwise city kids to come with a stranger, alone, at night?

Of course. He'd done it before. He didn't have to give them a choice of coming with him or not. No one knew how big the cult of Kreor was, or how much it might have grown since he was in prison. They hadn't managed to catch all his followers, and they could have converted more unhinged drifters. Maybe they'd even seen him in prison. Baltan should have asked about that when he'd called. Selkess spent at least one year in isolation, but that meant he had upwards of fourteen years to mingle with the other inmates.

And Stotsan said he'd gotten along with them, Baltan recalled. So he was able to talk to people, and he could have used that to increase his pool of devotees.

Ten days.

Before Baltan could say anything to Eureka, the phone rang, jolting all of them. Eureka settled Azzie down by wrapping a blanket around him and rose to answer the call, but Baltan waved his hand and said, "I'll get it. It's probably Stotsan calling back with a few choice words for me."

Maybe information on Selkess and what he's been up to since he was released, Baltan hoped.

He picked up the phone and lifted it to his ear.

"This is Baltan."

"It's so nice to hear your voice again, investigator."

Baltan's heart stopped, and all the blood in his veins froze with it.

"*Selkess?*"

He balled his other hand into a fist, clenching and unclenching, wishing he had a gun within reach and that it would do any good in this situation. Eureka was at his side in an instant, listening in.

"I don't mean to startle you, investigator," Selkess said, and Baltan could imagine the smug detachment of his smile. "Far from it. I mean to put your mind at ease. But this is... a little too impersonal, isn't it, considering our history? Why don't we meet somewhere for drinks? Don't worry, it will be somewhere public."

"How did you get this number?"

"Public records, of course. You aren't the only one who can read it, and I had a lot of free time to learn. Forgive my lack of social graces. I didn't expect you to be defensive of information that plenty of other people can easily obtain."

Baltan wiped a bead of sweat from his brow and tried to regulate his breathing. Eureka reached for the receiver, but Baltan shook his head. He didn't want Selkess to know how rattled he was.

Selkess continued, "I'm sorry to be forward, but I wish to discuss the specifics of a certain murder case with you. Let's meet tomorrow at the Gilded Gryphon, downtown. Midday works for me. I have a room there, and I've found the lobby is wonderfully spacious and the bar has a good selection of cocktails. There will be plenty of people around, but we should be able to talk openly all the same. I would invite our dear *friend* Eureka, but as I recall, he doesn't drink often. Is that still true?"

'Come alone,' is what he means, Baltan thought.

"I'll consider it," Baltan said, shoving the phone back down onto the receiver with enough force to make Selkess's ear ring.

Midday at the Gilded Gryphon, one of the ritziest hotels in Marina Delta. He certainly was making a show of himself, more than he ever would have dared to before. Although Baltan felt his heart start beating again, rapidly, he didn't feel any better. Selkess acting bolder didn't bode well for anyone.

He clenched his teeth and looked up at Eureka, whose brows had knit into a furious line. "I've got to go. We don't want him resorting to more extreme lengths to get our attention, and he is the best lead we've got when it comes to Evanne's murder. I'll check out the area first before I meet him."

There would be people around, even if they were only passing by on their way to check in and out. But did he say it to try to reassure Baltan that he wasn't going to try anything yet, or to remind him that he couldn't do anything him in front of witnesses no matter what Selkess said about his intentions?

"I'll go with you." It wasn't a question.

"No, you've got to stay with Azzie. We *can't* leave a child alone with him at large again."

The corner of Eureka's lip pulled back and showed a hint of fang. Baltan braced himself for an argument while Eureka weighed the options.

"Fine," he growled. "But I don't like it."

Azzie was still wrapped up in the blanket, eyes wide and ears lifted as high as they could go. Helpless. Dependent, on both Eureka and Baltan. Being so needed was a new feeling for Baltan. He looked out for Eureka and fought to defend him, but he always viewed him as an equal partner who could also fend for himself if he wasn't around. He wondered if Eureka saw the same in him, or if he felt the way Baltan did toward Azzie—like he was weak and hopeless without him. There was no way to know for certain.

"Still..." Eureka frowned, concern plain on his face, "Isn't there anything I can do?"

"Keep Azzie safe." Baltan walked with purpose to the hallway closet, and reached up to the top shelf to retrieve a sleek black case. He unlatched it and ran his fingers over the smooth steel of his favorite pistol. "I've got myself covered."

Baltan spent the rest of the day alternating between researching the cult and the area around the Gilded Gryphon in case he needed to make a quick getaway. In between reading and decoding, he did his best to reassure Azzie again that nothing about the situation was his fault, and Eureka did his best to keep Baltan from having a nervous breakdown.

It might have worked a lot better if Eureka quit tensing his hands out of stress, drawing attention to the knife-sharp claws at the ends of his fingers. Baltan had seen those claws tear through plenty of obstacles and, when absolutely needed, people. He almost reconsidered bringing Eureka with him to the meeting. Having some visible power standing behind him might be a better intimidation tactic than a concealed firearm, even if the pistol was ultimately more effective.

He didn't want to resort to that, though. He didn't want anyone to see Eureka as nothing but a source of brute strength to handle the dirty work.

"Why don't you take Azzie out tomorrow?" Baltan suggested, finding himself at Eureka's side without really meaning to. He had come into the kitchen to grab his sixth bottle of soda and Eureka was there, sorting through the pantry in search of a snack for Azzie. He was recovering quickly, but a full meal was still out of the question for the time being. He'd already had more food than he was probably used to in a day.

"Are you sure?" Eureka asked, nearly dropping the box of salted crackers. "That's a huge step for him."

Baltan could understand the reaction. Azzie was still weak and hadn't been with them very long, and there was no telling what his reaction to leaving the house would be. "I don't think he'll run away. He likes you, and it does seem like he was never let outside before the murder. I think, if anything, he'd be overwhelmed and want to come back to the house, not get lost trying to get away from you. And besides, if Selkess knows our phone number, he probably knows our address, too. It might be safer if you and Azzie aren't here while I'm meeting with him, in case he tries to pull anything while we're separated."

"I see your point," Eureka nodded. "And he does need some clothing of his own. He can't keep wearing my sweaters forever."

Baltan restrained himself from mock-gagging at the thought. "Take it easy on our bank account. And everyone else's eyes."

"They are not *that* bad," Eureka protested, tugging at the hem of his orange, green, and yellow zig-zag patterned sweater. "Besides, I'm sure he'll choose his own, *reasonably priced* clothes," he added with a glint of mischief in his eyes.

Let's hope his fashion sense isn't easily influenced, Baltan thought.

Eureka handed Baltan a small plate of crackers. "Eat something to settle your stomach."

"It isn't upset," Baltan said, though he accepted nonetheless.

"After that much soda, it will be," Eureka replied, making another plate to take to Azzie. "There will be more time to do research in the morning, too, and I'm sure you've already gone over everything at least twice by now. Why don't we take a break for a while? *The Night Train* should be starting soon."

We may not have as much time as you think.

Baltan wanted to put up a fight and insist that he needed to work until the sun came up. However, one look at Eureka settling down on the couch and gently rousing Azzie from his blanket nest was too tempting. A few years ago he would have rolled his eyes at the idea of domestic life, but pushing thirty was starting to change his viewpoint. The things that had appealed to him in his twenties, when he was young and had too much time on his hands, seemed pointless. Going to bars and clubs was weary work, especially when Eureka only joined him because he was too drunk to find his own way home but sober enough to make a slurred call. And there was nothing to do at those places *but* drink. He couldn't strike up a casual conversation with people his age without feeling like a fraud at best or jealous of their normal lives at worst. His social skills were abysmal, anyway.

For a while Baltan thought it was all good fun. He even managed a few dates that ended pretty well despite not quite having his bearings the next morning. But the allure faded sooner than he'd hoped, and he hadn't left the house for any considerable amount of time since early summer. He didn't want to think about how empty his time was while he watched other people enjoy themselves, didn't want to keep getting into relationships he knew would only last a night.

Baltan turned on the radio, which was already tuned to *The Night Train*'s station, and plopped down on the other side of Eureka. Within moments the jazzy opening music played, starting with a few sharp chords before fading out to a lively hum as the announcer came on. "Tonight, the murderous tale of a mysterious briefcase. What's in the briefcase, and why would it drive someone to murder? Some secrets are deadly, and some truths deadlier. Check your luggage carefully as you find your seat on... *The Night Train*."

"I'll wager the last slice of cake I can figure out who the killer is before the second act," Eureka said with a smile.

"I accept, raise you the first slice of cake, *and* I bet I can figure it out before they finish revealing the entire cast."

"Showing off a bit, aren't you?" Eureka laughed.

"There's cake on the line," Baltan responded with the utmost seriousness.

Baltan let the last bite of cake all but melt in his mouth while Eureka tucked Azzie into bed. It wasn't good to eat sweets immediately before sleeping, but he wasn't going to let anything stop him from claiming his prize.

The killer had turned out to be the detective investigating the case, covering his own tracks while he secretly made plans to run off with his victim's mistress, only for his rookie partner to figure out what was going on with by-the-book thinking and turn him in. Classic *Night Train* plotline.

Eureka had figured it out, too, but not before the host was done introducing all the characters, so the spoils went to Baltan.

If only it was so easy to feel that good about cracking a case in real life. If only it stopped at pointing to the villain, making the accusation, and having the justice system take care of the rest.

Baltan put the dishes in the sink and headed upstairs to bed. He nearly took the right door, but Eureka emerged as he reached the second floor landing, reminding him it was no longer his room. At least not for now.

Eureka had taken longer to put Azzie to bed than he had the night before, probably checking the lock on the window.

What little good mood they'd built up over the evening dissipated.

Baltan fell face-first onto Eureka's bed and waited for the tension to leave his body. It didn't.

"You shouldn't sleep in your day clothes," Eureka said.

"What difference is it going to make?" But it wouldn't be comfortable to sleep in denim jeans, no matter how old and broken-in. He kicked them off, leaving his undershorts and shirt where they were and falling onto his back once he was done.

Eureka didn't bother getting under the covers. He settled onto his stomach, hands under his pillow. If Baltan wanted, he could reach up and touch a rare unscarred patch of skin on his upper arm, but he couldn't find the motivation. He was tired enough without the reminder of what they weren't.

"I know there's no way for me to go with you, but I wish I could," Eureka grumbled. "I have... *questions* for Selkess. About where Azzie came from."

"You think you know who his parents are?" Baltan asked.

"It's only a theory. I could be wrong." His shoulders shifted and he stared off to the side, searching for the right words. "As far as I've seen, only my mother and my twin brother have the same eye color as me and Azzie. It's possible he could be my nephew."

Baltan ran the thought through his head, but for some reason it didn't add up. Just because it was possible didn't mean it was true.

Azzie was half-Eastern, which meant Eureka's brother would have left the tribe to meet his mother. That wasn't impossible—most Kwoltan Gera defectors ended up in the Marine cities, and Marina Delta was the most integrated of the three. Maybe he'd ended up somewhere else, but given that Azzie was *here*, it seemed like more of a stretch to place his parents in another city.

Baltan doubted it. He couldn't believe they somehow missed him, not when so many people knew Eureka's face. Word would have travelled, somehow, that someone with a resemblance was living in the area. It made much more sense that Azzie's father would be the brother they already *knew* lived in Marina Delta, rather than the one they had to guess at.

Eureka seemed entirely too quick to decide that Azzie was his brother's kid when, by his own admission, they shared the same odd eye color.

Baltan rubbed his forehead. It was late, and he was trying to connect dots that might have nothing to do with each other. Whatever the truth was, they didn't have nearly enough information about where Azzie came from.

"I'll get what information I can out of him."

"And if anything goes wrong," Eureka's voice was hushed even though there was no one to overhear them, "If anything doesn't seem right, *promise* you'll do what it takes to get out alive."

"I promise." Baltan rolled over so his back was to Eureka. He didn't want him to see how worried he was, and he knew he couldn't hide it completely. "Now get some sleep."

VIII

Breakfast was an uncomfortably quiet affair. Eureka was not one to hide his feelings, and watching them shift across his face was a near theatrical performance.

Azzie came down to join them on his own, letting a nervous look flicker between the two before refocusing his attention on the layers of sliced apples, oranges, and almonds on his plate.

"We're going out today," Eureka told him, keeping his voice low despite feigning enthusiasm. "Won't that be exciting? We'll find some new clothes for you. Maybe a few toys. We'll see."

Azzie's ears flicked up and down once and his eyes widened, then he nodded. Baltan filed the reaction away in his mind as something to analyze later. Given that Azzie didn't seem to know how to write and had limited speech, figuring out what his ear movements and facial gestures meant might be the only way to effectively communicate with him for a while.

Baltan let that go and concentrated on his more immediate and far more life-threatening task: figuring out how to talk to Selkess. Expecting him to be transparent about anything went straight from optimism to stupidity, and going into the meeting unprepared was downright crazy.

He didn't think bringing a paper with questions was a good idea, so he studied the list of pointers he'd written down that morning.

Play nice—'Why do you want to talk to me?' not 'What do you want?'
Ask specific questions. Don't give him room to twist your words. But also don't ask him anything directly about Azzie; the less he knows we know, the better.

Ask him to clarify what he means and pretend to not understand. Make him explain what he means so he can't play word games.

Treat it like a business meeting. Serious and professional. Detached.

Don't drink anything he offers. Even if you see it being poured.

There wasn't much use in trying to plan out an encounter with Selkess. Things were going to happen that Baltan could never predict, and this was the best he could do to prepare himself mentally.

At least he'd have his trusty pistol at his hip in case things went completely wrong. The cult members that no doubt surrounded Selkess day and night might take him down, but at least he could make sure Selkess never orchestrated another massacre if it came to that. He sincerely hoped it wouldn't. Being a vigilante and killing people had never appealed to him, and he'd rather turn Selkess over to the incompetence of the authorities than murder him in cold blood.

But if that was what it took to keep the children of Marina Delta safe, and to protect all he held dear, he'd do it.

He finished his breakfast, set his dishes in the sink, and double-checked that his pistol was loaded and the safety engaged before holstering it. It would be a while until midday, but he wanted to make sure he had plenty of time to survey the area in-person before he met with Selkess.

Azzie gave him a worried look. One ear tipped up.

Baltan hazarded a guess at what it meant and responded, "I'll be okay. You're going to have a fun day with Eureka, so enjoy it instead of worrying about me. I know what I'm doing." For added measure he tried to ruffle the kid's hair, but he flinched, so he stopped short of actually touching him and pulled his hand back. "It's okay. You're okay. Alright?" To Eureka he said, "I'd better get going. I don't want to miss the bus."

"We'll catch the next one," Eureka said. "To the Eirden shopping center, about two miles south of the Gilded Gryphon. If you need us."

Baltan frowned. *That close?* he wanted to ask, but he already knew that was why Eureka had chosen that location. Leaving at different times and taking different buses would have to be enough to throw off Selkess's allies, assuming they were being watched.

"Sounds like a plan," he said, leaving the safety and comfort of home behind.

Nothing was out of place near the Gilded Gryphon, but Baltan wondered if he would have recognized unusual behavior. The Gilded Gryphon was made of sharp edges and geometric patterns, and somehow so were all the people in and around it. They walked with their noses up and their shoulders spiked, every step calculated.

Baltan shook his head. He couldn't imagine himself living among these snobs who cared more about Eastern blood and money than they did about intelligence and integrity.

Selkess would stick out like a sore thumb.

He slinked around the hotel, checking every exit for ambushes that might be poised to strike once he made his escape. There were none. He glanced up, but there was no way to make a quick getaway there. Even if he took the unexpected route up and into the hotel, the windows from the second floor on were sealed shut to prevent 'accidents.'

He had a full clip and a wary mind. He'd have to trust those to get him out of any trouble he encountered.

The automatic doors slid open at the same time that the clouds parted, letting sunlight pour into the lobby around Baltan's shadow. Instead of making the room brighter, the light shone through the stained glass and gave everything a foreboding red glow.

He took note of how many people were in the lobby and at the bar. Plenty were coming and going, some were checking out of their rooms, but only a scant few were actually staying for any significant amount of time. Everything was as expected there.

His eyes scanned the bar for the midnight blue of Selkess's hair, but didn't spot it. He wondered if after all this time he would actually remember what Selkess looked like.

Then he remembered the mad glint in his eyes as they struggled, a knife edging closer and closer to his throat before Eureka recovered and rose up behind him like a tidal wave. The insane glee turned to panic in an instant when the pointed teeth that gave Eureka his goofy smile did what they were made to do and—

No, Baltan wouldn't ever forget what Selkess looked like.

"Sir?" a young woman dressed in a Gilded Gryphon uniform approached him.

"What?" he asked, bringing himself back to the moment. Selkess wasn't going to pull a knife on him here.

"Are you here to meet someone?" she asked. She looked nervous, a little scared, hands wringing around the hem of her blazer. Probably not one of Selkess's followers. "The man at the table next to the dwarf palmettos wants your attention. He says you have a scheduled meeting?"

Baltan looked over. The fronds of the mini palm obscured the man, but he could see enough skin around the lavish suit and greenery to know he was an Azure. In this part of town, there weren't likely to be two sitting in the same lobby.

"Yes, thank you," Baltan said to the hostess, smiling in an attempt to put her obvious anxieties at ease while he tried to keep his stomach from turning somersaults.

He took sure and steady steps on his way to the table, steeling himself more and more with each stride. He couldn't show weakness, couldn't let Selkess know he was intimidated in the slightest. He needed to take control of his meeting and hold onto it no matter what Selkess told him.

Baltan took the seat across from Selkess and sat as if he'd expected to arrive first. He did his best to ignore the pungent stench of cheap cologne and looked Selkess over with as blank an expression as he could manage even as he gripped the arm of the chair tight.

It took his eyes a moment to register what he was seeing. His facial expression held, but mostly out of shock, and all his words vanished.

"It certainly has been a long time, investigator," Selkess said. His voice was quieter than it was on the phone; he must have held it close to his mouth. That should have come as no surprise given the scar tissue plainly visible beneath his scarf. "I think time has given us both a turn for the better. Wouldn't you agree?" He leaned back in his seat. "The cocktails are excellent. I sampled a few last night, and I highly recommend the Ruby Dragon. Just the right amount of tartness to complement the sweetness..." A tight smile. "I think I remembered you being a man of more words than this. Silence doesn't suit you."

Selkess tilted his head, ever so slightly, so the sewn-open eye on his left side directly faced Baltan. His throat felt like it was closing, and he couldn't even choke out a response. *How* had he passed any mental examination looking like that?

"Oh, how embarrassing!" Selkess brushed his bangs to the side in an attempt to conceal it. Baltan wasn't fooled. If he was really worried about Baltan's reaction, he would have had it covered from the beginning. He wanted it to be seen. "I wasn't feeling well at the time. I was going through a... a rough patch, you could call it. But I feel so much better now. I really do. And I have you and Eureka to thank for that, don't I?"

"What do you want?" Baltan snapped. A flash of *something* crossed Selkess's face—satisfaction, probably—and he tried to save whatever chance he had at actually getting through Selkess's act by following up with, "Beyond thanking me, I mean. You could have done that on the phone. Are you looking for assistance getting a job, or something like that? Because we've been retired for a while now, and I'm not sure our names alone are going to be enough with your record."

"No," Selkess laughed. "No, I'm not looking for a job. It's actually the opposite of what you suggest. I brought you here to give *you* work."

Baltan's trigger finger itched. He could interpret that statement any number of ways, and he was sure that Selkess knew it.

Selkess slid a photograph across the table to Baltan. *Don't pick it up right away.* He forced himself to maintain eye contact, but he found it difficult even with that dreadful stitched eye hidden from view. He knew it was still there, still watching his every movement. *Two can play that game.*

He gave the photo a dismissive glance, then slowly picked it up, fighting to maintain control of his facial expression when he recognized Azzie. He looked so *miserable*, and the fact that Selkess had it was suspicious all on its own. What excuse could Baltan use to keep it as evidence?

The tension broke briefly when a waitress came over to take their drink orders. Selkess was careful to keep his mutilated eye covered long enough to place a request for a Ruby Dragon for himself and whatever the special of the day was for Baltan.

"I'm sure you heard about the peculiar murder that occurred a few days ago. The victim's name was Evanne."

"I read about it in the paper," Baltan shrugged.

"She was a dear friend of mine," Selkess went on. "She visited me regularly, and had offered to give me a place to stay once I was released from prison. We were finalizing the arrangement when she... Well, in any case, I suppose she did help me find a place to stay." He gestured to the hotel lobby. "She left quite a bit of money to me, and it's allowed me to book a room here for a few days. Then I'll move on to somewhere more permanent. But before I go, it's of the utmost importance that I find the child in the photograph."

"Why?" Baltan asked. "If you want to hire me as a bounty hunter to find your girlfriend's killer, you're out of luck. I'm not in that business anymore."

"Girlfriend's killer? You don't *believe* that ridiculous story, do you?" Selkess asked.

Don't let anything slip. "I believe what the Investigative Department decides based on the evidence they turn up is none of my business anymore."

"That is a disappointment," Selkess said, and he sounded almost genuine. "I am not interested in revenge, Baltan. Against you or anyone. What I want you to do is put your detective skills to work and find this boy. He's missing, and he's my responsibility. I'll spare no expense to bring him home safely."

"You're kidding yourself if you think I'm ever letting you near another child," Baltan spat. "And don't give me that crap about not being interested in revenge. You'd have no reason to contact me otherwise."

"I'm interested in hiring you because you're the best, though I admit the idea of you working for me is... satisfying." Selkess's good eye narrowed. "Regardless of how you feel, he *is* my responsibility, and I need him found."

"Do you have any proof?"

"Evanne left his custody to me. I think you'll find my claims are *perfectly* legal." To prove it, he slid a manila folder across the table and gestured for Baltan to look through it.

It didn't take Baltan's trained eyes long to find the words he was looking for.

In the event of untimely death, or otherwise incapacity to care for children and/or animals the named party SELKESS___ *will be awarded full custody of any and all of the living creatures under the care of the owner of this will.*

He took a moment to be rude and flip through the rest of the pages to make sure all the correct signatures were in place. They were.

Selkess had legal custody of Azzie.

"I don't believe it," Baltan gaped, and he drew his mouth into a hard line. "Alright, so the kid's your responsibility. That doesn't mean *I* have to help you find him. How did you lose him, anyway?"

"It would seem that he wandered off during a storm," Selkess answered coolly. "Or was he fleeing a crime scene? My memory isn't as good as it used to be, though I'm sure I could recall a strong alibi if I was pressed..."

Baltan's fingers twisted the edge of the photo as his grip tightened. "What's his name?" he asked through gritted teeth.

"Pardon?"

"What's his name?" Baltan repeated, slowing for emphasis. "You want me to find him? Give me something to go on. What name will he answer to? How old is he? Where does he like to go? Even the best detectives in the world can't pull answers out of thin air."

"He's fourteen, born at the beginning of Libra. He loves the ocean. He doesn't talk very much." Selkess gave those answers easily enough, but when Baltan didn't let up on his glare he began to look less sure. "He collects bottle caps and other small, shiny objects."

"Stick to what's going to help me find him, not random facts to prove you know him," Baltan cut in. "Like his *name.*"

"Evanne didn't give him one," Selkess conceded.

"Why not?"

"She was a strange woman, and she seemed to think that since he was a boy, a man should name him. Sometimes people do have such strange ideas."

"He lived with her for fourteen years. She had to have called him something." Baltan sat back in his chair, showing he was willing to let it go for now. "What about relatives? Biological parents are always given a chance to step up and claim their own before they're turned over to the court, or in this case, the will."

Something resembling anger flashed across Selkess's face. "If he wants him, he can come forward."

"You must have some idea of who it is, then."

"I suppose I do, but then again, I'm no detective. Though, if you can't figure it out, maybe I overestimated you."

Baltan did the math in his head. If Azzie was fourteen and born in early Libra, he'd have been conceived in late Capricorn, right around the time they'd brought Selkess to justice. There had been plenty of partying throughout the three marine cities at the time; ample opportunities for quick, drunken flings that might result in a half-Azure, half-Eastern child. Not *just* half-Azure. Azzie had one highly unique trait, even among Azures.

Either Eureka's theory was correct and his long-lost brother had defected to the city at least fifteen years ago and never sought out his brother, which seemed more and more unlikely the longer Baltan thought about it, or...

Baltan pushed his mind back to that night, but it was fuzzy at best. He stupidly accepted a few challenges to prove himself to the older investigators and drank way too much. Eureka had sworn off alcohol forever after a celebratory binge left him with a particularly nasty hangover and no memory of what had happened. He'd lost his only good shirt, too.

And it was absolutely possible a woman could have been involved in him losing it.

Don't react, Baltan urged himself. *It's still a theory. It could all be a coincidence. Don't let him gain the upper hand.*

He didn't expect Selkess would back down if Eureka was Azzie's father. If anything, it would make him more eager to get his hands on the kid. No matter how he denied it, revenge absolutely was a motive, but not everything added up. Not yet. He still needed to play into Selkess's game to get more information.

Before either of them had the chance to speak again, a waitress approached with a tray of drinks. She set a red cocktail down in front of Selkess—trying her best not to look directly at him—and handed something that smelled like caramel and had the consistency of cream to Baltan.

"Cigarette?" she offered, holding up a pack.

"No, thank you. I don't smoke, and my friend here quit... six years ago now, isn't it? Besides, those aren't his brand," Selkess answered, his tone confident and breezy as he took a sip of his drink.

The waitress nodded and hurried away, barely restraining herself from running.

Baltan narrowed his eyes, if only to stop them from widening in shock, and set his drink down a little harder than he meant to. The glass clanked harshly on the tabletop.

He figured Selkess had likely been watching them since he'd gotten out of prison, but for at least six *years*? Exactly how long had it been going on? How many people around him and Eureka were spying on them and reporting back to Selkess? How closely were they being watched? He glanced around the lobby again. How many of these people innocently milling about were really Selkess's allies, hiding in plain sight?

Selkess stirred his drink. "Come now, don't make me drink alone. I would think you'd have had quite enough of that by now."

"I've had enough, alright!" Baltan snapped. "Stalking is a crime, Selkess. I'll have you reported as soon as I can get to a phone."

"With mountains of evidence, too, I'm sure," Selkess chortled. "One conversation is enough to convict a man, is it?" He drained his glass, head tilted back slightly to expose the grizzled scars on his neck again. "Without much to go on, I'm afraid the Investigative Department won't be able to prioritize your complaint. After all, there *is* a dangerous killer on the loose..."

Baltan glared, not bothering to hide his animosity anymore. "I'm well aware."

"Then I sincerely hope you will help me find the boy," Selkess pushed. "If only to avoid more 'unfortunate incidents.'"

"How do you mean?"

"It's just a feeling I have, that my having custody of this child will prevent any ill fortune from falling on certain individuals. Like Eureka, for instance. Or yourself." He tilted his head, angling the stitched eye away from Baltan. The disappearance of that ever-opened eye made Baltan's chest feel lighter, though his threat doubled the pressure. "These little feelings I have usually end up being correct, of course. Otherwise I wouldn't bother with them. And this boy... I have a *strong* feeling about him. He's gifted, but disturbed. He could use the guidance of someone who understands him."

Unease slithered up Baltan's spine. *Disturbed.* Did Selkess know something about Azzie that he didn't? It was true he couldn't trust Selkess, but that didn't automatically mean Azzie was completely harmless either. Anyone could snap under the right circumstances, and with all they'd been able to piece together about his life so far, it wouldn't be far-fetched if Azzie did lose it someday.

"Someone like you?" Baltan barked out a laugh while he was still able and brushed an imaginary speck of dust from his shoulder. "I think we're done here. Thank you for the drink. My answer is *no*."

The room darkened. A cloud must have moved in front of the sun, Baltan reasoned. It definitely didn't have anything to do with the glower that flickered across Selkess's face. "What a shame. Do give my regards to Eureka, then. And Tolleu."

Baltan frowned. "Who?"

"Tolleu. You asked what his name was. That's the name I would have given him." Selkess took a quick peek over his shoulder to flag down the nearest waitress. "He reminds me of my son. And while that life may be behind me now, I had hoped to make a fresh start with him."

"We don't always get what we want."

"All the same, my regards."

Baltan stood. "You know, I've got a feeling, too."

"Do tell," Selkess leered.

"Come near me or Eureka, and your next 'feeling' is going to be a bullet in your head."

Baltan kept a brisk pace all the way to the bus stop.

Selkess wanted to take Azzie into his custody and he had a legal claim to that. Fighting it would require proving Eureka was his father, or potentially his uncle, but Eureka was one of a pair of *identical* twins. His DNA would match either way.

That presented a whole other can of emotional worms Baltan didn't want to open.

And if they won the custody battle, they'd still have to turn around and prove Azzie wasn't a killer. Then they'd have to fight for the rest of their lives to keep him, knowing they were surrounded by a network of insanity watching their every move.

Azzie reminds Selkess of his son, Baltan thought. There were dots to connect there. If Selkess killed his son, which seemed likely, then his criminal record didn't start in Marina Omega.

He needed to figure out what exactly Selkess was planning, and there was no better place to start than the beginning. According to his record, he had come from one of the tribes: Illdresil Gera, some distance to the north. Mystery and myth veiled the tribe as much as the fog that protected it from view.

Baltan took a deep breath and let it out slowly.

Maybe he should have taken a cigarette after all.

Once the bus came, Baltan took a seat in the back and rested his forehead against the cool glass. He could feel a headache coming on from the stress even as his thoughts gradually shifted away from the encounter, toward what he should tell Eureka, and then to home in general.

He wished he could pretend that he was coming back from a bar or the shooting range. That the past few days had all been a weird dream. That he would open his eyes and find himself in bed with a hangover instead of leaning on a bus window and feeling every bump it passed over. That everything was normal.

Was 'normal' something he would ever know again?

IX

Azzie kept his ears up to catch the sound of Baltan's footsteps as he walked away into certain danger. He didn't know who this 'Selkess' person was, but he sounded like one of the Bad people Evanne warned him about.

So they were real after all. Azzie must have gotten lucky enough to find good people before he came across one of the Bad ones.

He looked to Eureka, who was staring a hole through the door. He kept clenching and unclenching his hands and shifting on his feet. Azzie knew he probably wanted more than anything to follow after Baltan and make sure he was safe.

He wasn't so sure about having a 'fun' day. They would be too worried about Baltan for that.

"I suppose we ought to get ready to go," Eureka said at last. "First things first, we need to make sure you're alright to go outside. It shouldn't take more than a moment, but I will need you to take the sweater off. Is that okay?"

Azzie nodded and followed Eureka upstairs to the bathroom. Eureka tapped the countertop and Azzie hopped up, taking a seat and removing the sweater. His back was to the mirror, so he couldn't get a clear look at what Eureka was worried about, but when he glanced down he did see a raised section of raw-looking skin that startled him into a yelp.

Why is that there? he thought in a panic. *Did the Prophet do that to me? Why?*

Eureka steadied him with a hand on his shoulder. "It's okay. Trust me, it looks worse than it is. The cuts aren't infected." He leaned closer, examining the wound. "They're actually healing quite nicely. Better than I expected, even. But it is going to leave a permanent scar. Fortunately it shouldn't be hard to hide, as long as you don't wear any open-collar shirts."

He thought that might be a joke, but he didn't get it.

Eureka was quiet for a moment, probably trying to think of the right thing to say before continuing. "Where I'm from, scars are a badge of pride and honor. Every scar is evidence of something you've survived, and proof of your strength and willpower. If you showed this to your agemates in Kwoltan Gera, they'd all admire you for overcoming such an ordeal. Some might even be jealous."

Azzie tentatively reached up to touch the jagged scar running down his face. Eureka winced when his fingers made contact and his eyes clouded with sadness. "Not this one, I'm afraid. No one would admire this scar. But yours won't be like this. The cuts on your chest are a lot neater. They'll probably be thin lines you can hide with makeup, if you want."

If scars were something to be proud of, why would he want to hide them, and why wasn't Eureka proud of his most noticeable scar?

He must have gotten that one in some embarrassing way, Azzie thought.

Eureka opened the medicine cabinet and removed a bottle of clear liquid and a cotton swab. "This might sting a little, but it will help make sure your cuts stay clean and heal the way they're supposed to." He soaked the cotton swab in the solution and carefully dabbed the cuts with it. Azzie bit his lower lip to contain a hiss as they pricked with needle-like pain, but it was over in a few moments. "There you go. You're a good patient," Eureka said, handing the sweater back to him. "I suppose we'll need to find something that fits you a little better for now, if you're going to go outside…"

He helped Azzie off the counter and walked into Baltan's room. Azzie stayed in the doorway and watched as he opened the closet.

"We won't tell Baltan about this, okay?" Eureka said to him over his shoulder, searching through the hanging row of shirts to find something that would fit Azzie well enough. Baltan was closer to his size than Eureka, but he was still a little bigger than Azzie.

Eureka scoffed, "How does one person own so many black clothes? Wait, here's a gray one—oh, no, it's just faded."

The pants and long-sleeved shirt that Eureka picked out of Baltan's wardrobe were more or less the right size. A belt kept the pants from falling off altogether, even if the hems dragged along the floor whenever Azzie took an awkward step in Baltan's boots.

"I'm sure you'll feel a lot better after we get you something that fits right," Eureka said. "Baltan said not to go too crazy, but we'll see where the day takes us."

Azzie followed him to his room, and Eureka let him pick out what clothes he would wear that day. He tugged on the sand-brown pants and a purple sweater with orange rectangles, then knelt down so he was eye-level with Azzie.

"I understand this might be a little frightening for you. Remember, as long as I'm with you, nothing and no one can hurt you, and you can hold onto my hand if you have to. Okay?"

Azzie flicked his ears a few times to show that he understood. He really wanted to *say* so, but he had the feeling that if he opened his mouth, nothing would come out. Especially after seeing the cuts on his chest.

I'll get my voice back soon, he thought. *Then I can help Eureka and Baltan, somehow.* He'd start with telling them the Prophet had sent him to find Eureka, but he didn't know for sure how that would help, since he didn't know why. Maybe Eureka would know who he was talking about and be able to go further in the investigation with that knowledge.

"We'd better get going. The bus is pretty frequent on work days, but we still don't want to miss it."

He opened the door and stepped through first, giving Azzie the courage to follow after. The clouds were beginning to break as the storm passed, littering the street with patches of weak sunlight.

Dingy buildings stretched away from the ground, all clustered together so tightly there was almost no space left between them. Aside from the few bright flowers people had placed on their doorsteps, the world was a mix of gray and brown. The blue spots in the sky were so far away they might as well belong to another world.

Eureka led him slowly down the street, and Azzie stayed close to make sure the giant man took up most of his vision. The world was less scary when he could only see it around Eureka.

They came to a place where another road cut across their path and Azzie peeked to the side to see more dull, brown-and-gray buildings. Eureka stood at the corner which, though faded, had been painted blue.

There was one thing on the street that was different. It looked like a large beetle, but it had circles instead of legs. Azzie ducked behind Eureka, then tugged at his sweater and pointed to it.

"Hm? Oh, that's an auto. A bus is kind of like that, but bigger."

Azzie squinted at it. Were they supposed to sit on top of it? How did something so heavy-looking move?

They were at the corner for only a few moments before something definitely alive approached them. It was small, fuzzy, orange, had pointed ears, and chirruped in greeting as it trotted up to Eureka.

"Ah," he waved a hand at it, "No, Fire, not right now. No food."

Without pausing, Fire jumped onto Eureka's leg and started to climb. Despite wincing, he laughed as he removed the animal with one hand. He held it up in front of Azzie, and Fire slowly blinked its big, amber eyes at him. "Fire is one of the friendliest cats on the block, probably because I handled him so much as a kitten."

So *this* was a cat. Fire wasn't at all what Azzie thought a cat would be based on Evanne's descriptions. He didn't see any mats or bugs in Fire's fluffy fur, and he didn't have glowing red eyes or bloody talons either.

"You can pet him." Eureka carefully held the cat closer. Azzie tightened his grip on Eureka's sweater with one hand and reached for the cat with the other, letting his fingers briefly brush against a tuft of orange fur. Fire lifted his head with a purr and bumped his nose against his palm.

Azzie got so caught up in petting the cat, he hardly noticed when Eureka set him down and he had to kneel to keep stroking Fire's head and chin.

A deep growl made Fire dash away, and Azzie's ears flattened in alarm. A *much* bigger auto was rumbling down the street, and before he could process it the hulking beast spluttered to a stop. An acrid tang filled the air and he coughed. Azzie had to squeeze Eureka's hand to keep himself from running back to their house, if he could even find it.

A squeal split the air and doors opened on the side of the bus. Eureka patted his head reassuringly and helped him up the first step.

The bus was cramped and too warm despite the mild chill outside. Everyone on board—nearly every seat filled;

where were they all going, where did they all come from?—
had dull expressions and tired eyes. They groaned and shook
when they sat down, not lifting their heads as Eureka and
Azzie pressed through between the rows of crowded seats.
Most of them had blue skin like Eureka's, yet they were nothing like him. He was the ocean; they were dirty puddles on the
side of the run-down street.

Eureka found a seat for them near the back and let
Azzie sit by the window. He promised he didn't have to look
out if he didn't want to and put an arm around him so he could
hide.

"I'm sorry if this is too much," Eureka said quietly.
"We won't stay any longer than we have to if you're uncomfortable."

I want *to stay out,* Azzie thought. *I want to be brave
enough to handle this.*

But he wasn't. There was too much *new* everywhere.
And the people—how was it possible for them all to look so
defeated? Was it because they were Bad? How was he going
to help them all be good?

According to Eureka the bus ride wouldn't actually
take long. They were going uptown, not all the way to another
city. Azzie didn't know what made 'uptown' different from
the rest of it, except that the clothing store was there. If there
were other cities, they must be very far away.

In the span of time it took the bus to make five stops,
Azzie had seen more than he'd ever imagined possible. It
clanked through street after street and row after row of houses, letting some people off and some people on. Before long
there was an entirely different group of people on board than
when he and Eureka started. And there were even *more* outside, some walking, some driving their own autos. Eventually
the bus got onto a bigger street that was full of autos, all of
them rushing by with people inside.

All those houses had to have at least one person living
in them, and Azzie had counted one hundred not long after
they left their house.

The world was so big, which might be just right for someone as strong as Eureka, but Azzie was afraid it would swallow him up. He squeezed Eureka's hand tightly and hid his eyes behind his sleeve.

When the bus stopped, they were in a whole new world that was much more colorful and shapely than the hive of gray blocks they'd come from. Golden fountains sculpted in the shapes of large animals that Azzie didn't have names for watered vibrant flowers as big as his head. The fronts of the buildings were see-through to show off the items for sale inside. Sunlight gleamed off the glass and brightened the whole street. It was almost as if there was a fog hanging over Eureka and Baltan's neighborhood that was lifted here, where people who looked like Baltan walked like breezes, rushing from one place to the next.

And there were people *everywhere*. Dozens of them were walking around, and swarms came in and out of the shops. He was starting to accept there were more of them than he would ever know, but Azzie still kept hold of Eureka's hand in fear that one of those gusts of people might separate them and leave him stranded in this strange place.

"This is the Eirden shopping center," Eureka explained. "It's a little fancier than the places I normally go to, but we should be able to find some nice clothes for you here."

And it's closer to Baltan, Azzie thought. He hadn't forgotten that part of their discussion.

Eureka looked around to get his bearings before heading for one of the stores at the end of the street. Azzie followed behind him, placing his feet exactly where Eureka's had been. There was less risk of getting bumped into that way. Everyone took notice of Eureka as he passed by. A few gave a respectful nod or a polite smile, but all of them were quick to get out of his way. Even the few blue people in the crowd took wide paths around him.

Eureka glanced back at Azzie, who gave him a questioning look. "It's unusual to see a tribe-born Azure in a city like this," he explained quietly. "Those others grew up with the city. And there's nothing wrong with that! But even after all these years, I'm still newer than they are. It took me a long time to adjust, so I probably stick out." He glanced down. "That or Baltan has a point about my sweaters, but I don't care either way!"

Azzie lifted his ears. If Eureka could learn how to survive in the city after coming from somewhere totally different, after feeling so out of place and lost, then so could he. Maybe.

He wasn't ready quite yet, though, and he kept his eyes fixed on Eureka as they moved. If he looked around too much more he would be overwhelmed.

Being inside the clothing store was more difficult than being in the street. Everything was cramped and crowded together by display racks, and there were more people moving in the tight space. Azzie desperately wanted to go back outside almost as soon as they entered. He grabbed Eureka's forearm with both hands and his ears flattened again.

Eureka crouched down, cupping a hand around one of Azzie's ears to block out the noise. "It's okay. I'm right here." When Azzie dared to make eye contact, he asked, "Do you want to go home?"

Azzie swallowed and shook his head. *Be brave!*

"Alright." Eureka ruffled his hair gently. "Remember, you can let me know if it's too much at any time, and I'll find us a way home right then. You don't have to force yourself."

Azzie continued to cling to Eureka's arm, but he was at least able to walk. Eureka guided him through the gaggles of people who didn't get out of the way this time, moving carefully to make sure Azzie didn't get knocked into anything along the way.

Despite the horde of people near the doors, the area for Azzie's age group was totally empty.

"Most kids your age aren't back from school yet," Eureka said. "I suppose we should—" He sighed. "Let's pick some things out. You'll need socks, underwear, a few pairs of pants, warm shirts, and a coat."

Azzie looked around, waiting for Eureka to grab things and hold them up to him to see if they'd fit, the way the other parents were doing with their kids. Instead Eureka's eyes were on him, waiting for him to move.

I get to choose, Azzie realized, looking around at the different shirts that were stacked on shelves beside them. His eyes rested on a black one and he smiled a little. What if he chose all black clothes, like Baltan? Or if he picked the most colorful things, like Eureka?

He let the thought go. It would be funny, but he didn't like the idea of wearing only one kind of clothing. Not when he got to pick anything he wanted.

Azzie scanned the racks near them, then began to edge closer to another aisle. Eureka stayed where he was, standing head and shoulders over the racks, never out of sight. Gradually Azzie moved away from the shirts and toward the pants, then the socks and underwear, then the shoes. Eureka didn't follow closely, but did move so he could see Azzie no matter where he went.

Feeling more confident, Azzie returned to where they'd began and examined the shirts, paying attention to how they looked next to each other. He wandered back and forth between the rows, trying to get a good sense of what he had to choose from, occasionally looking back to make sure Eureka was still there. He would smile reassuringly and maybe wave, but never made a move to follow Azzie unless he motioned for him to come closer.

Azzie was starting to get the hang of being in a store by the time they were done picking out clothes. He darted behind Eureka when people walked toward them, but he didn't mind very much when they were standing still. And if he did get nervous, he could touch Eureka's hand.

It was hard to be nervous when he was so excited about his new clothes. He'd struck the perfect middle-ground: dark pants, a dark jacket, and shirts that were either brightly colored or black with large splashes of color.

As soon as they left the store, Eureka found a public restroom where Azzie could change into one of the new outfits. He hadn't minded wearing Baltan's clothes, but being in clothes that actually fit, that *he'd* chosen, felt better than he could have ever believed.

He smiled from ear to ear and held Eureka's hand loosely as they headed to a different store. They must have finished at the clothing store earlier than Eureka had expected. They were supposed to be out of the house until Baltan came back, but the sun had barely moved in the sky.

Eureka started for a store that was painted bright pink and green. One side of the window display was filled with things that looked like Fire, but didn't move or blink their shiny eyes. Azzie was pretty sure they weren't alive. The other side had a collection of wooden people moving on strings. Azzie covered his ears at the dull buzzing noise they made.

"You might be too old for some of these things, but—"

Azzie could barely hear him over the buzzing, which got louder and louder the closer they got to the door. He grabbed onto Eureka's arm to try to stop him from going further.

The moment he moved his hands away from his ears, the low buzzing became an intense roar. It wasn't just the grinding of the wood people anymore. He had blocked out the noise of the crowds, but now it hit him all at once: the click-clack of footsteps, the droning of conversations broken up by shouts and bursts of laughter, the roar of buses coming and going.

And worst of all, from inside the pink-and-green store, the shrill shriek of a screaming child.

Azzie clung to Eureka, burying his face into the softer, squishier part of his waist.

The next thing he knew, they were in the back corner of a different, quieter shop. The noise from the streets faded to a subdued hum. Azzie was in Eureka's arms. He must have carried him there.

Once Azzie could hear again and slowed his breathing, Eureka set him down and patted his head to comfort him.

Before he could even ask if he wanted to go home, Azzie pushed the panic aside and looked around at the store. *I can do this. I want to look around.*

The shop was smaller than the others, and almost empty. Azzie stayed near Eureka until he felt completely alright again, then browsed freely. He never left Eureka's sight, but there were so many interesting books on the shelves he hardly needed to move. He couldn't read any of them, but the dots and dashes on the pages were fun to trace with his finger.

Once he was done looking around he rejoined Eureka, who was flipping through a collection of thin cardboard boxes. With a triumphant, "Aha!" he pulled one of the cases free.

"This album is the new set of *The Night Train*," he said, showing Azzie the cover. "With this, we can listen to the newest episodes any time we want. I think there are a few on here that haven't even aired yet!"

Azzie looked at the artwork on the cover. Tan faces were carved out of the black background, all of them wearing either smart or shocked expressions. There were words as well, but Azzie couldn't tell what they were, so he assumed the sharp lines spelled out *The Night Train*.

"I bet Baltan will be glad to have this. He loves listening to them over again. You'll probably have them memorized before too long!" Eureka laughed, tucking the album under his arm. "Are there any radio shows you like? We can see if they have recordings."

Azzie shook his head. Evanne had occasionally listened to music, but he didn't know any of it by name.

With a determined look on his face, Eureka showed him to another selection of albums and put a pair of ear muffs over his head. They pushed his ears back so the insides of the pads were closer to the holes.

"Let's find something, then. There's all kinds of music here."

Azzie's eyes followed the wire that connected the ear muffs to a machine. Eureka fiddled with it for a moment, and he jumped when music started playing in his ears. The sound drowned out everything else. He made sure he knew where Eureka was, then closed his eyes and let his mind drift away for a moment. He imagined he was floating, the music gently pushing him along. Whenever the song changed, he pretended the current had chnged to take him in a new direction.

Azzie liked all of it more or less, mostly the melodious rising and falling sounds that Eureka told him were made by a violin, but only the sound of ocean waves brought him out of his daydreams. He tugged Eureka's sleeve and squealed, "Yes!"

At first Azzie thought he'd said something wrong when a look of pure surprise passed over Eureka's face, but it was almost immediately replaced with a warm smile. "You like that one?"

Azzie nodded. Eureka found the right album and put it together with *The Night Train* and an album of violin music.

"I think that's all we should get here for now," he said, showing Azzie the covers again. "This one is *Classical Music Collection Number Eight*—" it had pictures of musical instruments in different colors against a blue background, "— and this one is *Sounds of Nature: Water*." That one was all blue, with a few light ripples spreading across it. "When you want to listen to one, let me or Baltan know."

Oh, right. Baltan.

Eureka was always thinking of Baltan, but Azzie forgot about him as soon as he started listening to the music.

Just like he forgot about Evanne.

The albums would be a nice surprise. Azzie gestured that he wanted to carry them after Eureka paid for them and they were back out in the plaza again.

Instead of going anywhere else, Eureka asked, "You like the ocean, don't you?"

Azzie bounced on his heels and flicked his ears up to say yes. He didn't think he could muster another word for a while. He hadn't *meant* to say anything earlier; the word had come out all on its own.

"Why don't we go see it later?"

His eyes widened. Were they really close enough to the ocean to go there?

Eureka lifted the bags of clothing and the albums. "After we drop these off at the house, we should all go. It's been ages since Baltan and I went out anywhere, and I'm sure the beach is lovely after that storm. This late in the year it'll be quiet, too."

Azzie's memories of his first visit to the ocean were too hazy to picture it, but he trusted Eureka's word. He looked up. Would the ocean be as blue as the sky, or more greenish, like his eyes? Would the waves be big or small? Would they sound like the album up close? He was so excited he nearly stumbled over a loose cobblestone on the path as Eureka began moving again. His stomach grumbled when he bounded forward to keep up, despite having eaten breakfast not very long ago. Over the past few days he'd found himself getting hungry more often, and he wondered if it was because of Eureka's cooking or because he knew he could eat more if he wanted.

"Let's head back home and get you some lunch. I doubt Baltan would have stayed out for very long," Eureka said, leading Azzie back to a blue corner where a bus would soon appear.

He didn't feel as scared getting on the bus a second time, and Azzie watched everything as it passed by the window. The world was so much bigger than he'd ever known, and he wanted to see as much of it as he could.

One roast tomato sandwich and a glass of citrus juice later, Azzie was curled up in his blanket on the couch again, listening to the sounds of rain and the ocean through the radio. He was amazed he could rest at all, as thrilled as he was about seeing the ocean. Listening to it was holding him over until Baltan came home.

It crossed his mind that they probably wouldn't really go to the ocean once Baltan came back. He'd be tired. He and Eureka would have important things to talk about. Eureka would probably forget all about even bringing it up, and if Azzie tried to ask he'd be met with a swift and brutal, "No."

He focused on the rhythm of the waves crashing over each other and tried to imagine the ocean instead. He remembered it was big, and cold, and wet. He remembered it wrapping around his calves and pulling him closer.

At the moment Eureka was quietly reading a book, sweeping his right foot against the carpet in time to the album. Like a wave.

Azzie stretched out his own foot and gently tapped Eureka's leg with the tip of his toe. When he received no reaction, he did it again, holding it there this time. Eureka flipped the page of his book absently.

He stretched out his foot even more, pushing Eureka's leg slightly. The longer he went without reacting, the more he pushed. Eventually Azzie couldn't press any harder, and he slowly uncurled and shifted so he could get into a better position.

Once he abandoned the safety of his blanket, Eureka reached out and tapped Azzie's nose with one finger. He squeaked and covered his nose with his hands, eyes screwed shut, only to peek them open again when he realized it hadn't hurt at all. Eureka was smiling, a spark of humor in his eyes.

Azzie wasn't sure how to respond. He flicked one ear, then the other. He didn't know if it was okay for him to attack back, but he didn't want to curl up and make Eureka think he'd taken the playful gesture the wrong way.

A moment later he didn't have to worry about it. The door opened.

Baltan was back.

X

Even when he was standing in the doorway, Baltan still didn't feel like he was home. He couldn't help scanning the room for bugs and wires, wondering how closely they were being monitored. The phone would have to go, which he didn't lament, but he was a little more reluctant get rid of the computer. Even though he rarely used it anymore, owning a computer had once been a big deal to him, a sign that he was a *true* professional investigator making his way in the world. But, if it had been tapped somehow, it couldn't stay.

He decided not to think too hard about *how* it had been tapped. If Selkess's followers had done it once, they could do it again. Debugging wasn't an option.

"I need to talk to you," he said to Eureka as soon as he walked in.

"I know," Eureka answered, already closing the distance between them. He glanced at Azzie, who was curling into a ball on the couch and clutching the blanket tightly. "Should we talk about this in the bedroom?"

Baltan wondered if the city excursion hadn't gone well for them, but he'd have to ask about that later. "Yes, definitely." He knew Azzie was listening and he didn't want the poor kid to be even more traumatized by anything he had to say. Part of him was worried he might confirm some of what Selkess had said before he had a chance to fully explain it.

Behind the safety of the closed door, Eureka asked, "How bad was it?"

"*Bad*," Baltan seethed. "He's trying to act like he's not insane, but I don't trust a person who sewed one of their own eyes open to give an accurate assessment of their mental state."

Eureka opened and closed his mouth a few times, trying to come up with something to say before settling on, "He did *what*?"

"At least he gave me some useful information," Baltan went on, trying to relay it all in as few words as possible. "He's been watching us for a long time. He knows things about me that he shouldn't, so that means he knows things about you, too. And he knows we have Azzie, who is apparently fourteen—"

"*Fourteen*?"

"—recently fourteen. Evanne was one of Selkess's followers. She transferred her guardianship of Azzie to him in her will, and he's pretty desperate to get his hands on the kid."

Eureka tried not to look like that news made him want to break things, and Baltan admired him for that. He was probably doing a better job of it than Baltan was, because he definitely *felt* like he wanted to break things. Maybe he should have actually gone to the shooting range after the meeting.

"Did he say anything else? He can't have brought that up without intending to do something with it, and somehow I doubt he wants to take us to family court."

"Not much about Azzie, I'm afraid. And I didn't want to push it too far, since we don't know what he's up to yet." Baltan folded his arms, dropped them at his sides, and folded them again. "He had a son, apparently. I think it's safe to put the emphasis on *had*. And he's determined to have Azzie now to, I don't know, make up for killing his last one?"

A low growl rumbled through Eureka's words. "When and where? That has to be significant. If we can dig up more information on his past, maybe it'll lead us to some idea of where he's going. He might go back to wherever he lived with his son to commit another massacre."

"I think you'd know better than I would," Baltan said. "I don't trust using our computer to do more research given the amount of information he has on us already. I don't like someone looking over my shoulder while I work." He reluctantly met Eureka's eyes. "The last time I checked his public record, it said he came from Illdresil Gera. I suggest we start there."

Eureka's face hardened. "That won't be easy."

"It's just a tribe village."

"*Just* a tribe village?" Eureka retorted.

"It's on the map, which means we can get there somehow," Baltan said with a shrug. "We've cracked tougher nuts, I'm sure. I mean, you can still speak the language fluently, and I'm decent enough with it, so that won't be a problem. This is going to be the easiest part of this investigation."

"You're very wrong about that." Eureka flexed his fingers, examining the sharp claws. "Illdresil Gera has survived on reclusion from the rest of civilization for decades now. Their kind haven't been seen outside of their village since... well, since Selkess. They aren't going to like strangers walking in, *especially* not an Easterner and a Kwoltan Gera Azure."

Baltan tensed. Eureka hadn't raised his voice, but he could tell with every word how unhappy he was. Then again, he didn't expect Eureka would smile again until they found a way to take legal custody of Azzie away from Selkess.

The look of disappointment and frustration was too much, and Baltan broke eye contact first. "We'll figure something out. We always do."

"I'll do my best," Eureka offered, easing his shoulders a little.

"I know it won't be easy. I didn't mean to imply that it would be."

Eureka shifted his shoulders, getting rid of any remaining stiffness. "I know you didn't mean anything by it, but it's a sore subject. Not all Azure tribes are the same, and I don't know a lot about Illdresil Gera, other than the stories my grandparents used to tell me."

Which could be a problem in this case, Baltan thought. *Reclusive, closely guarded, and not friendly.*

"Any chance we can use a disguise?" he asked. Eureka had managed to blend in seamlessly with their targets a few times before when dealing with Azure gangs.

"None," Eureka answered, almost laughing. Almost. "I'm a head taller and twice as wide as any Illdresil Gera Azure."

"We will still need to go there, possibly to warn them if nothing else," Baltan said. "It's just a matter of figuring out how we can get in without being chased off."

"Or chasing them off," Eureka added.

"I'll have to do some research at the library. And we should be careful what we say on the phone if we use it again before this is over. I don't know exactly what he's using to monitor us, or who."

Eureka placed a hand on his shoulder. "Don't let it make you too paranoid. There are still good people out there who we can trust."

Those incompetent morons at the Investigative Department, you mean? Baltan thought.

At least they were starting to form a clear plan of action. Do research on Illdresil Gera, figure out the best way to get there, and go. As tedious as that would be, at least they'd be getting out of the city for a while to dodge Selkess and his followers. If it was going to be hard for Baltan and Eureka to get in, then it would be just as hard for them, too. Baltan couldn't imagine Selkess left Illdresil Gera on good terms.

"What do we do with Azzie in the meantime?"

"Take him with us," Baltan shrugged, giving Eureka the answer he knew he would like best. "Selkess wants him for nefarious purposes. Right now the safest place in the world for him is wherever we are, even if that happens to be marching up to the door of an Azure village that isn't going to like us being there."

"They probably won't be looking for a fight," Eureka said. "They'll defend themselves, but they won't attack us first unless they feel like we're a legitimate threat. As long as we keep a respectful distance, we should be okay. But that's not really the same thing as getting them to talk to us."

Baltan tried to think up a more tactful icebreaker than, *Hey, did someone from your village go crazy and kill a bunch of kids? Sorry about that, but can you help us stop him from doing it again?*

"It does still bother me that he mentioned having a son, specifically," Eureka said.

"Possibly to goad us into checking out Illdresil Gera. You don't think it's a trap, do you?"

"I think it's concerning, that's all." Eureka shook his head. "Then again, the idea of him being a parent at all is concerning. I'm sure no judge would want to hand Azzie over to him, but if Selkess passed his psych evaluation, there isn't a strong enough legal reason to designate Azzie as a ward of the state instead. We don't exactly have any claim to Azzie ourselves at this point."

"We might," Baltan pointed out. "*You* might."

"Baltan—"

"I'm not saying it just because!" Baltan was too tired to hold it back any longer. "Selkess brought up the possibility too, and I don't believe that's a coincidence. I don't think your brother left the tribe, and neither do you."

"You really think...?" Eureka asked, trying and failing to mask his hopefulness. He rubbed his palms together, and Baltan saw his hands were shaking. "I'm not... I mean, when it comes to women, I've, ah... never had much luck. With this face? No. It's not—it can't be. He can't be mine."

"You had a night of heavy drinking right around the time he would've been conceived." Baltan wanted to reach out to Eureka, take his hands and steady them, but he refrained. He couldn't, not now. It was too intimate. "It's not impossible, at any rate."

"I…" Eureka looked around the room, searching for answers. "I don't know."

Stone-faced, Baltan pointed out, "Supposing he is your brother's kid, you two are identical twins, aren't you? So that gives you a DNA match. Unless his mom comes forward and says your brother is the father instead—which would still make you his uncle and give you at least some claim over Selkess—then you absolutely could say you're his father and the courts would have to believe it based on medical evidence."

Baltan shifted his weight from one foot to the other. He could see the logical arguments weren't working, but he didn't want to resort to the emotional ones. "I don't know why you're so against the idea. Haven't you always wanted a family?" he pressed, trying desperately to not sound bitter.

It was impossible.

"I wanted to *be there* for my family!" Eureka focused his gaze rigidly on a discolored patch of carpet the way he always did when he was trying not to cry. "If Azzie is my son, it means that I missed fourteen years of his life! Fourteen years where I could have taken care of him. Instead he went through… through who knows what kind of abuse! He can barely talk now, let alone read or write or—" He stopped to take a shuddering breath, "Baltan, everything is going to be so *hard* for him! And all the while, I could have done something about it. But I didn't."

Baltan reached up and guided Eureka's chin so they were facing each other again. "Stop it. You didn't know."

"But I should have!" Eureka's voice cracked. "I'm not sure I'm ready for this. I'll give Azzie the best life I can now, but if I really am his father, then a good part of this is my fault."

Baltan could tell he wasn't only talking about the years of torment Azzie had endured. If Eureka hadn't been his father, Selkess probably wouldn't have taken an interest in him. Assuming his birth mother was alive and had given him up, he would have grown up in the state system. While that wasn't the best option for a kid it was still a whole lot better than being mistreated by one of Selkess's insane followers.

That reinforced the idea that he *was* Azzie's father in Baltan's mind, but he decided to let it go for the time being. Eureka needed time to accept it. There was no need to beat it in.

"Do we tell Azzie?" Baltan asked.

Worry clouded Eureka's features. "Not yet. Life is already confusing enough for him right now. Let's let him adjust a little more and once things calm down we'll have a talk with him about the possibility."

Nervous he'll resent you for not being around? Baltan wondered.

"That sounds like the best plan. I'm sure he'll be happy about it, but we can wait for now." He waited for Eureka to smile. When he didn't, he asked, "How awful is the clothing you got for him?" He hadn't gotten a good look thanks to the blanket.

"Not half bad," Eureka said after taking a brief pause to collect himself.

"And the other half?"

"You'll see," he answered flatly. "Soon, in fact. I was thinking a trip to the ocean would do us all some good. He'll love it, and you need a break before you pick up your research again."

"I don't need a—"

"You had to talk to Selkess today. You need a longer break than you're getting."

Baltan considered it. How long had it been since he'd last gone to the beach? Living with it nearby for so long had done little to endear it to him. It was always there, and he always figured he'd have another day to go whenever it came up.

Then he thought of Azzie and how he had been locked up inside for most, if not *all*, of his life. He could put up with spending an afternoon at the beach to give the kid a handful of good memories.

The sun was beginning to set, dyeing the clear sky bright shades of red and orange. Despite the cool breeze rolling over the waves and onto the beach, Azzie didn't slow down one bit once his feet touched the sand. He wasn't the best at running and stumbled a few times as he sank into the damp grit, but he got right back up and kept rushing around the shoreline to chase after gulls and the tide.

Baltan fluffed his coat and folded it over his chest. The zipper had broken a few years back, but he liked it too much to get rid of it.

Azzie picked something up and ran back to where Eureka and Baltan were standing, near the seawall that elevated the city and protected it from floods. He waved his closed fist excitedly before holding it out to Baltan, and after a nudge from Eureka he held out his own hand.

A wet, sand-covered starfish fell into his palm. He cringed internally at the sensation before forcing a smile. "Thanks, kid. It's great. I love dead sea creatures."

Azzie smiled and raced back toward the waves. Baltan started to lower his hand to drop the starfish before Eureka muttered, "Don't you dare."

"But it's…" Baltan squirmed, "I don't think it's dead."

Eureka took it from him. "I'll hold onto it, then. It's not going to bite you."

Azzie came racing back with another gift, and Baltan held out his hand, wondering if this time it was going to be a crab.

A sand-crusted bottle cap bounced onto his fingers and he made a fist to keep it from falling. Then he flipped it over to see which brand it was and nodded to Azzie. "Hagen's Grape Cooler, very nice."

Smiling even more brightly than before, Azzie darted away again.

"Oh, a sea star is too icky for you, but you'll accept a grungy old bottle cap?" Eureka teased.

"Hush. We're bonding."

Baltan watched as Azzie scoured the beach, no doubt looking for more bottle caps. He hadn't given anything to Eureka, and Baltan wondered if that was because they'd already connected. Azzie might be trying to please him because he wasn't sure how Baltan felt about him yet. In an abusive home, his survival probably depended on having the favor of his caretaker.

There could be more to it than that, Baltan considered.

He thought back to Azzie's confession. He hadn't had any idea what he was confessing to; he was merely reacting to the guilt and confusion the way an abuse victim would: blaming himself. Baltan had expected that getting him out of that mentality would be a tougher fight. A few days ago the kid cowered at the sight of him. Now he was bringing him gifts and seeking his approval.

The fact that he had given them his trust so rapidly could mean, despite everything, he was an optimistic child making the most of his situation.

Or it could be a sign that his will was so broken he would do anything an adult told him. He might be nothing more than a puppet being manipulated by someone far more sinister. How much did Azzie know about the cult? Was it something Evanne had kept secret from him, or something he'd been raised into?

Baltan didn't believe Azzie was deceiving them, but they needed to be mindful about what they discussed around him.

"Careful!"

Eureka bolted from his side and scooped Azzie out of the way of a sleeper wave. Baltan's eyes naturally followed, only to be briefly blinded by the orange glow of the sun on the horizon. Was the sun really starting to set already?

That meant they had nine days to figure out and thwart Selkess's plans. Nine days until the first night of Capricorn, the winter solstice, and the possible end of all of all of their lives.

Before panic could set in, he heard Azzie laughing. He blinked the sun out of his eyes in time to catch Eureka proudly lifting the child—maybe *his* child—onto his shoulders.

Let him have today. Just for now, just for today, let everything be alright.

XI

A warm hand on his shoulder roused Azzie from his latest dream of diving in and out of ocean waves. He yawned and shifted, tucking his nose into his pillow to see if he could get back to sleep. He was sure the sea had been trying to tell him something important.

"It's time to wake up," Eureka said, giving him a gentle shake. "If you want to eat breakfast, you need to get out of bed and get dressed now."

Excitement jolted him awake. Baltan and Eureka had spent all of the previous day doing research about Illdresil Gera, and Azzie couldn't be more anxious to see what life was like outside the city.

As Azzie understood it, Illdresil Gera was the opposite of the city. There was no ocean, no beach, and thankfully no crowded buildings. They would be going north and east, away from the shore and into the wide fields where farmers grew all the food they ate. Once they went far enough north they would find a cluster of tall hills with waterfalls flowing down into a mist-filled valley. That was where the Illdresil Gera Azures lived, hidden by the mist and fog.

The waterfalls excited him most. He had seen rain, of course, but there was as much difference between rain and a waterfall as there was between the ocean and a puddle.

The people both interested and scared him. According to Eureka and Baltan, they probably wouldn't be very friendly, and Azzie was not to leave their side for a moment in case things took, "a turn for the worse." But he wanted to meet them all the same. Were they good or Bad? Would they act like Eureka, or Baltan, or Evanne, or some other way that he couldn't imagine?

Azzie got up after Eureka left the room, changing out of his pajamas and stuffing them into his suitcase. They were going to be gone for a few days and he hadn't been able to decide what to take with him, so he'd crammed almost everything in. He pulled out the clothes he wanted to wear that day, then forced everything back down into the suitcase and closed it tight.

Baltan spotted him from the couch as he came down the stairs and rolled his eyes in Eureka's direction. "One of *your* shirts today."

Eureka leaned around the corner of the kitchen to see what Azzie had chosen and responded, "No, black stripes means one of yours."

Azzie laughed, a quiet sound that he wasn't sure either of them caught. He'd chosen his clothes to be a mash-up of their styles, but he hadn't anticipated Baltan and Eureka picking up on it. He was glad they had; it was fun to have this little game to themselves.

He sat at the table just as Eureka was setting down the last of the fruit, and he struggled between shoveling it into his mouth as quickly as possible and savoring each bite. He hadn't figured out how to do both yet.

If he ate faster, would they leave faster?

Azzie hurried his breakfast down, but that didn't make Baltan and Eureka speed up. He should have thought of that before he cleaned his plate. There was nothing worse than watching other people eat when he didn't have any food of his own.

Their pace slowed more when they started to talk.

"It's going to take all day to get there," Baltan complained. "And we'll be going through the most boring crop fields possible the whole way."

"Boring is exactly what we should be looking forward to right now," Eureka responded.

Boring was *never* what Azzie was looking forward to. He'd had years and years of boring, broken up with moments of scary and upsetting and painful. But it would be worth it once they got there, and he got to see something so completely new that even Eureka and Baltan had never seen it. They were going all the way to the edge of the world, and Azzie couldn't wait to peek over.

It was going to be dangerous, but Evanne had spent Azzie's whole life telling him how dangerous the world outside their house was, and now that he was in it he was handling himself fine. The dangers were overwhelmed by all the ways he was finding to be happy. Eating delicious food, curling up next to Eureka for a nap, listening to Baltan explain a mystery book or an episode of *The Night Train*, going for a walk to feed the stray cats in the neighborhood, *cats*—there were way more good things than Bad.

Maybe Baltan and Eureka were there to teach him how to be good.

Azzie glanced at Baltan. He was cloudier than normal today, and that made him nervous. Had he done something to make Baltan mad? He knew he had taken his bedroom, but Baltan liked spending time with Eureka so much, wouldn't he have preferred they share a room anyway?

He kept the bottle caps, which was a good sign. Azzie had been tempted to store them away for himself. He missed his old collection, which must still be in Evanne's home somewhere.

That was a sacrifice, wasn't it? He gave up the happiness of collecting the bottle caps to make Baltan like him.

Don't forget what else *you've sacrificed for this.*

Azzie rested a hand over the cuts on his chest, but the stab of guilt he felt was more painful. He ought to miss Evanne more than a handful of colorful tin pieces. She was *dead*. Maybe the fact that he forgot about her so easily was proof he truly was Bad.

He thought of the Prophet's words and a cold, creeping feeling crawled over his back.

I need to do more than have fun, Azzie thought. *I have to figure out how to make the world a better place, and find the Prophet again now that I've found Eureka. He'll know what to do next.*

He wondered if the weight on his shoulders was what characters on *The Night Train* called 'destiny.'

It was an awfully heavy feeling.

The bus ride was long and dull. Azzie was full of excitement at the start, amazed by all the new types of animals and plants... until he saw the same types of animals and plants for almost the entire day, with only a few rest stops to get out and walk around. Even those offered nothing to do but go to the bathroom and then back to the bus.

Eureka and Baltan tried to talk to him about things they read in the newspaper, but his voice had tucked itself away somewhere. He listened and nodded along, unable to actually say anything back. He was too anxious for what was to come. When would they see the hills? When would they get there?

When would they get off of this boring bus?

After the third rest stop they almost had the bus to themselves. Despite that, Baltan and Eureka kept him closer than ever. The Bad person Baltan had gone to meet— Selkess—was out there somewhere.

Azzie hoped he would never meet him. He knew from the way Baltan and Eureka spoke about him that he was terrifying, and he was certain they were trying to make him *less* scary for his sake. He must be the most vile, sneaky, dangerous Bad person to ever live.

That must be why Eureka kept staring at him, and why Baltan wouldn't relax his shoulders even when he was trying to tell a funny story.

Maybe helping Eureka and Baltan stop Selkess was how Azzie would make the world better. He liked the idea of that, standing beside them against the evils of the world and making it a safer and happier place for everyone. Maybe he was supposed to learn how to be an investigator and go into crime-fighting the way they had, solving mysteries and putting the Bad people in jail. It would take a lot of work, but it sounded like something they could do together.

There was only one Eastern man left on the bus with them. Deep wrinkles and dark spots surrounded his bright eyes. A bag full of books sat at his feet, and he looked as if he was barely resisting the urge to strike up a conversation— about the books, if Azzie had to guess. Azzie guessed most everything about this man had to do with the bag of books. If this were an episode of *The Night Train*, the books would be unexpectedly important, and Azzie was trying his best to expect things before they snuck up on him or Eureka or Baltan.

Baltan was definitely expecting something. His suspicious glare was probably all that kept the man silent.

Azzie flicked one of his ears against Eureka's arm. The man didn't seem like a dangerous cult follower to him, and maybe talking to him would be a good idea. If he was going anywhere near Illdresil Gera, he might know more about it. And anything he had to say must be more interesting than sitting there in dull, dull silence.

Eureka took a break from keeping an eye on everything around them to smile at Azzie. "We're almost to the last stop. Then we'll have a bit of a walk."

The friendly tone of his voice invited the old man to speak at last.

"You lot headed to the Azure village?"

Baltan shot back, "Why would it matter to you if we were?"

"Whoa, there," the man said, putting up his calloused hands in defense. "Didn't realize the curiosity of a humble farmer was an offense to you city folk."

"Calm down," Eureka whispered to Baltan. To the old man he said, "We are going that way. Are you?"

"My farm is close by. Name's Turnap. Yours?"

Azzie could almost feel both Eureka and Baltan wonder if they ought to give fake names. That's what detectives on *The Night Train* did sometimes when they weren't sure of someone. But if he was working for Selkess, he'd know already.

"I'm Eureka, this is Baltan, and this is Azurite."

Azzie's ears twitched at the sound of his full name. He liked it a lot even though he'd only heard it a few times. Then again, he had only had it for a few days.

So much had changed, and so quickly. Would changing the world be that fast?

"Nice to meet you all," Turnap said. "But if you react like that to a harmless old man, you won't get far in the village. They'll have a spear at your throat before you know it, and they won't hesitate to cut you up if you give them that attitude."

"We'll have to chance it," Eureka responded while Baltan did a very close impression of Fussy's face when Eureka had tried to give the old tabby chicken instead of tuna.

Turnap regarded them with a trained eye, though what it was trained to see Azzie couldn't know. He must have liked what he saw, though, because he added, "There won't be any chance of getting in after sundown. The night guards attack first and ask questions later."

"So you know them?" Baltan pressed.

"Not personally, not most of them," Turnap answered. His smile made his face crinkle up in the most pleasant way. "But yes, I know most of their names, and I'm on good terms with a few. That might help you if you need to speak to them."

"It would," Eureka said before Baltan could make a remark about not needing anyone's help. "We don't mean any harm to the village and we won't stay long. All we'll do is ask a few questions, then leave."

"I don't know if I can get you that far," Turnap admitted. "There are a few things those Azures are cagey about. How important is this?"

"It's a matter of life and death," Eureka answered.

Turnap frowned. "Sounds like a cagey matter, then, but I'll do what I can."

The conversation ended there until the bus stopped. Turnap picked up his book bag and motioning for the three to follow him once they retrieved their luggage. "My farm's just up the road, about three kilometers as the crow flies. We'll have to go around for a bit, though."

Azzie wanted to ask around *what*. He didn't see anything but black—until his eyes adjusted. Stretched out in front of them wasn't a dark valley and a starless sky, but a towering hill that was barely visible thanks to its own shadow.

Baltan whistled and whispered to Eureka, "I'm starting to get what you meant about this place being secluded."

"It's a little less steep around this side of the hill," Turnap explained, taking the lead. "Still takes some doing to climb up, though, so I hope you aren't against hiking."

Azzie didn't know if he was or wasn't. How far was a kilometer? He was already tired out from the bus ride, and it wouldn't be any easier carrying a bag full of clothing. The cold air stung his chest, and his breath turned to fog in front of his face.

Sacrifice, he reminded himself. They weren't there to have fun or be comfortable, they were there to stop an evil man from doing something horrible.

Azzie could hardly see anything and had no way to tell how far they'd gone, other than the ache in his legs. He was only able to follow Turnap thanks to the moonlight shining off his white hair. Baltan grumbled every now and again and took smaller steps, like he was feeling his way forward with each move, but Eureka's stride was confident as he guided them from behind.

Azzie looked back once and was struck by the eerie glow of light from Eureka's eyes. He wondered if his own looked the same, but he doubted it. If they did, he would be able to see as well as Eureka.

They walked for a lot longer than Azzie thought they should have before Turnap led them up a ridge that wound along the side of the hill.

"Careful, now," he said as he marked out their trail. "It's slippery with moss and wet grass. The stones are slick, but their ridges make good footholds if you can avoid the green bits."

Azzie urged a bit of the previous days' excitement into his legs. They were almost to Turnap's farm, and the next day, they'd be as far into Illdresil Gera as they were allowed. It was difficult to be enthusiastic about something he couldn't see yet, but he let his imagination pick up his feet.

He struggled to make it up the hillside, stumbling once when he lost his footing on a patch of moss. Eureka caught him before he could fall and gently set him on firm ground again. He patted Azzie's back. "Keep going. We must be nearly there by now."

The trail curved and Turnap stopped at a gaping hole in the side of the hill. "You're right. The farm is beyond this tunnel. It's going to be pitch-black, and tight, but keep walking and you'll make it to the other side in no time."

Turnap vanished into the mass of pure black, and Azzie coughed a few times to hide the thumping of his heart.

He didn't want to go into the darkness. He would get lost and it would swallow him up. Wasn't there any other way?

"Let's stay close together," Baltan said, disappearing after Turnap.

Eureka reached a hand up, feeling around the edges of the tunnel. "I'll have to duck. Hopefully it doesn't get much narrower." He nudged Azzie. "I'll be right behind you."

Sacrifice.

Azzie forced his way into the blackness, feeling forward with his hands the way he'd seen Baltan do. He could trail his fingertips along the stone walls when he stretched his arms all the way out to his sides. He whimpered, and Baltan called from ahead, "It slopes down a little here. Don't be scared."

Azzie reached the slant, but Baltan didn't say anything about the roaring, rushing sound from above. He stopped, curling up like a clam closing its shell.

"We must be under a waterfall," Eureka said. "So we're very close. If you keep going, you'll be out soon."

Azzie took a deep breath and a cautious step forward. His foot sank through the dark, jolting him for a moment before cold stone stopped his fall. He whimpered again, reaching back to cling to Eureka's legs. All he could think about was being trapped there in the dark, unable to see the stars or the sea ever again.

Eureka lifted him onto his feet again, but let go as soon as Azzie was standing. He handed him his bag and nudged him forward again. "You can do this. I'm right here, so you don't have to be afraid."

Baltan's voice echoed through the tunnel. "We're outside now! You have to come see this!"

Just try to think of what it will be like, Azzie urged himself, closing his eyes to the dark and pushing forward.

What he saw was far better than anything he could have imagined.

The tunnel opened up above a wide valley surrounded by tall peaks. The sky was more white than black from the swirling clusters of stars, more than Azzie would ever be able to count. A big cottage sat in the valley, and a few large, feathered animals ambled through the fields.

Turnap gestured to where the path continued up the hill. "The village is that way, but as I said, you'd do better to rest up and try your luck in the morning. Odds are good we've already been spotted and their guard will be up. It'll be worse if we try to sneak in at night, and camping on their border is out of the question."

"No need to convince us," Baltan grumbled, casting a look back at Eureka to see if he thought Turnap was trustworthy.

Azzie was close enough to feel Eureka shrug his shoulders.

"Stay close," Eureka whispered to Azzie, and together they followed Turnap down the slope.

XII

The cottage was surprisingly bare despite its size. It had clearly been built for a family, like most farmhouses, but there was little evidence anyone lived there other than Turnap. The front room was sparser than theirs when it came to furniture—just a couch and a table set for one. It was almost colder inside than out, even with Turnap rushing to turn on the lights and the heat.

Baltan and Eureka took their seats on the couch, keeping a half-conscious Azzie between them. The kid hardly talked, but Baltan still appreciated that he hadn't complained even though he was clearly exhausted. He wasn't sure he could have resisted the urge at Azzie's age.

"Tea?" Turnap offered, setting a kettle on the stove.

"Please," Eureka answered amicably, but like Baltan he kept his eyes on Turnap as he prepared their drinks. The farmer had no opportunity to slip any poisons in, unless they were in the tea itself—but he'd taken his own from the same tin and only hesitated to cool it. Still, Baltan waited to drink until Eureka gave the tea a discerning sniff and nodded.

"I suppose we ought to talk about this 'life or death' business," Turnap said. "I'll start with a confession. I knew who you were before you told me."

Baltan kept his hands steady on his teacup. No need to reach for his gun yet.

Eureka calmly slipped an arm around Azzie, who leaned into his side. "How's that?" His voice was curious, but breezy. Baltan thanked his lucky stars for his partner's charm; if he'd said it, it would have come out demanding and harsh and probably set Turnap on edge.

Not that he wasn't already. Despite his friendliness, the way the old man wrung his hands told Baltan he had something to hide.

"Can I trust you to hear me out?"

Baltan kept his mouth shut and let Eureka's firm nod be their response.

"After all..." Turnap waved his hand in the general direction of the village, "... all of *that*, I, well... I wanted to know what happened to Selkess. I started picking up papers, asking around, seeing if I could find where he might have ended up. Wouldn't you know it, about a year later your faces were all over. The heroes who brought a child murderer to justice." He smiled apologetically while drawing a finger across his face from his right brow down. "Not easy to forget a face like that."

The mention of Selkess made the hairs on Baltan's neck rise, but Turnap's explanation wasn't implausible. There were plenty of total strangers who knew his and Eureka's faces. They'd been in all the big papers often enough to be minor celebrities.

Which probably made it easier to get information on us.

But more pressing still: what was "all of that?"

"Then you must have an idea of why we're here," Eureka said before Baltan could ask.

Turnap took a long drink. "I do. And I must tell you again: no one in Illdresil Gera will be keen on giving you the information you want. Some things are too painful to remember, and this is one of them."

"Perhaps you could help us, then?" Eureka hunched his shoulders in an attempt to look less intimidating. "It seems like you know a lot about what's gone on around here. We may still have to go into the village, but if we're turned away, at least we'll have something to go off of."

"I don't know." Turnap cast his eyes downward. "It hurts me, too."

His body language and tone led Baltan to believe he was being sincere, but that didn't mean he still might not be a part of the cult. The pain he felt might have nothing to do with murdered children and more to do with the 'mistreatment' of his leader.

"Take your time."

"I'll be just a moment." Turnap stood and headed down the hall. Baltan calculated how quickly he, Eureka, and Azzie could get to the door in case Turnap came back with a weapon.

He may as well have.

Turnap's eyes misted with sorrow as he handed them a framed picture. If not for the fact that he'd seen him recently, Baltan wouldn't have recognized the man in the photograph as Selkess. His downturned gaze dampened his smile and in his arms was a laughing child who must have been his son at three or four years old.

"Selkess asked me to take a photo of him and Lleuwellyn before he left for the East," Turnap explained. "He seemed worried about something. Scared. I tried to get him to tell me what was going on. I told him if anything was wrong, he could talk to me about it. I *tried*. But then he was gone." He shook his head. "I know what he did. I've spent far too much time these past years wondering if there was anything… if I'd done *something* different, then it wouldn't have happened. I should never have let him go."

Baltan could tell tears were on the way, and to his relief Azzie looked like he'd already fallen asleep. He wouldn't shy away from telling the kid what he needed to know, but there wasn't any need to upset him.

"I wanted you to know it wasn't always that way. And in a lot of ways, that makes it worse," Turnap said, shaking his head before brushing the corners of his eyes with a thumb. "This is how I remember him. He was a good person. I taught him how to read and write when he was a youngster.

He was so *bright*, and his visits kept me from getting lonely. Then when he grew up he started bringing his son with him, and asked me to teach him, too." He rested his forehead in his hand, then shook his head again. "I never would have thought..."

Baltan sighed. He'd heard plenty of lines like that before, and he never believed them. "There's nothing you can do to change that now, but you *can* help us make sure it doesn't happen again."

"What do you mean?" The wrinkles on Turnap's forehead deepened. "I thought you were here to... hasn't he passed?"

Eureka shook his head slowly. "No. He survived his sentence."

"Then... the child with you is...?"

"We believe Selkess is targeting him," Baltan answered. "We suspect he's already killed again, but we don't have enough evidence to prove it, and even if we did I doubt we'd be able to prosecute before he does something worse."

Turnap's face reflected horror that Baltan, for all the terrible things he'd witnessed, couldn't imagine. He could relate plenty to the fear that an evil person would rise from their grave; Selkess had given him a taste of that already. But he couldn't possibly know what it would be like if Selkess was someone he had *loved*.

"Then you *must* go to the village," Turnap said, "All of Illdresil Gera will want to stop him from killing again. If there's any help to be found, I'm sure you'll find it there. After what he... well," Turnap spared a glance at Azzie, "No need to go into detail. If you haven't already guessed, then I'm sure you'll hear everything tomorrow."

"We can only hope." Eureka rose to his feet, leaving Azzie to squeak in protest when he slumped against the empty cushion. "Baltan, why don't you and Azzie get settled wherever we'll be sleeping? I'd like to cook dinner, since you're already offering us so much, Turnap."

"Accept the offer," Baltan said. Cooking dinner might be an Eureka-like thing to do in general, but it would also be the best way to make absolute certain that they weren't poisoned.

"I'll admit, I find myself not much in the mood to cook right now," Turnap nodded. "There's some poultry in the fridge that should be thawed, and there's fresh thyme and carrots in the pantry, but you're welcome to anything you find." He motioned for Baltan and Azzie to follow him. "Guest bed's this way."

The room was mostly filled by a large bed, but there was enough space for a small bookshelf with a few almanacs and travel guides. A vase with a few sprigs of lavender and mint sat on the top shelf, giving the room a fresh, pleasant aroma. There was a washroom off to the side, just big enough for a toilet and shower.

What Baltan wouldn't give for a warm shower—but that would have to wait until Eureka was available to watch Azzie. He set his bag down at the foot of the bed and tested the mattress. It wasn't as soft as Eureka's bed, but it would do.

Azzie stared longingly at the bed. He was trembling and his eyes were listless, yet he stood still in the doorway. He only moved when Baltan motioned to his bag and said, "You won't sleep well if you go to bed in dirty clothes."

The kid nodded and changed into his pajamas, but he was slow and shaking the whole time. Worry flared in Baltan's mind. Had they pushed him too far, too soon? Baltan had assumed that if he managed in the city, he would be okay on a long bus ride through the countryside, but maybe he'd been wrong. Or maybe the strain of walking in the cold for so long had taken a physical toll on him. He had likely never walked for so long at once before, and days ago he had been feverish.

Baltan felt his forehead, ignoring his visible flinch. He was cold. His jacket may not have been enough to protect him from the chill while he was still recovering.

Dammit, a sick kid is the last thing we need right now! Baltan thought. He took off his own coat and put it around Azzie's shoulders, then sat him down on the bed. "Try to get some rest. We've got a big day tomorrow."

Azzie did as he was told and curled up in the coat as best he could. Baltan sat with him until he fell asleep again and found that he was rooted to the spot, watching him. He couldn't shake the dread that if he left the room, something awful would happen.

What if Azzie got too cold without him there and stopped breathing?

Baltan knew it was ridiculous. Azzie was just cold from being outside.

But what if? Baltan's mind nagged. *What if he needs you? What if you leave him all alone and he loses his trust in you forever?*

This is why I didn't want kids! Baltan snapped at himself.

'Didn't?' Not, 'don't?'

Baltan had never given it much thought. He had never considered settling down or starting a family. It always seemed like something for other people, not him. Then again, he'd hardly been able to think beyond the next day until recently.

He still didn't think he would ever be a family man in the traditional sense—but nothing about this was traditional, and he knew Eureka would fight tooth and nail to keep Azzie after this was over.

Oddly enough, Baltan wasn't bothered by that.

Had knowing the kid for a few days changed him that much?

Or did he only want to please Eureka?

Azzie's breath hitched ever so slightly and Baltan's heart nearly stopped, only for him to recognize the sound as light snoring. Baltan sighed and forced his attention away from the sleeping child, selecting a random magazine from the bookshelf to study instead.

Eureka couldn't come soon enough with dinner.

The night dragged on. Baltan could hear dishes being moved in the kitchen and Eureka speaking softly to Turnap about mundane things like the weather and animal care. Finally the familiar cadence of his footsteps started down the hall, accompanied by the mouth-watering aroma of herb-roasted poultry and vegetables.

Eureka took one look at Azzie, handed the plates to Baltan, and headed for the bathroom. The sound of running water filled the silence and Eureka came back moments later with a cloth that had been soaked in warm water. He sat Azzie up and set about scrubbing his arms, neck, and chest.

Warmth gradually worked its way back into the kid. He yawned and his gaze focused, alert and curious.

"What was wrong with him?" Baltan asked.

"Worn out. He's been pushing himself for the past few days. Today might have been a little too much on top of it all," Eureka replied, flipping the cloth and wiping Azzie's face. He squirmed away, but Eureka was persistent. "A quick wash, a warm meal, and a good night's sleep is all he needs."

"I had no idea what to do," Baltan admitted.

Eureka blinked at him. "I'm doing what makes me feel better when I'm off-kilter. You did the same, and I appreciate you trying."

As if to prove the point, Azzie grabbed the plate and started shoveling down carrots.

"Still, I..."

"You're too hard on yourself," Eureka said. "You know, maybe you'd be a good parent someday." His face darkened almost as soon as he said it. "Not that I'm suggesting anything! I know how you feel about, ah, about that idea."

It was Baltan's turn to blush and he hid it by stabbing his fork into a carrot.

Eureka wanted a family. He didn't. It was one of the main reasons why they wouldn't work out.

Yet, he could admit he was warming to the idea of it.

Azzie didn't seem like the type to be defiant for no reason, to stay out late and make them worry, to make rude remarks every chance he got. But he wouldn't be that way forever—not if Baltan had any influence on him. He could clearly recall his rebellious teen years, and he was grateful for them. The world was a tough place to be and a little belligerence, used right, could go a long way.

Eureka would probably disagree. He'd want to shield Azzie from all hardship. He'd been through enough already without knowing how difficult life outside his bubble could be.

If they kept Azzie, how would they raise him? Would they try enrolling him in school? Eureka would likely insist on homeschooling, but Baltan knew first-hand how stifling that was. The last thing Azzie needed was being locked up in a house all day again.

Did he dare have those conversations with Eureka?

The proud gleam in Eureka's eyes as he watched Azzie eat told him he wouldn't have a choice soon. Whether or not Azzie was Eureka's biological child hardly mattered; they were bonded, and Baltan loved Eureka too much to deny him anything.

Eureka met Baltan's gaze at last. Anxiety replaced pride as he nodded toward Azzie.

He knew what Eureka was thinking. After all, he'd been thinking it himself. But there was a world of difference between thought and action.

He didn't have the heart to stop Eureka. Taking Azzie in was the right thing to do, what any morally good person *would* do—when it came to thoughts, anyway. Eureka had always been a man of action, though. He never left his good deeds in his head even though about half of them belonged there.

As much as Baltan griped, it was one of the reasons he'd fallen for him in the first place.

And he didn't know when they'd have another quiet moment together.

Subtly, he nodded. Whatever he felt or thought, this was Eureka's call to make. If he thought now was the right time, Baltan had to trust him.

"Azzie?" The kid didn't stop eating, but his ears flicked once. "I want to ask you an important question. It's alright if you don't answer now."

Baltan refused to look up despite the hesitance in Eureka's voice.

"What I want to ask is, well..." He swallowed. "Are you happy? With us?"

"Yes."

Eureka swallowed again. "That's good, because..."

Baltan braced himself. This was it, the moment he'd secretly been waiting for.

Everything was going to be different. Eureka was finally going to be a father, and he was going to be—what, exactly?

His whole body tensed in anticipation and fear. He always thought Eureka having a family would mean the end of their time as roommates. They would still be friends, but there wasn't room in their home for a wife and a child *and* Baltan. But without Azzie's mother in the picture, where did that leave him?

Eureka looked at him again, just for a heartbeat.

"Because... because we're happy with you, too! I just wanted to, you know, check. It's important to speak up if you're having a problem, but it's also good to say if everything is okay. That way we know we're doing the right thing." He forced a smile. "Now, let's finish eating and get to bed! Big day tomorrow. We need our sleep."

Azzie must have picked up on the dissonance between his words and his tone—it wasn't hard to miss—but shook it off and dug into the meat.

For once, Baltan needed to force himself to finish his meal, and Eureka barely picked at his own.

He shouldn't be so frustrated. This was Eureka's choice to make.

But why didn't he do what he obviously wanted to? Did he realize making that kind of commitment was out of the question until they solved the case and cleared Azzie's name? Had he, for once, decided to set aside emotion for logic? Was it that the timing was bad and he couldn't let the chance that Azzie was his son distract him from the case?

Or did he pull back *only* because he thought Baltan wouldn't be happy with it?

Don't make me *responsible for you missing out on your dreams!*

He was tempted, so tempted, to take that final step and offer Azzie their home permanently. He wouldn't, though—not because he still wasn't sure, but because he'd never forgive himself for being that spiteful toward Eureka. Baltan waited until Azzie was settled under the sheets to sigh and shake his head. He didn't say anything. He couldn't. Instead, he got into bed on the other side of the kid, turned his back to Eureka, and clenched his jaw.

"Good night," Eureka offered.

"Yeah," Baltan muttered back. He hoped he didn't sound too bothered, but he knew he did. He'd never been any good at hiding things from Eureka.

"G'night," Azzie murmured.

XIII

Morning came quietly.

Baltan took a moment to appreciate the sight of Eureka and Azzie curled up together before the guilt and frustration of the previous night caught up to him. He needed to talk to Eureka about it, but he didn't know what to say. He wanted to confront him about being too selfless for his own good.

Yet, Eureka acting selfishly had gotten them into the whole situation. If he hadn't brought Azzie home, Baltan would probably have spent that morning sleeping off a hangover in someone else's bed. Instead he was in an old farmer's cottage, about to walk into a dangerous village, chasing after a killer who should be dead, and trying to justify saying no to a child in need.

Eureka yawned and stretched, arching over Azzie, who reached his hands out and gripped the blankets to work the sleep out of his limbs. Both were well-rested, but Baltan had spent the night coming up with plans and mulling over the case. Selkess had yet to say or do anything that could incriminate him in Evanne's murder, other than having a convoluted motive that would never fly in court.

Waiting for him to do something horrible was almost as bad for Baltan's nerves as the aftermath. He wished he'd packed more soda, but the last of the bottles already decorated the bookshelf.

Illdresil Gera might be a good lead, if they could get anyone to talk. Turnap certainly thought they would, and it would be worthwhile, but Baltan still couldn't shake the feeling that they were grasping at straws.

"Is Turnap awake?" Eureka asked.

"He's a farmer, so I would think he got up a while ago," Baltan replied. He reached into his bag on instinct, once again faced with the sad reality that there was no soda.

Azzie got up, and Baltan noticed the hesitance in his movements. He waited for Eureka to get dressed before he so much as looked at the door, with the occasional glance back at Baltan to see what he was doing. He always checked to see if his actions were okay, always waited for punishment for doing something wrong. Baltan wondered how long it would take for Azzie to gain some of the confidence and brazenness a fourteen year old boy should have. If he *ever* did; Azzie might second-guess his every action for the rest of his life.

Counseling, Baltan decided, as soon as Selkess was no longer a threat and Azzie's custody was settled. They knew plenty of grief counselors from their days in the Investigative Department, so it wouldn't be too hard to get a recommendation even if he did end up with the state.

Baltan lingered in the room to pack up their things, allowing Eureka to show Azzie out.

Eureka paused at the door. "Baltan?"

"It's fine," Baltan said. "Go. I'll catch up."

Eureka placed a careful hand on his shoulder, gave a light squeeze, and was gone.

Usually Baltan tried to pack neatly to maximize space, but there was something innately therapeutic about throwing every piece of clothing back into its suitcase as hard as he could.

The inviting smell of buttered toast met Baltan in the living room. Turnap had indeed gotten up before them and set out toast, butter, jam, and juice to get them started. Baltan did his best to stay alert, offering a terse, "Thank you," for breakfast, but it was getting harder and harder not to like the old farmer.

They ate in silence, and Turnap only spoke once they'd finished.

Apparently he'd had a long night of mostly unwanted thoughts, too.

"It won't be easy for you," he said. "They tend to be a skittish lot already, and bringing up Selkess's name isn't going to help."

"We'll phrase everything as gently as possible," Eureka said with a nod at Baltan. "Right?"

"As gently as we're allowed," Baltan answered. "If we have to rip the bandage off, then that's what we have to do."

Turnap told them the best route to the village—turn right at the mouth of the tunnel, climb up to the next path, and follow it in. A guard would be posted, and they would have to negotiate their way from there, since Turnap would fare no better trying to go inside the village itself than they would.

Baltan hoped the company of two Azures might grant them easier access, but if Illdresil Gera and Kwoltan Gera had quarreled in the past, he might have to think of something else, and soon. His trusty pistol was still holstered at his side, but taking the guard hostage at gunpoint was probably not the best leverage to use when they were asking for help and drastically outnumbered.

Azzie tried to dart ahead as soon as they left the cottage, but Eureka blocked his path with one outstretched hand. "Stay close to us."

Baltan started to smile. It was nice to see a little boldness out of the kid, but his timing was off.

Focus.

The path looked shorter in the daylight, though the tunnel was still dark enough to stand out against the grassy hillside. The air was moist from a waterfall just out of sight, probably flowing down the other side of the hill from a different tunnel. Baltan shook himself to warm up, but the damp air sunk into his clothing.

They veered away from the tunnel and began to climb with Baltan leading, Azzie behind him, and Eureka taking the rear in case either of them lost their grip. The hill was too steep to walk up, but enough boulders and rocks jutted out for them to use as footholds.

Baltan looked around with each meter he scaled, trying to find the path they were supposed to take into the village. He almost missed it—'path' was a vast overstatement. They would have to walk single-file along the narrow passage, and Baltan wondered if Eureka would fit at all.

He pulled himself onto the ledge, tested his balance, and then reached down to help Azzie and Eureka up. Eureka dug into the hillside with his claws, but still had to take each step carefully to avoid slipping back down.

"Let's hope it gets wider," Baltan grumbled. The morning dew made the grass slick, and he had to take deliberate steps to progress along the ridge.

"Please," Eureka agreed, the tips of his fingers pulling out clumps of grass when he moved his hand to its next hold.

Azzie kept their pace, since he had enough space to walk normally. He still looked nervous, watching them both closely.

This is the least of our problems, Baltan reminded himself.

The path didn't widen until they curved around the side of the hill, where it dipped down and revealed the valley—though perhaps that, too, was an overstatement. The fog was so thick they could hardly see anything other than the tops of a few exceptionally tall trees.

Baltan leaned back. The mist obscured everything beyond and made the way down look like a steep drop. He had to remember that his feet were still on solid ground as birds flew through the hills beneath them.

"Where's the guard?" Baltan asked, glancing around the path briefly before staring hard into the mist to see if he could spot movement.

"I doubt we'll see them before they see us," Eureka said. He brought Azzie closer again and the kid shrank against his side, ears up and eyes alert.

Azzie's ears twitched and Eureka darted forward, shoving Baltan out of the way. A spear planted itself in the ground where he had just been. A shout in Azure followed, and Eureka gave a rapid response.

The guard slipped out of the fog as if it was a cloak, invisible one moment, then standing in plain sight the next.

Her oval face was framed with navy blue hair that, even braided and tied up, nearly reached her knees. It swayed with her long, plumed tail as she grabbed the spear and held it with the blade pointing skyward. She was slender, but her short tunic revealed muscular legs that could probably break bones as easily as a kick from a horse. Baltan would rather get kicked by a horse; at least it wouldn't be *aiming* for his vital organs.

Her youthful appearance was accentuated by her small nose and downturned eyes, and Baltan considered the various reasons why someone older wasn't keeping watch. Then again, there very well could be a more advanced guardsman still hiding close by.

Eureka started the conversation, and Baltan pretended not to understand what they were saying. She might let more slip if she thought it would go over his head; they'd gotten plenty of extra information out of witnesses and informants that way in the past.

Judging by the way her jaw clenched when she looked at him, playing dumb was the best thing he could do for the investigation.

"That was an excellent throw," Eureka said. "I presume you meant to miss my partner as a warning, but I couldn't be too sure."

"That's correct." She regarded him with the darkest blue eyes Baltan had ever seen. "Your reflexes are quick. A warrior, if I'm not mistaken?"

"Hardly, though I consider it an honor that one of the famed sentries of Illdresil Gera would call me that."

Baltan could *see* her warming up to him. She leaned against her spear and held her tail low, the tip waving smoothly back and forth with interest. "My name is Keldiwellyta," she offered. "What are you doing so far from home, warrior?"

"My companions and I need your assistance," Eureka said. "The Easterner and I are investigators. We believe your tribe might be able to help us save innocent lives, including the child who's travelling with us. You can call me Eureka, my partner is named Baltan, and our young friend is Azzie."

"Save lives?" Keldiwellyta repeated, her tail coming to a stop. "But what does that have to do with us? Why should I believe you?" She stood up straight. "Both your tribe and the Easterners have been our enemies before. How can I be sure you're telling the truth?"

"It's frightening to trust strangers with something so precious to you," Eureka said, "But you must believe that we are not here to hurt you. If you don't want us to enter the village, we'll wait here. We only need to get some information."

Keldiwellyta considered for a moment before asking, "What do you need to know?"

"To start with, what does the name 'Selkess' mean to you?"

Baltan couldn't see much of the village through the fog. Occasionally they would pass by someone and Keldiwellyta would give a short explanation of why she was walking three outsiders through the valley. They didn't look hostile enough to attack them if they wandered off, but Baltan wasn't going to take that chance. He stayed within reach of Keldiwellyta's tail, which she occasionally waved in their direction, presumably to make sure they were still behind her.

Unfortunately the villagers didn't look like they wanted to talk, and Keldiwellyta didn't wait long enough for them to try. She seemed intent on taking them around the entire valley, showing them all the sights that occasionally appeared in the fog.

The sound of water pouring down the rocky cliffs permeated the air as much as the mist itself. Sprawling trees covered in globes of glowing amber reflected the light of dozens of fireflies trapped in paper lanterns. The branches were draped in jewel-toned fabric hammocks big enough for whole families, a few of which greeted their guide when she passed and then glowered down at them for intruding on their beautiful village.

There weren't many children. The few that Baltan did spot were swiftly nestled away again, which was no easy task given they were likely older than Azzie.

Baltan couldn't help but find the fog more than a bit claustrophobic. Even living in as closed-in an area as Marina Delta, he could still see the sky from his bedroom window, and the wide expanse of the beach was a short bus ride away. Nothing was pressing against him, but Baltan still felt as though he was trapped by walls he couldn't see.

The farms they had driven through on the bus had once belonged to Illdresil Gera, but they had gradually been pushed back by Eastern settlers. Now they were confined within the misty flatland with nowhere else to go.

Maybe they felt as boxed-in as he did.

Keldiwellyta finally stopped in the middle of a ring of trees. Silky banners wove through the space overhead and dozens of glowing lanterns hung from the surrounding branches.

Some kind of meeting pavilion, Baltan surmised. It was probably best to let the tribal Azures come to them on their own terms instead of trying to hunt them down through the fog, but he didn't like the idea of being cut off from escape routes.

Keldiwellyta lifted her chin with a smile and trotted over to a woman whose face may as well have been chiseled from stone.

That must be their leader.

They leaned in close as they spoke, making sure their conversation stayed private. Baltan didn't need to hear them to know the woman wasn't pleased. Keldiwellyta hurried to respectable distance as soon as their conversation ended, her gaze as low as her tail.

The woman raised her spear into the air. The lanterns' glow glinted off the blade, casting sharp pinpricks of light through the fog. Her commanding voice resonated through the clearing and cut through the haze.

"To me, my brothers and sisters!"

Shapes formed out of the mist and shadows. They all looked like Keldiwellyta, more or less—tall and lithe, with pale skin and long, dark hair. The only immediate difference was the length of their robes and the complexity of their embroidery.

Baltan held his ground as the woman approached.

"I am Sheria." Her sneer skewed into a grimace as her eyes travelled from Eureka to Baltan to Azzie. "Why have you trespassed on our territory?"

Eureka dipped his head as a show of respect. If she was expecting the same from Baltan, she was going to have to live with the disappointment of not receiving it.

Eureka spoke first. "We've come for information that we believe only you can give us."

"We know that," Sheria said, raising an eyebrow. "The question is, what would a savage, a red-blood, and that *creature* want with it?"

Baltan gathered all the Azure vocabulary he'd picked up from living in Marina Delta and said, as clearly and eloquently as he could manage, "Being a bitch isn't going to make us leave, and we aren't your enemy. Selkess is."

It had been a long time since he'd spoken Azure, let alone insulted someone in it, and he didn't know if he said the right thing. Sheria's scowl was briefly overtaken by confusion before returning, so he hoped he'd gotten the message across well enough. Eureka was in no hurry to add any comments or corrections.

Being rude to a woman with a bad temper and a spear wasn't the best decision he ever made, but he'd rather be skewered than let her get away with disrespecting Eureka and Azzie.

Baltan's anger dwindled from a fire to a few smoldering embers when he saw the gathered Azures curling their tails around themselves and huddling closer together. "Selkess?" they whispered, some of them barely managing that. "Selkess is back?"

"Do not fear!" Sheria drew their attention with a quick wave of her raised tail. "We have trained many excellent guards. He will not cross our border. We will be safe."

Keldiwellyta shrank when a few of the older sentries threw glares her way.

Eureka spoke up again, his tone grim. "He might not get that close if you would cooperate with us. We suspect he's already planning to commit more murders, and the sooner we act, the more likely we are to stop him before he kills again. The last time he was free, thirty young boys and girls—thirty sons and daughters—were taken from their families. You lose nothing by helping us save them."

A shocked cry rippled through the gathered Azures.

"Thirty? Did he say *thirty*?"

"That makes *forty*!"

Baltan's gut twisted. He had expected as much, but he hadn't wanted to think about the numbers. Some part of him had hoped that maybe Selkess had *only* killed his son and been banished for that.

"Anything you can tell us could help us prevent that number from increasing," Eureka said. "Is there anyone willing to talk who remembers what happened?"

"I know what happened!" A girl not much older than Azzie bounded forward. She wore the shorter tunic of a sentry, but didn't carry a spear.

"He said he wanted to talk to people who *remember* what happened," Keldiwellyta said, beckoning the younger girl back with her tail.

She wasn't the only one who had approached. Several of those gathered around the trees stepped into the circle, their eyes wide and wary, as if Selkess would emerge from the fog and slaughter them all at any moment. Two adults with flowers prominently embroidered into their long robes surrounded the girl, much to her apparent annoyance. The teenage boy near her received the same treatment from his parents, one of them holding his spear at the ready.

The last few embers burning in Baltan's chest extinguished themselves. These weren't tight-lipped suspects resisting interrogation. They had lost everything dear to them and were trying desperately to protect what little they had left against a threat that made them feel powerless.

It's our job to help them feel empowered, Baltan reminded himself. He'd never been the best at dealing with victims' families, but this was different. He even felt bad about his earlier outburst in light of all they'd suffered. Even Sheria temporarily let go of her pride and tilted her head down, her tail brushing the grass.

This was always Baltan's least favorite part of the job, but he was determined to give it his all and not leave the interviewing to Eureka for once.

The process was simple, in theory. Get the claimant's name and relation to the victim, then ask them to say a little bit about the incident: where it happened, when it happened, the names of possible witnesses, etc.

In practice, it was a far more grueling ordeal.

Eureka and Baltan split the clearing down the middle and got to work. Baltan had to be careful not to accidentally reveal his holster when he reached into his back pocket for a notepad and pen.

Not that he was likely to forget.

The first woman he interviewed kept her hands clasped tightly together. She stared at them with an intensity not uncommon in those who survived their loved ones.

"My name is Lleuta. My son, Tolollyn, was murdered by Selkess. I was gathering healing herbs for him—no. No, he hadn't told me to do it. I just did it. I thought I was being useful. So many of the children were ill, and I thought, well, Selkess will need all the help he can get, won't he? I shouldn't have done it. I should have stayed by my son's side until he was better!"

It was hard to leave her so upset, but there was nothing Baltan could do for those wounds and there were more parents to talk to.

The next one tapped Baltan's shoulder gently to get his attention. He wore a long robe and a gaunt expression.

"My name is Aianak, and this is my wife, Hatora. Sergillyta, my daughter, was…" He couldn't finish and leaned against Hatora for support. She held his hands to her heart, but the numbness in her eyes told Baltan all he needed and more than he wanted.

Keldiwellyta shuffled her feet. "I don't have much to say. I survived because I didn't get sick and my parents wouldn't let me visit the others until they were better. I was so mad at them, and I was sound asleep in my hammock while all my friends were killed! But I guess I'm still alive, so I should be happy." She lashed her tail. "I was going to be a weaver like my father, but that day I decided to become a sentry."

The voice of an elderly woman rose above the rest and Baltan saw Eureka and Azzie standing with a sentry so old she had to use her spear to hold herself up. "He didn't stop at killing our children—he killed our *future*. Our *hope*. Who will we tell our stories to? Who will carry our spears?" She broke off into a fit of coughing. "What good is an old woman with no one to pass our heritage down to?"

Baltan turned away to face another sentry, one much fiercer than the feeble elder.

"My name is Letoulile. My son was Valhallyn, and he was going to be a sentry like us before he was killed. He was named for that, and he lived up to it! You would never meet a braver boy. He didn't cry when he got sick. He didn't complain. He said he'd fight the sickness with all he had, because he had to get better and train with us and he was going to win back the valley outside for us, too. He thought he could do anything if he willed it. I wish... I wish he'd gotten the chance. I should have been there!"

"I'm Lleuaset!" the girl who had tried to rush forward spoke before either of the adults with her could open their mouths, eager to be a part of such an important moment. "These are my parents, Lleua and Klaidkalik. Keldiwellyta has been like my older sister since Selkess killed my *real* sister, Kallyta, but that happened a few constellations before I was born."

Lleua and Klaidkalik didn't look any better than the rest of the parents despite still having their younger daughter. Not even the joy of new life could take away the pain of losing a child. Though Lleua hid her face in Lleuaset's hair, the shudder of her shoulders betrayed that she was crying.

The whole tribe is still in mourning.

Sheria met Baltan's eyes and approached him before Eureka could take her statement. She held his gaze, as if *daring* him to say anything. "My name is Sheria. My son, Nalallyn, was murdered by Selkess. He was best friends with Selkess's son, Lleuwellyn. They were never apart, and when Lleuwellyn was called on to help Selkess with treating the sick children, Nalallyn decided to help out, too. He was selfless, and kind, and wonderful, and he paid for it with his life. His father and I were on guard duty. We didn't find out our son was dead until morning."

Baltan broke eye contact first. "I'm sorry for your loss."

She seemed to be putting all her concentration into maintaining her stony expression. She was one of the only tribe members who hadn't broken down into tears, and all the others looked like they had died years ago. Before she could leave, he lifted his notepad and said, "I've noticed that several of the others also mentioned sick children, and that Selkess was treating them. Can you tell me more about that?"

"Yes. It was an illness we had never seen before. We all felt a bit weaker and a little nauseous for a few days, but the children were affected the most. Selkess was our seer, so it was his duty to care for them."

"Forgive my ignorance. What does a seer do?"

Her eyes widened briefly, as if she couldn't believe he would ask such a ridiculous question. Then she nodded to herself in a sort of 'ah yes, ignorant Easterners,' kind of way and explained, "They're *supposed* to connect us to our ancestors in Lleu Gera. They read the stars for signs to guide us, and they protect us from death with medicine and prayers. Selkess was…" she sighed. "He was brilliant. We had no doubt that he would make our children well again. We trusted him!"

"I see. And the illness—you were fatigued and nauseous? Were there other symptoms?"

Sheria paused to remember, and in that moment she must have seen something she didn't like over Baltan's shoulder. Her glare returned, deadlier than ever, and she tightened her grip on the spear.

"Sheria!"

Another Azure bounded into the clearing.

Baltan's hand flew to his holster. Eureka leapt to his side, shoulders tense and teeth bared.

Selkess!

He nearly drew his pistol and took aim, but Eureka's snarl died in his throat and he stood back, forcing his muscles to relax.

No. Not Selkess.

Even Selkess wasn't arrogant enough to waltz into Illdresil Gera after what he'd done, but they couldn't be blamed for making the mistake.

Baltan gave the newcomer a thorough once-over. The visible half of his face was a dead ringer for a young Selkess; long bangs obscured the other half. Although he had called out Sheria's name with confidence, his posture was anything but. His tail nearly dragged on the ground, his shoulders slumped forward, and he kept his head down.

"You shouldn't have called a tribe meeting without me," he went on, trying to mask the slight tremble in his voice when he realized how surrounded he was. Baltan didn't get the feeling that it was because of the outsiders. Why was he so nervous with his own people?

Baltan glanced around the gathering. All of them looked at the young man with narrowed eyes and whispered curses.

It wasn't hard to imagine why.

Sheria denied him the dignity of a response, facing away instead of answering. She slipped out of the clearing without another word to anyone, but the others followed her lead in unison, each making a point to turn his or her back on him before departing.

Soon it was just the four of them left.

"I see you've met our chief sentry," the newcomer said. Just as Baltan thought, he sounded more at ease without his tribemates around. "I hope she's been hospitable while she kept you from me, but if you have received injuries, I can treat them."

Eureka tilted his head. "Who *are* you?"

He took a moment to respond, as if he hadn't expected them to pay much attention to him.

"I am Lleuwellyn, seer of Illdresil Gera."

XIV

The medicine hut reminded Baltan too much of his room as a teenager.

At first it seemed as mystical as something called a medicine hut should. A bundle of firefly lanterns hung down from the center of the roof, casting a warm glow not unlike a lit hearth. Shelves lined the walls, holding all manner of dried herbs, broken-open geodes, and iridescent potions, some of which gave off their own odd, blue-green light.

But upon closer inspection, the awe and wonder of the place all but vanished. The firefly chandelier hung over an ordinary, if lumpy, mattress. Notepads, pens, and travelogues occupied their fair share of space on the shelves. A pile of presumably unwashed tunics and robes lay on the far side of the hut.

Eureka took a deep breath and smiled. "Reminds me of home."

They had decided to talk to Lleuwellyn where he was most comfortable. The more distance they put between him and his tribe, the more relaxed he became, eventually lifting his tail from dirt-level and looking forward instead of down.

They had been followed. Eureka said nothing but stayed alert, eyes piercing through the veil of fog at the sentries barely visible around them. No doubt a guard was posted outside the medicine hut.

"My apologies for oversleeping," Lleuwellyn said as soon as they were inside. He looked at Baltan and added in accented but fluent common language, "If I had known we had visitors, I would have greeted you sooner. Welcome to Illdresil Gera. What do you need from us?"

"We're investigators. This is Eureka, I'm Baltan, and the kid is Azzie. We're here for information on Selkess."

Lleuwellyn flinched and tugged his sleeves down over his wrists. "Oh. Him."

"Your tribemates had a lot to say," Eureka offered. "But they didn't get into specifics. No one would say exactly *how* he..." He glanced at Azzie, who could now understand what they were saying, and cautiously finished, "... what he did to the victims, or why."

The fur along the top of Lleuwellyn's tail stood on end and his lips drew a tight line.

"We know he was your father," Eureka continued. "You must have some idea—"

"No, I don't!" Lleuwellyn's tail whipped up, knocking a bottle of clear liquid onto the floor. "I don't know why he killed my friends, I don't know why he spared me, I don't know what he was thinking at all!"

"Don't get angry at Eureka," Baltan snapped. Lleuwellyn glared at him and he glared back, ready to make a sharp retort before a whimper from Azzie broke them up.

At that they stepped back—when had they moved toward each other?—and Lleuwellyn brushed his tail flat again. Lleuwellyn might have been ashamed of himself for startling the kid, but he still had to drag an apology out through clenched teeth. "I'm sorry. I was very young when it happened. I might have forgotten a few of the details, and I don't know how useful I can be. But I guess I can try."

"It's alright," Eureka said as if nothing had happened. "Take your time."

Lleuwellyn put the bottle he'd knocked over back on the shelf. He seemed to have an easier time talking when he wasn't directly facing them. Baltan wondered if that was why he kept one of his eyes covered, but he doubted the reason was that benign.

"When I was three or four, Selkess began leaving the village for constellations at a time. He said he was looking for a cure, but he wouldn't tell me what it was for. I always assumed he was talking about my grandfather's dementia. He was probably running away from the stress of dealing with him. After he died, I thought Selkess would stay, but... it isn't like he had a choice after what he did."

"The others mentioned an illness of some kind," Eureka pointed out. "Could you tell us more about it?"

"Silver poisoning," Lleuwellyn replied with a shrug. "He brought silver back with him. Lots of it. I'm not sure how he managed to carry it all the way from the East, but the entire village fell ill." He shook his head slowly, careful not to shake the bangs covering his eye loose. "We were secluded for so long we forgot the symptoms and thought it was some new illness. The children were affected worse than the adults, so it was agreed that they should stay in the medicine hut for supervision overnight."

"And you were there?"

"Yes, of course. I was already training in medicine and spiritual healing by then."

Eureka's eyebrows rose. "Wouldn't you have been a bit young?"

"According to Selkess, I showed an innate talent for it at an extremely young age. He wanted to start my training early, in case my abilities became overwhelming," Lleuwellyn sniffed. "That went about as well as you would expect."

Baltan did his best not to snort. He knew most Azures believed the stars were their lost ancestors who could speak to them in visions; Eureka had talked about it from a theoretical standpoint a few times. But hearing him discuss it like it was *real* gave him whiplash.

Of course, he should have considered they *were* in an Azure village, one that Selkess had been born and raised in. They were bound to hold those beliefs more closely than he was used to. Selkess had traded one form of religious zealotry for another.

He had to keep their perspective in mind. It didn't matter if it was real or not; it only mattered that Selkess *believed* it was real.

Lleuwellyn continued. "I didn't have his stamina, and I was affected by the poisoning, too. Eventually I had to sleep. Then he struck. When I woke up, everyone was already dead, and my eye was..." He paused and waved his tail in Azzie's direction. "Can you make him look away?"

The kid didn't fuss when Eureka held up a hand over his eyes.

Satisfied, Lleuwellyn tucked the bangs covering the left side of his face behind his ear.

Even after so many years, the skin around the sutured eye was an angry mess of discolored welts and twisted burn marks. Baltan could make out the mark that had been cut onto Azzie's chest etched into the warped skin if he squinted.

"Acidic venom," Lleuwellyn said by way of explanation, quieter now. "The others were spared that suffering, at least. He injected them with a neurotoxin derived from spinerat venom. Very quick, very clean. They were probably gone before they ever had a chance of waking up." The note of bitterness in his voice betrayed jealousy as well as guilt. "Keldiwellyta and I were the only survivors of our generation."

Baltan lowered his head. He understood too well what Lleuwellyn must have gone through, and it didn't take a genius to see that his tribe hadn't helped at all. Keldiwellyta would surely have struggled with survivor's guilt as well, but she didn't resemble the worst monster the tribe had ever seen.

"I'm sorry," Eureka offered.

Lleuwellyn nodded distantly in response and moved his bangs back in front of his burned eye. "That was the last I saw of Selkess, and I hope to keep it that way."

The hut quieted until only the faint buzzing of the fireflies was audible. Azzie startled himself by coughing and Eureka rubbed his back to soothe him. He was a bit paler than normal. Maybe the investigation was too much for him, but that couldn't be helped. They had to have answers and Baltan was not going to leave empty-handed.

"Why didn't your tribe kill him?" Baltan asked. "They'd have been more than justified."

"He was our seer. By law, we *couldn't*." Lleuwellyn folded his arms. "No one was happy about it and we all would have loved to see him die, but we couldn't. It would be a greater taboo than cutting our hair or eating meat. We would have been no tribe at all if we broke our most sacred belief and executed him." He directed his accusatory gaze at Eureka again. "You could have, though. Your tribe has no law against killing the sacred people of other tribes."

"It does have laws against killing when there are other options open to us, and I was hardly beholden to *tribe* laws at the time," Eureka responded in the same sharp tone he used when people commented on his size.

A revelation flashed through Baltan's mind. "If the guards aren't allowed to kill seers, even when they've done something awful, then what's stopping him from coming here with a group of violent devotees and finishing off the rest of the tribe?"

Lleuwellyn nearly turned white, but Eureka shook his head. "No, I doubt Selkess would attack Illdresil Gera now. It would be too much hassle and doesn't suit his M-O. There aren't any children left here, remember?" He paused. "Except for one that got away from him before."

"I'm an adult now," Lleuwellyn said, his tail fluffing up again with indignation.

"But not to him," Eureka countered. "He'll always see you as a child, because you're *his* child. And with that burn distinguishing you from the rest..." He frowned. "I doubt you've seen the last of him now that he's free."

Lleuwellyn held his tail and ran his fingers through its soft fur, but it didn't smooth out under his touch this time. "Do you think he'd do that? Come back here just to kill me?"

"Maybe." Baltan weighed the odds in his mind. It was hard to say what Selkess might do at any given time, but it wasn't *un*likely. "He hasn't gotten any better since he left, that's for sure. You could be in danger."

Eureka leaned down to whisper to Baltan, and he was sure he was in for it about scaring Lleuwellyn, but instead Eureka said, "I hear movement. Be ready."

He hardly finished speaking before an older sentry entered the hut. His eyes were narrowed at them, Lleuwellyn included.

"You are wanted for counsel, seer."

"Has something happened?" Lleuwellyn breathed.

"In a way."

Eureka motioned for Azzie to stand behind him, reaching back to hold his hand for comfort. Baltan didn't miss that his other hand was flexed, readying his claws for battle.

Baltan would have preferred to run, but who knew if they'd ever find their way back to the pass through the fog without help?

Outside, all of the sentries had gathered in a semicircle, and every single one was armed.

"Sheria, is something wrong?" Lleuwellyn asked. Hesitation made his voice shake.

"Yes," she said. Her tone was stern, but there was something else underneath that Baltan couldn't identify. "I have listened to your conversation and heard enough. If what the intruders said about Selkess having followers is true, then we are all in danger should he come here."

"Your sentries will protect us. They won't make it into the valley." It came out less as a statement and more as a question, which made the feeble defense too easy to tear apart.

"And how many will die in the process?" Sheria challenged. "These are the disciples of a murderer. They will no doubt carry weapons, and they will have his knowledge of secret passes that are not often patrolled. The risk to our tribe is too great." She stamped her foot into the ground. "The sentries *will* do what we must to protect Illdresil Gera!"

She pointed her spear at Lleuwellyn.

"I speak for the people of Illdresil Gera, who are one in this decision. Seer Lleuwellyn, your bloodline is dead. You are hereby banished from our tribe. You and these intruders must be gone from the valley by nightfall or you will be forcibly removed."

"But... but you *can't!*" Lleuwellyn gaped. "There's no one to take my place!" His voice cracked. "Lleu Gera will never allow this!"

"Lleu Gera allowed a madman to murder our children!" Sheria snapped, her tail lashing so fiercely Baltan expected it to crack like a whip. After realizing she might have committed heresy, she went on in a calmer tone, "It is not ideal, but Lleu Gera will send us a new seer. They have in the past. And once we have a new seer, we can start to live again—it is not too late for many of us to have another child."

She rammed the blunt end of her spear into the soft earth. "If anyone wishes to speak for this outcast, do so now."

The gathered sentries remained silent. Lleuwellyn turned his head slowly to examine them each, stopping when his eye rested on Keldiwellyta. His tail lifted a centimeter and he called out with the tiniest amount of hope, "Kel?"

She recoiled as if he'd spat at her, her nose wrinkling in disgust. She said nothing, not even deigning to insult him, and turned away.

Baltan caught the tip of Lleuwellyn's tail disappearing into the mist as he fled the scene. If Eureka hadn't gasped softly as he passed by, Baltan might not have seen him at all.

He hadn't meant for this to happen. He hadn't meant for Lleuwellyn to be exiled from his tribe. All he had done was propose an idea, a possibility, of something Selkess *might* do, the way he always did when he and Eureka worked together.

Now the air was thick with betrayal, fear, and heartbreak. Eureka was trembling, and not from the chill of the mist that seeped into everything.

Baltan reached for his hand to reassure him, and paused.

The hand that should have been holding Azzie's was empty.

Azzie was gone.

XV

Azzie hadn't been able to think straight from the moment they set foot in the village.

At first he thought the voices all around him were the tribe members whispering to each other, but when they came forward to talk to Baltan and Eureka, there were far too many voices. And they seemed to be talking directly to *him*, in a language he didn't understand.

None of them spoke a language he understood. Not until Lleuwellyn led them away to talk alone. The whispers didn't stop, but at least he knew what Lleuwellyn was saying.

He wished he didn't.

Once he realized Selkess and the Prophet were the same person, his mind wandered off somewhere else that was as dark and horrible as the first night he'd spent in Eureka and

Baltan's home. Confusion and fear plagued his every thought until it was all he could do not to beg Eureka to take him home.

He might have learned what goodness was, but he also knew that he was thoroughly Bad for agreeing to help Selkess. Evanne's death was at least half his fault.

But if he was helping Eureka and Baltan catch him, that meant he was doing something good, didn't it?

Was it really good if someone as terrible as Selkess wanted him to do it? After all, he had told him to find Eureka in the first place.

Why?

Azzie chased an answer to that question around his head all day, and like the shell in his dream it got away from him every time he thought he'd caught it.

If it came to a stand-off between his guardians and the Prophet, Azzie knew which he would choose. But did Eureka and Baltan know that? They couldn't take chances on who they gave their trust.

You haven't done anything yet, he reminded himself, Baltan's words rising from the back of his mind. *You didn't pull the trigger. You didn't kill anyone.*

Eureka trusted him. Baltan must, too. And he would prove to them that they should.

That started with following Lleuwellyn.

They'd been distracted. They hadn't seen Lleuwellyn's feet kneading the ground, getting ready to run, or the uneasy way the tip of his tail flicked. Their attention was on the woman and her guards.

But Azzie saw, and he didn't waste a heartbeat, slipping his hand out of Eureka's and bolting after the seer.

Azzie lost sight of Lleuwellyn immediately, but it didn't matter. He knew, somehow, where he needed to go. The voices in his ears urged him onward, guiding him around trees and up a rocky slope with a well-worn path, until he stood above the fog, alone with Lleuwellyn.

The top of the hill was a pointed peak, but the side facing the village was flat enough for a small group to stand comfortably. In the center was a pool that sparkled with star-light despite the shadow of the peak falling across it.

Azzie looked up. It was still daytime.

He probably should have been scared. Lleuwellyn was a stranger, and not like anyone he'd met before. He wasn't like the sea or the sky. He was something new that Azzie didn't have words for yet.

Still, Azzie couldn't help but feel that Lleuwellyn wasn't *so* different. He had been attacked by Selkess and left alone, like Azzie—so whatever he was, maybe Azzie was that thing, too.

It was a calming thought, but something about the hill itself helped slow Azzie's rapid heartbeat and fill his aching lungs with air. The voices were quieter but clearer there, and their words were more than words. He could finally understand exactly what they were telling him.

Be at peace.

Maybe that was why Lleuwellyn had come.

He didn't look peaceful. He sat at the edge of the pool, his hands gripping the stone for support. His head was bowed low enough that some of his hair touched the water's surface.

Lleuwellyn stared into the pool with so much focus that he didn't realize he was no longer alone, and Azzie wondered if he should leave. This place was different from any other he had seen so far. He shouldn't interrupt, especially if Lleuwellyn was there for an important reason. But, at the same time, this place made Azzie *feel* different. The voices that whispered to him were welcoming. He had to know why.

Finally Lleuwellyn noticed him, jerking himself upright and staring in alarm. "How did you get here?"

"I followed you." Even Azzie's own voice came to him easier here. "What is this place?"

"It's, well... how to put it..." Lleuwellyn ran his fingers through the wet strands of his hair, thinking. "Every seer gives it their own name. When I was young, I called it the To-gether Place. Selkess called it the Starpool. My great grandmother called it the Eye of the Stars, which is what I've always liked best. It's where we come to commune with Lleu Gera and seek guidance."

Lleu Gera. The term had been thrown around earlier, but it felt more familiar than that. Did the whispering voices belong to them?

Lleuwellyn moved closer, circling Azzie once, his expression thoughtful. "You should not have been able to follow me here. Even members of Illdresil Gera can only find this place if I bring them. It's sacred, and protected."

"You did bring me," Azzie said.

"No, I didn't. Unless..." Lleuwellyn's tail waved from base to tip in a long, fluid movement. If Azzie had to guess, that meant he was interested in something. "Come sit at the water's edge with me. Tell me what you see."

He returned to the place where he had been sitting, and Azzie saw the stone there was worn smooth. Many seers must have sat in the exact same spot over years and years. He settled beside Lleuwellyn, copying him as exactly as possible, and stared into the water.

At first, all he saw was the dark, sparkling surface. He still couldn't understand how it was possible for the water to look like the night sky. Maybe it was perfectly clear, and he was seeing speckled rocks at the bottom of the pool.

He didn't see anything special, but when he closed his eyes, he *heard*.

Welcome, young one.

Welcome, gifted one.

Welcome, seer.

He opened his eyes. The water looked the same as before, but he had definitely heard the voices of children talking to him. He had never been able to tell the age of the voices before, or if they were boys or girls. Here, he thought he could pick out each one and give it a name.

"There are children."

Lleuwellyn drew in a sharp breath.

"Did I do it wrong?" Azzie asked, ears pinned back despite himself.

"No. It's fine. I suppose they *would* rather talk to someone who isn't related to Selkess," Lleuwellyn sighed. "Wouldn't everyone?"

"Why can I hear them? What does 'gifted' mean?"

"It means you can perceive things beyond this world," Lleuwellyn said, his voice still sad. He reached down to touch the water. It didn't ripple at all. Azzie almost expected to see little glittering stars on his skin when he drew it back, but it was just a normal sort of wet. "I see my great grandmother. When I was born, Selkess called upon her spirit to watch over me. She has always helped me when I'm having trouble. As much as she can, anyway..."

As far as Azzie knew, no one had ever called upon a spirit to watch over him. Maybe that was why he heard instead of saw.

"Will Ll... Lle... will your grandma tell us how to stop Selkess?"

"It's never that simple." Lleuwellyn narrowed his eye and slapped his hand against the water, but it didn't even make a splash. His hand passed through the water and out again like it wasn't even there, though his sleeve still got wet somehow. "Tell me something useful!"

Azzie flinched back, and so did Lleuwellyn.

"I'm sorry. I shouldn't have done that, I'm sorry." Lleuwellyn touched the pool again, stroking it almost like a cat. "I'm not a very good seer. They wouldn't have cast me out otherwise. Selkess was the one they all thought was great, before he betrayed them. I'm just a cheap imitation compared to him." He smiled, but he didn't look any happier. "You'll probably be better than me, too. Please, try again."

Azzie took a deep breath and closed his eyes. He pointed his ears as far forward as he could, doing his best to listen to the voices of the spirits. It was a little like adjusting the radio, pinpointing the right voice and ignoring the static hum from the rest.

He had to quiet himself and let the calm in; otherwise he couldn't focus right. That must be why Lleuwellyn wasn't very good. His sadness was almost deafening, but Azzie tuned it out enough to get through.

Be open to new teachings, young seer.

Selkess did not lie to you. Your choices could change the world one day.

You must have the courage of a warrior and the cunning of a hunter if you are to succeed.

Azzie frowned. If his choices really did matter that much, he would have to be careful to make the right ones. He was pretty sure coming to the Together Place was one of them. He was pretty sure *Lleuwellyn* was one of them, too. He only needed to glance at his reflection to be overwhelmed by the seer's loneliness and his own desire to do something about it.

Neither of them had families. Both of them had grown up alone, away from the world. But they could be each other's family now, together with Eureka and Baltan. Lleuwellyn could teach him more about Lleu Gera, and he could teach Lleuwellyn how to hear better.

"You know what I see in the water?" Azzie shifted closer. He didn't think Lleuwellyn would like a hug, so he brushed their arms against each other instead. "I see you."

Lleuwellyn started to lean away, stopped, and curled his tail around Azzie. "Thank you."

Looking closer, Azzie thought he could see the stars mirrored in Lleuwellyn's eye. It must have been a trick of his reflection.

Walk your paths together, and you will find your burdens easier to bear.

Then the voices were quiet, and Azzie knew they would not speak to him like that again.

The calm gave way to a crackle of energy. He could run all the way to the ocean and back! Every part of him was alive, intense, like he'd been struck by lightning. If Lleu Gera trusted him, then he *must* be good!

He tried to jump up only to find that his knees and elbows were stiff. He thought they had been there for a short time, but the sun was starting to set.

Lleuwellyn got to his feet, stretching his long legs and arms. "We had better get you back to Eureka and Baltan. We won't have any chance of finding them in the village without running into the sentries, so we should wait for them at Turnap's cottage instead."

Rather than go back into the valley, Lleuwellyn led Azzie across the hills, up and down in an uneven, twisting route toward the pass. Azzie was pleased his voice didn't disappear when they left the Together Place. "Did your great-grandmother say anything to you?"

"A lot of things. Some that I still need to think about before I share," Lleuwellyn answered. He looked down at Azzie and they slowed their pace. "That's important, too. You should always think carefully about what Lleu Gera tells you before you say anything to anyone else. Sometimes they hide their real message, and you don't want to tell people the wrong thing."

Azzie didn't understand why they wouldn't say what they meant. What they said to him was plain enough, but maybe he hadn't thought about it enough yet.

"Sometimes the ocean talks to me like that. In my dreams. But I don't always know what it says." Azzie replied. Maybe now he would. "I think it helped me find Eureka, but that might have been the... I mean, Selkess."

Lleuwellyn's expression hardened. "Let's keep going."

As they wound through the hills, Azzie's thoughts turned to Eureka and Baltan and the trouble he would be in. There had been no time, no way, to explain to them what he was doing. They probably figured out he was following Lleuwellyn, but they would still be upset with him for running off.

He wasn't looking forward to the punishment. What would they do to him?

There were the usual things: hitting him, shoving him into a dark room, putting food in front of him and not letting him eat. But Eureka and Baltan weren't Evanne, which meant they might have *other* punishments he couldn't imagine.

Lleuwellyn stopped, his tail bushed out in alarm. His eye glistened with the same starlight as before, but the sky was still dull and dusky. "We have to hurry. Something terrible has happened!"

He set off running. Despite the growing ache in his stomach, Azzie followed him the rest of the way to the pass. He managed to keep up, Lleuwellyn's tail never disappearing from his sight. "What is it?"

"Turnap!" Lleuwellyn called back. "I didn't see exactly what, but he's in danger!"

They arrived at the pass and emerged from the fog to see that Eureka and Baltan were already in the valley beyond the hills.

Azzie's legs shook. Eureka and Baltan were waiting for them. He tried to see their faces, but they were still too far away and the mist made it impossible to get a good look. How mad were they?

Lleuwellyn kept going, so he did, too.

Baltan's voice was tight when he saw Lleuwellyn and called out, "Where's Azzie? Is he with you?"

Oh, no. They were *really* mad.

Azzie considered running back into the hills and hiding for a while. Sometimes that made things worse, but if he timed it right he could come back after their anger had burnt out and they stopped caring that he was gone.

"Azzie!"

Too late. Eureka saw him, and his legs were trembling too much to run. He would never be able to get away from Eureka anyway.

Eureka folded Azzie into a tight hug and didn't let go until Azzie started squirming for air. "Why did you run off like that? We were both worried about you! Don't frighten us like that again. If you have an idea, you need to tell us. Okay?"

"O-o…" Azzie's heart was still beating fast, and if he tried to finish the word it would probably come out of his chest. He nodded instead and didn't hesitate when Eureka offered a hand to hold.

A shout reminded him that there were other problems to deal with.

Baltan grabbed Lleuwellyn's arm as he passed, but he shook him off and continued toward the cottage. By the time Eureka and Azzie caught up he was already inside, the door flung wide open. Eureka motioned for Azzie and Baltan to stand back while he went in, but Lleuwellyn half-carried, half-dragged Turnap out before he could.

The old man didn't look good. His side was bleeding badly through the bandage torn from Lleuwellyn's robe. Baltan stopped Azzie from getting closer, but even from a distance he could hear how Turnap struggled to breathe.

"Hang on," Lleuwellyn said, keeping pressure on the wound despite the blood coating his hand. "I'll have you patched up in no time, Turnap. Focus on breathing. *Don't* fall asleep." He looked up as Eureka kneeled beside them, eye wide with desperation. "Can you carry him? We need to get him to a hospital. We might still catch the late bus to the city."

Turnap choked out a bubble of blood and Lleuwellyn pushed him toward Eureka. "Now! Hurry!"

Eureka put his hand to the wound and his frown deepened. "Lleuwellyn, he's…"

"He can't die! I won't let him!" He lowered his face to Turnap's, touching their foreheads together. "You hear me? You will not die tonight!"

Turnap's lips quivered as he opened his mouth, but only blood came out.

And yet, somehow, Azzie heard him perfectly. He broke free of Baltan's hold and stepped closer.

There had to be a reason why he heard words, but Eureka and Lleuwellyn didn't.

If he really was gifted, he should share it. He might not be able to talk on his own, not as often as he liked, but he could borrow Turnap's words so Eureka and Lleuwellyn could understand. There wasn't time to think about what he heard. He needed to say it *now*.

"Don't be afraid, Lleuwellyn." Azzie tried not to get distracted by Lleuwellyn and Eureka's shocked faces. He needed to listen. "It's time to move on. There's nothing left for you here. But, if you can face the future with courage, there is still so much ahead of you."

"There is *nothing* ahead of me!" Lleuwellyn sobbed, wrapping his arms around Turnap. "Please, please don't leave me alone."

"You won't be alone. You'll have them." Azzie paused. "*Us.* You'll have *us.*"

Lleuwellyn lifted his head, regarding Eureka, Azzie, and Baltan, his eyes resting on the Easterner. His voice was hollow with doubt. "Will I?"

Baltan's gaze was made of storm clouds barely containing lightning. Azzie had wondered if Baltan didn't like him; he knew Baltan didn't like Lleuwellyn with one look. He grit his teeth, but his words still had a bite. "Why not? I've *always* wanted to see how many people we can squeeze into a two-bed, one-bath house."

"Baltan!" Eureka snapped. "Now is not the—"

Azzie tried to drown out the noise of Eureka scolding Baltan. The voice got quieter and harder to distinguish from the endless murmuring in Azzie's ears. Turnap was dying.

He knew seeing someone die should scare him. This wasn't just death, it was *murder*. But when no words could get through, feelings still did, and Turnap wasn't scared or angry or upset. Azzie could felt nothing but peace from the old man. He was ready to move on.

He was...

"He was..."

... good, once.

"... good, once."

Then the voice was silent, and Turnap lay still.

Lleuwellyn fell, weeping, onto Turnap's chest.

Eureka stood and reached for Azzie, his eyes still wide not with fear, but wonder. He placed his hand on Azzie's shoulder, but it was so large that his palm rested over his heart. "What was...?"

Azzie didn't feel like explaining. He doubted he could. Instead he leaned against Eureka's side with a whimper. He wanted to curl up and hide from the world for a while. For now the best he could do was nestle his face into the woven threads of Eureka's sweater.

Baltan's voice came from far away. "We can't stay here. The killer could still be close by."

"You can't leave him like this!" Lleuwellyn protested, shielding Turnap's body from the wind. "And what about the animals, and—"

"We'll call someone out to investigate," Eureka said softly as he helped Lleuwellyn to his feet, "But Baltan's right. We're putting ourselves in danger."

"So go, then. Leave me," Lleuwellyn said in less than whisper.

Azzie shook his head. "Not alone."

Eureka put an arm around both of them and pulled them close while Baltan looked on, keeping an eye out for anyone who might hurt them.

They let Lleuwellyn grieve for as long as they could, but it wasn't long. It wasn't safe, and the bus stop was still a long walk through the cold night away. Eureka stayed close to Lleuwellyn, murmured soothing words to him every so often, but Azzie couldn't tell if Lleuwellyn was listening.

He stopped Lleuwellyn from running back to the cottage twice, once soon after they left and once when they reached the bus stop.

"I can't get on that thing," Lleuwellyn cried out, struggling against Eureka's arms. "If I get on that thing, I can never go back!"

"Lleuwellyn," Eureka sighed, his voice a perfect echo of the former seer's grief, "There's nothing to go back to now."

Lleuwellyn stood in the entryway of Eureka and Baltan's house with shaking knees. The living room was smaller and more cluttered than the medicine hut, and the bedrooms weren't much better. It took a good deal of coaxing from both Azzie and Eureka to get him inside, while Baltan walked in breezily, dumped his bag in the walkway, and charged up the stairs to bed without a word.

Azzie winced when the door to the bedroom slammed shut.

"I'll talk to him. He won't stay mad long." Eureka yawned and maneuvered his way around boxes of old bottles to a small door under the stairs. He pulled a few blankets and pillows out of the closet and threw them onto the couch. "It's not much, I know, but it ought to do you for now."

Lleuwellyn approached the couch like it might come to life and eat him, a cautious hand testing each cushion. "For now?"

"Until we can find somewhere for you to stay," Eureka said. "I'll ask around the neighborhood. I'm sure someone has a bedroom available. While I don't appreciate Baltan's attitude, he is right. This house isn't big enough for four people. It's hardly big enough for two."

A shiver ran down Azzie's spine. Did that mean they intended to send him away somewhere, too?

"And you don't trust me," Lleuwellyn added.

"I didn't say that."

"You don't have to." He waved his tail, though that didn't stop it from bristling, and shirked off his robe to reveal a lighter tunic beneath. "The couch is lovely. Thank you. Good night."

Eureka frowned, and Azzie thought he might say something almost Baltan-like, but he let it go. "The bathroom is upstairs, first door to your left. I'll make breakfast in the morning and we'll go get you some city clothes. What you've got won't last you long, and the less you stand out, the better."

Lleuwellyn muttered something in acknowledgement that Azzie didn't quite catch, but he was really too tired to listen anymore. With that done, Eureka patted Azzie's head and guided him up the stairs.

Once he was tucked into bed, Eureka asked, "Azzie, what you did earlier, when you were talking... was that on purpose? Did you know what you were doing?"

Azzie gave a sleepy nod.

"Have you always been able to do that?"

He wasn't sure how to answer, so he yawned and nestled into his pillow.

"You must be exhausted." Eureka tugged Azzie's favorite green blanket up a little higher over his chest and rubbed his ears. Louder than he needed to, he added, "I'm going to lock the door before I go to bed, so if you have to go to the bathroom, make sure you go soon." Then, quieter, "Wish me luck with Baltan."

Azzie nodded again and closed his eyes, sleepiness seeping into his bones and making his body heavy against the cloud-soft mattress.

He thought he drifted off to sleep right away, but when he opened his eyes again he could still see light from Eureka and Baltan's room in the hallway and hear their hushed voices as they argued back and forth. Even if Azzie couldn't make out what they were saying, it wasn't hard to guess that they were probably talking about Lleuwellyn.

He heard another sound under their heated whispers, drifting up from the first floor.

Gathering what little energy he had left, Azzie tested the door. It was still unlocked. Thinking on it, he was pretty sure it didn't have a lock at all.

He opened the door quietly and headed down, staying close to the wall where the stairs were less likely to creak, blanket trailing behind him.

Lleuwellyn was lying on his side, his dark hair making him nearly invisible in the unlit room. As Azzie crept closer, he saw Lleuwellyn was holding his tail to his chest, the tip of it wet from tears. Judging from his still shoulders and even breathing, Azzie deduced—something people did often on *The Night Train*—that he cried himself to sleep. Or he was *really* good at pretending not to cry.

Either way, Azzie unfurled the green blanket and draped it over him. It barely covered him from shoulder to toe, but it *did* cover him.

Azzie slipped back upstairs and into his bed, a smile on his face when he felt a little bit of Lleuwellyn's sadness ebb away.

As long as we walk our paths together, we can carry any burden.

And they would have plenty of burdens soon enough.

Act Two

DOWNPOUR

XVI

There was a time when Baltan loved libraries. He could have spent a whole day combing through bookshelf after bookshelf of reference materials and mystery novels. He used to carry out stacks of books taller than himself because they *might* have something to do with his interests, knowing he'd read them cover-to-cover regardless. However, after getting used to computers and their near limitless access to the world's encyclopedias and databases, libraries seemed tedious and ineffective. He didn't have days to spend on research anymore.

Rumor had it the government was going to renovate some of the more popular libraries with computers, but Baltan doubted they'd see such luxury in Marina Delta.

And to top it all off, Baltan wasn't sure where to start with the reference shelf. Did he continue studying up on Eastern religion and hope he stumbled across something useful? Did he look into cult ideology and methodology, criminal psychology, Azure mysticism?

He'd read most of those books before, and if memory served, there was no chapter for how to stop a serial killer from committing mass murder.

He wished he could have access to the recordings of Selkess's therapy sessions at the prison, but that was restricted to current members of the Investigative Department. Reenlisting was the second to last thing he wanted to do, but he would endure another few years in the Department if there was a remote chance that Selkess let something slip in those interviews.

Figure it out, Baltan urged himself. Eureka and Azzie were counting on him—and so was Lleuwellyn.

Try as he might, he couldn't bring himself to care as much about the *new* newcomer. Not so soon after accepting Azzie and not with him looking like the man they were trying to hunt down.

It wasn't Lleuwellyn's fault. He knew that. But he still made Baltan jump every time he caught a glimpse of him. Wandering downstairs half-asleep and nearly drawing a gun on the young man sleeping on the couch hadn't been a pleasant way to start the morning.

Eureka was trying harder to accommodate Lleuwellyn, who was, after all, just another traumatized kid after his father's identity was removed from the equation. But Baltan knew it wasn't the easiest thing Eureka had ever done either.

Baltan gave his head a short shake to clear his mind. He couldn't get distracted and start thinking about Eureka or how much fun he was probably having with their charges at the moment.

Or maybe he could.

Illdresil Gera, the Delta Omega massacre—both crimes had been mass murders of children, but they'd been *Azure* children specifically. There was nothing in the lore he'd read about Kreor that specified a need for Azure children. In fact, given that he was an Eastern deity whose cult predated the Eastern settlers crossing the mountains to the West, it would be incredibly inefficient for his followers to sacrifice Azure children.

So Azure children had to be targets particular to Selkess, which meant he would target Azure children again.

Where was there a large group of Azure children that he could gain easy access to? Being an Azure might have lowered his targets' suspicions in the past, but now that his face looked like *that*, Baltan doubted he'd gain anyone's trust this time.

He'd have to go through some kind of official channel, like a legal custody form, to spirit them away from their parents.

Or present himself as a doctor treating a mysterious illness, like he'd done in Illdresil Gera. If there was some kind of outbreak and he took care to hide his stitched eye, people might be desperate enough to not look twice.

Newspapers. Baltan rushed with single-minded determination to the stacks of recent newspapers in the reading section, combing through every column for any sign of a large number of Azure children suddenly falling ill. Health and Science, Special Interest, Education... nothing. Nothing out of the ordinary from the usual reports on funding issues, school sports, and extracurricular activities that parents and friends were invited to.

Unless Selkess wasn't planning anything in Marina Delta at all. He *had* said he was only staying for a few days until he found somewhere more 'permanent.' At the time Baltan assumed he meant he was staying in the hotel until he found an apartment or house, but what if he had meant leaving the city altogether? That seemed more likely.

So, a place where there were lots of Azure kids, not in Marina Delta—and certainly not Marina Omega or Illdresil Gera again. The parents were still too wary in those locations.

Where could he go?

Baltan left the newspapers for the time being and found a map. His eyes traced the length of the Kwoltan River until he spotted two dots, nearly side-by-side. One, on the West side of the river, was for Kwoltan Gera. The other, on the East side, marked Vinez.

The city was established only a few decades ago. It was unclear for some time if it would remain due to heavy protesting from Kwoltan Gera that, on more than a few occasions, got violent. Eureka commented on it over the years, but not often enough for Baltan to have committed the name to memory.

Baltan went back to the newspapers, found copies brought in from Vinez, and picked up a few of the most recent editions.

Health and Science, nothing.

Special Interest, nothing.

Education—a group of Azures ages ten to sixteen were transported out of the boarding school to be treated for a sudden illness. They were released to the care of medical professionals certified to treat Azures, including tribal doctors.

Baltan tugged at the collar of his sweater, which was suddenly a little too tight against his throat. His trembling fingers took two tries to find their hold.

He checked the date. *Seven days to the first of Capricorn. This happened* two days *ago.*

The article didn't give an exact number on how many children had come down with the illness, but it was definitely more than a dozen.

Baltan's mind leapt to thirty.

How long would Selkess keep them alive? Would he wait until Capricorn, or would he start killing off a few each day? What if he couldn't treat the sickness and they died from it without him even intending it yet?

Baltan steeled himself for a long discussion. Eureka hadn't been thrilled about going to Illdresil Gera, but he was going to *hate* crossing Kwoltan Gera's territory to get to Vinez.

He found every reference he could on the situation, but all he found was a yearbook featuring the school's eighteenth graduating class.

Baltan had hoped for information on exactly *who* the students had been discharged to, which might give him a lead on where to look for them. Assuming Selkess hadn't covered up his crazy eye and gotten them himself, his followers would have posed as medical staff and transported the kids to another location, which would still require an official-looking vehicle at least. Some school official must have seen it and could give them more information.

Unless Selkess had spies in the boarding school.

Boarding school. The phrase left a bitter taste in Baltan's mouth, but it was the best lead he had. It didn't take long to find multiple articles on it in the small section of the library dedicated to Vinez.

Baltan skimmed through the records. "Prince Anekhm Memorial Boarding School for Azure Youths, established roughly twenty years ago... open enrollment for Azure children but built specifically for tribal children… Frequent conflict with Kwoltan Gera over teachings and removal of students from tribal lands…"

So most, if not all, of the kidnapped children were from Kwoltan Gera itself.

Great.

Baltan read up as much as he could about the areas that were still under construction or less likely to be frequented by the general public. There were a few places—half-finished factories and warehouses, mostly—but nothing that leapt out at him as a sinister cult's evil lair.

He would need Eureka's help brushing up on his Azure language skills. He managed well enough in Illdresil Gera when he was only supposed to listen, but talking to the members of Kwoltan Gera was going to be a must. With any luck they might rally some support from the warrior tribe. Baltan would feel a lot better about charging into near-certain death if he had a platoon of trained fighters behind him. Usually he felt sure of victory as long as Eureka was by his side, but the last time it had been the two of them against Selkess, both of them had barely come out alive.

Besides, if Selkess got to have a group of bloodthirsty monsters on his side, Baltan saw no reason why they shouldn't have some righteously pissed off parents on theirs.

There was no way they could leave Azzie and Lleuwellyn at home, and no way they could be a part of the confrontation. They'd have to get a hotel room in Vinez, which wouldn't be cheap, but at least it would give Azzie and Lleuwellyn somewhere safe to stay while they handled everything.

He examined a map of the city and tried to scope out which hotel would be the best to stay in. It had to be somewhere near the boarding school, as he didn't think the cult had gotten their captives too far away from it. The further they went, the more conspicuous they would look. He'd have to make a copy of the map and draw out a radius around the school. It shouldn't be too hard to figure out the distance they'd likely been able to travel. Then he could look into locations within that circle where the cult might be able to hide a group of ten to sixteen year olds without drawing much attention.

Focus! The hotel first. There were a few small ones near the school, closer to the river, and not as grand as all the tourist attractions near the center of the city. The Seashell Inn & Spa looked promising. It advertised itself as a 'staycation getaway,' and it was a stone's throw from districts that were still under construction or recently completed.

He slid his finger around the dial to the first digit on the phone number, then put the note in his pocket and the handset back on the receiver. He couldn't book the reservation without at least telling Eureka. They had to act fast, he knew that, but it wouldn't matter if they weren't united. The only reason they survived Selkess the first time was because they got over their differences and worked together.

Baltan mulled over what he hoped was a compelling speech in his head. If he couldn't convince Eureka to act immediately, they and a bunch of Azure kids were doomed for sure.

Eureka brought Lleuwellyn and Azzie to the library some time in the afternoon. Baltan tucked his printed map into one of the books he was checking out before getting on the bus with them.

The ride home was quiet and tense. Baltan couldn't risk talking about anything in public. He wasn't even sure he could risk talking about it in the house. All he'd said to Eureka when they arrived was, "I need to talk to you, privately, later," and a heavy silence followed. He didn't even complain that Eureka had *three* large shopping bags full of clothes slung over his shoulder.

They got off the bus a few stops early to swing by the local grocery store and pick up some frozen dinners and a head of lettuce. That was a crime in and of itself, but Eureka was not going to have time to cook a meal that night. They would have to analyze Baltan's findings, follow up on what they already knew, pack, and possibly interrogate Azzie or Lleuwellyn if they were up to it. They'd be lucky if they got to bed before dawn.

Baltan wasn't looking forward to it, and he avoided looking at Eureka, which was making it all worse. Lleuwellyn and Azzie were keeping themselves distracted, at least; in the store, Lleuwellyn deemed it necessary to explain the medicinal values of every herb and spice they walked past to Azzie, who nodded along in understanding.

Baltan doubted Lleuwellyn's diversion was actually working. Azzie was too observant not to notice the unease between him and Eureka, and too curious not to wonder what it was about.

By the time they got home, Baltan had been clenching his jaw long enough and hard enough to give himself a headache. Once the groceries were in the kitchen and the oven on preheat, he marched straight up to the master bedroom. Eureka followed so close that Baltan barely had to wait to close the door behind him.

"What did you find?" Eureka asked.

"A group of kids in an Azure boarding school came down with a mysterious sickness and were transported out of school grounds," Baltan answered. "There's no way it isn't Selkess's doing, especially considering what happened in Illdresil Gera."

Anyone who didn't know him would have missed the subtle shift in Eureka's shoulders, the briefest dart of his tongue soothing suddenly dry lips and the way his jaw clenched after. But Baltan didn't miss anything.

Baltan rubbed his temples to try to ease some of the soreness. Both of them were steeled against what they knew was coming next. "We have to go, and we'll have to cross through Kwoltan Gera territory to get there. If possible, I'd like to stop there and talk to them, maybe get some backup if we can. I know it's going to be hard for you, but—"

"I'll go," Eureka said, standing at his full height with shoulders squared.

Baltan blinked. "What? Just like that?"

"I need to talk to my brother. I have to know if there's any possible way he could be Azzie's father, because if he's not, and I *am*, then..." He swallowed hard. "I *have* to know. It's a huge risk, but this mystery deserves to be solved, too."

"Well, that's that, then. I'll book a room for us at one of the local hotels."

"No, that won't be necessary." Baltan could tell Eureka was the one measuring his words now. His spoke slowly, like he was trying to string together the exact right phrases. "I said *I'll* go. You, Azzie, and Lleuwellyn should stay here for now."

Baltan narrowed his eyes, but before he could say anything, Eureka said, "You saw how Sheria reacted to you. Kwoltan Gera will be worse. It's a warrior tribe. They won't suffer trespassers lightly."

"I know," Baltan replied, straightening his back. "But I can't let you to go into danger by yourself. It's better that we're there to watch each other's backs."

"And leave Lleuwellyn and Azzie with no one to look out for them?" Eureka shook his head. "No. I can't risk that."

At the mention of Lleuwellyn, Baltan set his jaw to hold back a nasty remark. He had made his disdain for the situation known, and that wasn't the point. "I thought you said Kwoltan Gera Azures didn't kill needlessly."

"Driving out an intruder *is* just cause," Eureka growled, resting one claw on the long scar that divided his face. "Believe me, I am not underestimating how much danger I'll be in, but I'm the only one who has a chance of getting in undetected. If I can contact Keida, I'm sure he'll at least hear me out about the investigation—and Azzie."

"If you get hurt or killed, we won't know until it's too late." Baltan folded his arms. They had to stay together. This wasn't separating for an afternoon to get two different tasks done. If Eureka went to Kwoltan Gera by himself, he might never come back. Quietly, he added, "I won't let anything bad happen to you."

Eureka faltered.

"*You* could get hurt, Baltan."

It was such an *Eureka* thing to say that for a moment Baltan couldn't come up with anything to say back.

He certainly hadn't anticipated the sudden rush of anger. Baltan thought years in retirement might have left Eureka a little more reasonable about these things, but clearly he was wrong.

"Why do you always do that? Why do you always have to be the one to get hurt? You dragged me into this, dammit, you're not kicking me out now!"

"Baltan—"

"No. I'm going with you, and where we go, Lleuwellyn and Azzie go too. We'll make it work. We always do."

"You sound certain."

"I am," Baltan answered, meeting his eyes, "Because when I say that I won't let anything bad happen to you, I mean it." His eyes were starting to sting. This was getting too personal, too close to things that mattered too much and thoughts that had kept him awake too many nights.

"I'm not going to say you can go," Eureka said.

"It doesn't matter what you say," Baltan shot back. "I'm going. End of story."

Eureka made a noise that was half-groan, half-growl. "Promise me you'll protect Azzie and Lleuwellyn *first*, no matter what happens to me."

"Okay, I promise."

He didn't know if it was a lie or not.

XVII

Getting onto another bus was one of the last things Azzie wanted to do.

As far as he could tell, Lleuwellyn was sick of them, too. The former seer sat with his tail in his lap, absently stroking the fur to keep it from puffing out whenever the bus ran over a bump in the road. Their trip to the shopping center hadn't taken that long, and he had been too lost in grief over Turnap to pay much attention during the journey from the hills back to the city. Now, with nothing to distract him from the never-ending ride, he fidgeted and chewed on his lower lip and couldn't stop crossing and uncrossing his long legs.

The movement jostled Baltan's seat. Up front, there was plenty of room for passengers to stretch their legs, but they and the rest of the Azures on board were seated in cramped rows near the back

"Would you stop that?" Baltan snapped, not bothering to whisper. The moment he turned to face the window, Lleuwellyn crossed his legs again—left over right—and glared at him.

For the rest of the bus ride, every time Baltan looked over, Lleuwellyn readjusted his legs and shot him a mean look. Azzie stifled his laughter at first, but even that got old as the morning dragged on.

Baltan assured them it wouldn't be as long as last time. They were traveling about the same distance, but the road didn't have as many winding paths around or over hills. It still *felt* like it was taking forever.

After the way Illdresil Gera had treated them, Azzie didn't know whether to be excited or terrified. He wanted to see Kwoltan Gera and meet more Azures like Eureka, but Eureka told him Kwoltan Gera was a warrior village and they might be angry. He and Baltan might get hurt. Even Lleuwellyn could be attacked.

Eureka and Baltan were busy for most of the previous evening, so Azzie spent his time with Lleuwellyn in his room (but only with the door open; Eureka was *very* clear about that). It was easier for Lleuwellyn to talk away from the adults.

"Kwoltan Gera are the fiercest warriors to ever live," Lleuwellyn told him. "They're fearless, they're strong, and they don't question orders. They won't hesitate if their king tells them to attack, no matter the odds." The end of his tail curled in. "They're dangerous. All of Illdresil Gera's sentries wouldn't stand a chance in a fight against a single warband. If the Easterners didn't have guns and silver, they would never have settled on this side of the river, and they still leave Kwoltan Gera alone if they can help it."

Azzie didn't want to think Azures like Eureka could be so violent and mean, but Eureka was an outcast. What if he'd been sent away for being too kind? How much pain could someone his size cause if they didn't hesitate to use their claws and fangs?

The thought followed him for the whole journey, keeping him alert despite his boredom. Every time his eyelids started to get heavy, he imagined the warriors rising out of the river to wipe out everything in their path, starting with Eureka, Baltan, and Lleuwellyn.

The bus jerked to a stop. The doors hissed as they opened.

After an entire morning of waiting and wondering, they had arrived.

Eureka and Azzie stood first, though Baltan made sure to move between Azzie and the exit once he was out of his seat. "Can't have you running off again."

I won't, Azzie wanted to say, but his voice must not have caught up to them yet. He shook his head instead and waited, very still and patient, until it was their turn to finally get off the bus.

The first thing Azzie saw was the river.

The clear water flowed smoothly, skimming against the sandy banks and running over worn stones without changing its path. He thought it would be like the ocean, lapping against the shore with a steady rhythm, but it bubbled along without a care for anything beyond its edges. It didn't bother to reach out to him the way the tide did, but he felt compelled to go closer and listen to the light, playful sounds it made.

Baltan steered him away with a steady hand, toward a small building with archways almost too tall for it. The same late autumn sun that shimmered across the river glinted off the steel beams and glass of the ferry station, but the cold, gray metal felt out of place against the vibrant plant life that grew along the riverbank.

Azzie frowned as Baltan hurried them into the station to check in, his eyes wary for signs of movement along the river. When he was satisfied that no Kwoltan Gera warriors were going to attack, he instead eyed everyone in the station with suspicion. The attendant handed him the boarding passes for the next ferry and assured him that their luggage was already being taken from the bus to the cargo hold.

Azzie didn't see anyone around them who looked suspicious, but he carefully tucked the boarding pass into his pocket.

"You should stay here," Eureka said to Baltan, casting a nervous glance across the valley, to the huts visible in the distance, "You can keep an eye on things and let me—"

"No."

Azzie lifted his ears at Baltan's harsh tone. He had heard him raise his voice the previous day. Were Eureka and Baltan fighting?

Baltan went on with the same sharpness, "The next ferry won't be here until nearly sundown. That gives us plenty of time to talk, and we'd better get started, because there's a lot to go over."

"It's not safe," Eureka growled.

Baltan ignored him and left the station, leaving the rest of them to follow. Eureka caught up in a heartbeat, walking stiffly beside Baltan with Lleuwellyn and Azzie hidden behind him. His movements were different. In the city he hunched himself down and did his best to make himself less bulky. Now he was like a riptide, calm on the surface but dangerous beneath, ready to attack any moment. Baltan, too, looked less like he was watching out for danger and more like he was a hawk searching for a mouse to swoop down on.

The road that led to the station turned into gravel and dirt after a few steps. To the right was a line of trees wearing thick coats of ivy, the river, and the wonderful sound of the water swirling around the stones. In front of them was a field of grass almost as tall as Azzie, dotted with small yellow flowers and bushes with purple fronds.

He looked down at the ground, where the line between dirt and grass was as clearly defined as the scar across Eureka's face. He took a step into the field, then back onto the dusty soil, hopping between them. Grass, dirt, grass, dirt, grass, dirt...

"*Azzie!*" Lleuwellyn hissed, grabbing his hand and tugging him into line behind Eureka. He pointed at one of the several signs posted above the grass. "We have to be *discreet.*"

Azzie wasn't sure what that was or what the sign said, but he walked as quietly as possible, bending his knees a little more so he was invisible from his eyes down.

Eureka stopped so suddenly they nearly crashed into him.

Baltan turned back with a glare that disappeared when Eureka grabbed his arm and pulled the Easterner behind him.

Azzie didn't think anyone Eureka's size would be able to hide in the tall grass, but the three Azures that emerged from it were not as big as Eureka. They still looked as strong as Lleuwellyn said they would.

The leader was a woman, smaller than Lleuwellyn, but her exposed arms were all hard muscle. Her ears were like Azzie's, the left nicked at the end. She flicked them twice and the other warriors got into formation at her sides. To her right was a lean man whose dark blue skin and hair reminded Azzie of Lleuwellyn, but everything else about them was different. He curled his lip back, revealing teeth as jagged as the scar on his chin. To the left was another woman, smaller, who moved like liquid and had longer claws than the other two.

The warriors' pupils disappeared into white as they approached, and Azzie couldn't tell what they were thinking at all anymore.

Their eyes looked less human. More animal. More dangerous.

They were close enough for Azzie to see each of their scars, to hear the growls in their throats.

He would have lowered himself further into the grass to hide if he could move at all.

Eureka charged forward, getting away from the others so they wouldn't be caught in the fight.

The three scouts lunged at him, their claws tangling in the threads of his sweater. He turned, trying to throw them off, but they held fast and dug their claws in deeper, dragging him down.

Azzie's stomach turned at the smell of blood. *Whose blood?*

Eureka managed to land a blow on the lead scout's shoulder, but she only pulled back for a heartbeat, leaping onto his back and stabbing her claws into his shoulder blades as he fell to the ground. He struggled to stand, but like a whale breaching the surface, he fell back down into the churning tide of snarling bodies.

Azzie curled his lips and tensed his legs. He didn't care if he was outmatched or outnumbered. Doing nothing would hurt more than any bite or scratch.

"No!" Lleuwellyn grabbed his arm the moment he dashed toward the thrashing warriors. "They'll kill you!"

A thunderclap caused more birds than Azzie could count to take flight from the trees.

The fighting stopped as quickly as it started.

Baltan stood with his arm raised, pistol in hand, a glower fixed on the scouts.

He snarled something in Azure and the warriors reluctantly let Eureka up. His sweater was torn and he was bleeding from scratches on his chest, back, and a cut above his right eye. He shook it off, pressing the tattered remains of his clothes to the wounds like it was nothing.

Aside from the head scout's shoulder wound, the warriors didn't have any noticeable injuries. Although Azzie's heart wouldn't stop its pounding, he was glad to see Eureka hadn't hurt them. He wasn't cruel, no matter where he came from.

The white film vanished from their eyes, but two of the warriors looked ready to restart the battle the moment any of the outsiders made one wrong move. Their leader was hardly paying them any attention, turning her head away to wipe away the thin line of blood trickling down her forearm. She flicked her ears at them again and they stood back

Despite Lleuwellyn squeezing his arm, Azzie forced his trembling legs to lift him out of the tall grass so he could flick his ears in return. He hoped that was some way to say, 'we aren't going to hurt you.'

"Strange group," she commented in near-perfect common language.

"Strange times," Baltan responded. "We need to speak to your king. It's important. Can you escort us?"

The long-clawed warrior edged forward. "What business do an Easterner, an exile, and a prey animal have with our king?"

"Life-saving business." Lleuwellyn kept his head and tail low in a show of respect, and maybe to hide the fact that it was still bushed out in fear.

Eureka continued with a longer explanation in Azure. Azzie wished he could understand it, especially when the warriors' eyes widened and the man's mouth dropped open.

The leader snapped an order and the other two scouts raced back to the village, disappearing into the grass again. "You will be expected at the village. I will take you there." She looked to Eureka, her fierce eyes softened by a smile. "You still fight like you used to."

"I never had to fight harder than that against my tribemates," Eureka replied. Her scratches were already closing, but his still bled into his sweater.

She started toward the village, staying at Eureka's side while Azzie, Baltan, and Lleuwellyn were left to follow. Baltan and Lleuwellyn seemed content to walk further back and let them talk in private, but Azzie wanted to hear what they were saying.

Her chin was lifted with pride. "My name is Kariet-*Loloa* now."

"You've become a fine warrior." Eureka nodded, smiling as if she hadn't left deep scratches down his back. Maybe that was how things worked in Kwoltan Gera. "How are the others?"

"The same, mostly. You would think getting older and having kids would change them, but..."

"Has it changed *you*?"

Kariet-Loloa's laugh was unrestrained. "I suppose not, aside from giving me more to worry about." In a moment her cheer faded, her ears drooped, and she looked too much like the Azures of Illdresil Gera. "If what your companion said is true, I have two daughters who are in danger. Can you really help us save them?"

"I suppose that depends on what Egrieak-Kouran decides."

Kariet-Loloa nearly stopped walking and shook her hand to get some of the fresh blood off of her claws. "Let's hope your allies are persuasive, then."

XVIII

It had taken all of Baltan's self-control not to shoot the warriors that attacked Eureka.

They had known from the start that coming into the tribe's territory was a major risk. They were lucky the patrol had let up, and luckier still to be allowed into the village. He would have made everything worse if he had fired at the warriors.

But it was cowardly to do nothing but watch while Eureka fought for him.

He should probably be paying more attention to what the head scout and Eureka were saying, but they only spoke briefly and then continued on toward the village in silence. Hopefully her now-friendly demeanor boded well for how the rest of Kwoltan Gera would react.

Maybe they'd finally forgiven him for whatever he'd done to be banished. Baltan wasn't going to stake his life on it.

It crossed his mind that she might be an old flame of Eureka's. He hardly ever talked about his life in the tribe, and Baltan rarely thought about it. The unspoken agreement between them to not bring up painful memories had stood largely untested for fifteen years; Eureka didn't talk about Kwoltan Gera, and Baltan didn't talk about why he'd been living on his own as a teenager when they met.

The idea that he didn't know what Eureka was like before never bothered him. He'd always thought of *before* as dead and gone. Neither of them had anticipated it coming back to life and smacking them in the face like this.

Baltan considered the easy laugh that Eureka coaxed from the warrior despite what hung over them. Had he been popular in the tribe? Were there warriors who would be happy to see him again? He couldn't imagine Eureka had many enemies, but they had still cast him out.

There was one warrior in particular that occupied his thoughts.

Keida.

He clenched his fists briefly and forced himself not to start up with theories and speculations. He would meet Keida soon enough and know for sure what kind of person he was. Still, he couldn't help wondering if Keida would welcome his brother back, or chase him off with more than a few scratches.

Eureka only ever spoke of his family on his worst days, those rare occasions when he was the one to suggest going out and getting a drink. He'd never been any good at holding his liquor, and after a few drinks he'd sink his head onto his hands and mutter words of regret, longing, and the closest thing to hate Baltan ever heard from Eureka.

All of it was centered on Keida.

Eureka never said why he was exiled, and Baltan never asked. Some things were better left in the dark, away from prying eyes like his, but he couldn't help but piece together what little he did know. Keida had something to do with Eureka's banishment.

The closer they got to the village, the more Lleuwellyn's tail swished back and forth nervously. Baltan wished Azzie would slow down and walk with them, if only because Lleuwellyn settled down around him and his twitching was putting Baltan even more on edge, but he didn't dare raise his voice loud enough to call him.

The entire village halted at their arrival.

Old men and women stopped their gossiping; young adults talking over the fish they were eating swallowed their last mouthfuls and set the morsels down. A group of older warriors, who were standing in a circle with their heads bowed, looked up at them with narrowed eyes as the head scout joined them to make her report. Many others lingered by huts made from stone and wood, not hiding, but hanging back and watching in case they were needed.

Eureka scanned the faces present, but his eyes didn't linger anywhere. Keida must not be there. Baltan wasn't sure if that was good or bad.

They waited for someone in the tribe to say something. The gathered warriors waited for them to speak. The silence dragged on until all Baltan could hear was the pounding of his own heart as he struggled to ignore the hateful glares sent his way.

Another group entered the village, including one of the patrol members who had attacked Eureka. Only one of them had needed to bring the message to the tribe; the other must have gone off to fetch another scout troop.

At the front of the group was a large man, who stopped dead once he saw them.

It was like looking at a reflection of Eureka in a fun-house mirror. His face was younger-looking, free from the corrosion of life in the city, but he lacked the laugh lines around his eyes and the softer, kinder features that so defined Eureka. He was harder, less forgiving, and three crooked scars tore down the right side of his face. His left eye was the same sea-green color that Eureka and Azzie's were, but his narrower right eye was milky white and sightless.

His good eye searched through Lleuwellyn and Azzie, each of them standing up a little straighter to try to meet his gaze. Lleuwellyn brushed his bangs away from his face to briefly reveal his own scar before letting the natural veil fall back into place.

Keida was hesitant to look at Eureka, but when he did, the change in both of them was instantaneous. Eureka stood tall and proud, more than twenty years of weight lifted with the smallest smile and nod of acknowledgment from Keida. Whatever happened between them was forgiven.

Then Keida's eye settled on Baltan. His lip curled back slightly, revealing the barest hint of fang. He forced his contempt through those gritted teeth with one word. "Eureka."

Eureka stepped between him and Baltan, raising his chin and shoulders against the weight that crashed back onto them. "Keida."

Keida took a step, but paused his advance when a sharp, barked command drew the attention of everyone in the village.

The circle of warriors parted to allow their king through.

Baltan's eyes widened for a moment. The king was as big as Eureka and covered in battle scars that made him look older and meaner, though he certainly needed no help on either. A crown of woven grass and reeds sat on his permanently furrowed brow.

Aside from his dark blue eyes and cat-like ears, he was a dead ringer for an older Eureka.

Eureka looked back to Baltan for a moment, and Baltan caught his gaze.

Couldn't you have mentioned the king was your father sooner? Baltan hoped he received the message through his brief glare. Eureka opened his mouth, closed it, and returned his attention to the king, so Baltan trusted he did.

One more reason for Eureka to be reluctant to talk about his family, Baltan supposed. Being banished was bad enough. Being banished by your own father must have been unbearable.

And worse, he didn't look happy to see Eureka at all. He was nothing short of furious to see the rest of them.

"For what reason have you dared show your cursed face here?" he growled at Eureka, extending a claw accusingly.

Eureka explained as best he could, but he was stammering and stumbling over his words. "I... *we*, I mean... have come to help you. We have an enemy in common, and we can help—we can tell you more about him, come up with a plan..." He swallowed hard, "... s-sire."

The other warriors examined Eureka, whispering quietly to each other. If their king gave the order, they would tear Eureka to shreds, but there were sympathetic faces among the crowd. Some of them must have known and liked Eureka well enough when he was still with the tribe, and the woman from before kept trying to wipe her claws clean. She couldn't be too eager to draw blood again, and those around her looked equally as hesitant. A few nodded encouragingly to Eureka, and one even mouthed something to him.

They could be our allies, Baltan thought, *But only if Eureka convinces the king.*

The odds of that did not look good. He was listening as a formality; he made up his mind the moment he laid eyes on Eureka.

"We're here to help," Eureka repeated, breathless. "The tribe's children are in grave danger. They've been kidnapped by a murderer, and he will kill every single one of them if we don't stop him."

"Egrieak-Kouran," Keida cut in, standing side-by-side with Eureka to address the king. He didn't waste a moment between words, and even the more hostile members of the crowd leaned in and paid attention to what he said. "We should allow them to help us. If what Eureka says is true, and we have no reason to doubt him, then we will need assistance from those who know our foe better than we do." He tilted his head to address the riveted warriors. "It may be our only chance to save the children. A brute force attack will not help us in this situation. We need strategy, and for that we need knowledge we don't currently have."

The tribe's reaction wasn't lost on Egrieak-Kouran. He appraised the crowd to see how many were actively on his side versus how many were listening to Keida and saw that he was outnumbered.

One of the other warriors in the now split circle spoke up. Baltan made a mental note of his nose, which looked like it had been broken and set poorly some years ago. "Does it matter who helps us, as long as we get our children back? I'd fight beside rabid foxes if it meant keeping my son and daughter safe!"

More and more of the warriors started to nod and talk among themselves. Relief washed over Baltan and he let his shoulders relax. They wouldn't take much convincing after all.

Egrieak-Kouran cleared his throat, and immediately the chattering ceased and the warriors looked to him. The hope that dared to flutter in Baltan's chest sank back down to the earth. No matter how they felt, only Egrieak-Kouran's decision really mattered.

The king motioned for the outsiders to follow and headed for the southernmost hut, a massive structure that was nearly empty aside from a few brightly colored cloths hanging on the walls.

A sense of unease crept over Baltan. With the way the tribe was leaning, he didn't like being almost entirely alone with the one person who was dead-set against them. And with the size of the hut being what it was, he got the distinct feeling there ought to be more people in it.

Then again, Egrieak-Kouran seemed to take up all the empty space in the hut. Being in his presence was suffocating.

The king said something, and Keida reluctantly stood at his side. "I will translate," he growled.

Baltan almost winced on his behalf. That was certainly one way to silence opposition—making Keida say everything Egrieak-Kouran wanted, unable to speak his own mind on the issue, despite the fact that Baltan could understand well enough on his own. It was ingenious, and profoundly cruel.

"I can speak Azure," Baltan said.

The king looked at him as if he was a rotten fish and spoke so quietly only Keida could hear him.

"Your wife hurts my eyes."

At once, Eureka stood taller, squared his shoulders, and set his jaw. "Then my eyes must be stronger than yours; they aren't bothered at all."

Baltan couldn't help smiling, and he caught Lleuwellyn stifling a laugh. Eureka's hands might still be shaking, but he didn't break eye contact with Egrieak-Kouran.

"You should not have come back," Keida frowned, the wrinkles on his face mirroring the king's for a moment. "You have broken tribe law by setting foot on our land, and now you demand our help to fix a problem created by the Easterners."

"I don't demand anything," Eureka challenged. "We have information that can save the tribe's children—like the fact that Easterners *aren't* responsible for this. Isn't it more important for us to get the children back, unharmed? You can settle whatever score there is with me later, once they're safe."

"Our plan is already made. We can find and rescue them ourselves, without the help of rogues and red bloods."

"That's stupid," Baltan cut in. "You have no idea what you're up against. You could be leading your people to slaughter!"

"Insolent Easterner!" Egrieak-Kouran roared. He raised a hand to strike Baltan with his claws, but Eureka was faster. He lunged between them and parried the blow, then landed a slash of his own on the king's shoulder.

Baltan grabbed Lleuwellyn and Azzie and pulled them out of the way. Egrieak-Kouran's momentum led him to an unsteady stop where they had just been.

Eureka's voice was too cold. "If you respect power more than reason, then I'll convince you with power instead."

"You think *one* counterattack makes you powerful?" Egrieak-Kouran laughed.

"No. It makes me *merciful*."

Tension cracked through the air like static before a storm. They both stood completely still, Egrieak-Kouran not bothering to look at the bleeding wound on his shoulder. One wrong move from either of them and a full-blown brawl would break out.

Baltan didn't miss Keida's reaction as he watched with uncertainty, ready to fight but not sure who to fight for. It was obvious he disagreed with Egrieak-Kouran, but would he dare cross his king for the sake of his brother?

Egrieak-Kouran didn't risk it. Despite his bared teeth, he relented, crossing his arms to conceal his claws.

"They can help," the king grunted stiffly to Keida, "But *you* are in charge. What you say, they will do, not the other way."

Keida stood up a little taller even as he dipped his head in respect. Baltan wanted to cheer; they'd managed to get Kwoltan Gera's support without too much bloodshed or pushing, and the warrior most likely to cooperate was leading the rescue effort.

The king didn't stay in the hut for a moment longer. Baltan wondered what the other warriors would think of his scratch, but that didn't matter as long as they listened to orders and assisted them.

Free from the prying eyes of the tribe, Keida's expression softened with sympathy for Eureka. "You've come at a bad time, but it's good to see you. I did not think I would again in this life."

"Likewise," Eureka responded, "What are you called now?"

"My full name is Keida-Boitrat." He looked at the whole group again, and once more Baltan felt his searing gaze as his eye raked across him. "I never expected you'd be in the company of one of them."

"Baltan is my closest friend. He is as noble and brave as any warrior in the tribe." He gestured to the other two. "Lleuwellyn and Azzie have seen more suffering than either of us will ever know, but they still stand ready to help save Kwoltan Gera's children. As do I. Under your direction, of course, Keida-Boitrat."

"Has so much changed, for you to be formal with me?"

Eureka took so long to answer that Baltan wondered if he would say anything at all. "I have missed you every day. But I have lived a life outside the village, too." His voice was more solemn than Baltan had ever heard. Eureka placed one arm around Baltan, the other around Azzie and Lleuwellyn. He did not hold them tight, but Baltan could feel how tense he was anyway, still ready to fight.

A dozen emotions—jealousy, pain, betrayal, guilt—washed over Keida's face, before finally settling on begrudging acceptance. "If they are as courageous as you say, then they have a place here."

Eureka relaxed, but Azzie and Baltan stayed near him. Lleuwellyn alone moved away with uncertain steps, one hand touching the place where Eureka's arm had been.

Keida did not approach despite the longing in his eye. He spoke only in the detached tone of a strategist.

"We need a plan that the tribe can follow. I suggest we take a small group, including myself, to find the children. Our efforts should be focused on getting the children away from the kidnappers, so stealth is preferable to force. Once we find them, we'll sneak them out, and call in reinforcements only if completely necessary. You have some idea where they are, I hope?"

"I've narrowed it down to a few different places. We'll need to do more reconnaissance to figure out which is the most likely and find out if we can actually connect the kidnappers to that location," Baltan answered in Azure, puffing himself up a little.

Keida blinked at him, and Eureka translated the words that he must have gotten wrong. Then Keida nodded. "I'll choose warriors who know the city. They should be able to help with this... re-con-nuisance. Most of them speak common language better than I."

"You're doing better than I thought you would," Eureka said. "How did—"

"The school," Keida spat as if he'd tasted poison. "We speak our language with our children as much as we can, but they learn to speak common language and use it more now. And we must take jobs outside the tribe to pay for their school things, so we must speak our job's language, too. I picked it up faster than others my age, but the young of the tribe are better. They will help the most."

Eureka didn't look convinced, and Baltan could see both the merits and potential dangers in that decision. Having younger warriors who were more or less fluent in common language might make them inconspicuous and help them get around Vinez, but it also meant they were taking an inexperienced group into danger.

Keida sighed, "Egrieak-Kouran wants me to fail. He wants to prove he knows better and the old ways are best. But his plan—waging a war on Vinez—will get us all killed. We are warriors, but fighting is not always the answer." He hesitantly extended a hand to Baltan. "Tell me what you know of our enemy, and I will choose the best warriors for the mission."

Baltan took his hand and gave it a firm shake.

By midday, the warriors' hut was packed full of volunteers.

Baltan stood at the center of the room with Eureka and Keida. Lleuwellyn and Azzie were off to the side, close enough to keep an eye on but far enough that no one mistook them for a part of the mission's leadership.

Baltan lifted his chin, steadied his footing, and spoke with as clear and confident a voice as he could manage when his stomach was tying itself in knots.

"Several of this tribe's children were taken from the Prince Anekhm Memorial Boarding School two days ago for treatment of a mysterious illness. We believe this is not a natural illness, but was directly caused by a dangerous killer in order to get access to his victims. If we're correct, we only have a few days to find and rescue them before they're murdered."

A few of the gathered warriors gasped, and others leaned against each other for support, but they all kept their gaze firmly on Baltan as Keida translated for those who didn't speak common language well.

Baltan continued, "We're going to start by taking a small group with us to Vinez to do more research. Once we're ready, we'll assess the risks and possibly send for backup. If we do, we'll most likely need a full war party. We don't know yet how many allies our enemy has or the size of the location the children are being held in. Once we know, we'll be able to decide how many warriors we need to take them back. Eureka and I will be fighting, too. Anyone who agrees to joining this mission needs to understand and accept the high chance that we might not all make it back."

He paused for translation, and again was met with the unwavering focus of every warrior in the hut.

"To start with, we need younger tribe members who know the area and common language well."

That got a reaction out of them. The older warriors shouted their dissent, and Baltan couldn't blame them. They were most likely the parents or grandparents of the kidnapped children, and they had every right to want to be a part of this plan. Especially when they were being passed over for less experienced warriors.

"They have to prove themselves at some point," Keida said, soothing the crowd enough to get them listening again. "Would any of you doubt the teachings of their mentors? I will not select anyone without complete faith in their abilities. The young warriors are the right ones for *this* part of the mission. Take this time to sharpen your claws and practice your battle skills. You may have your chance to join the rescue effort soon enough."

There was no denying Keida was an eloquent speaker, and he probably would have sounded a lot better if Baltan was fluent. However, he couldn't help but question if maybe they ought to be taking along at least one senior warrior besides Keida.

He didn't have any say in that. Keida cleared his throat.

"Filhi-Viriar, Teirik-Viriar, and Erisolus-Ashail will join us."

The three chosen warriors struggled to the front of the gathering. They didn't look like the most intimidating bunch; Filhi-Viriar and Teirik-Viriar barely looked older than those they would be saving. That might be the point, but it would also mean Eureka and Keida would stick out more and be bigger targets. Erisolus-Ashail wasn't much better, and Baltan recognized him as one of the warriors who had attacked Eureka.

Not a single one of them refused the mission, each nodding to Keida in acknowledgment of their roles.

"What about them?" a young girl asked, coming forward from behind Erisolus-Ashail to point at Lleuwellyn and Azzie. "Are they going?"

Keida looked to Eureka and Baltan. They hadn't had a chance to discuss it, but Baltan almost wanted to leave Lleuwellyn and Azzie in the village. They would probably be safer there, surrounded by trained warriors who were ready to fight the cult with all their might. Then again, Baltan wouldn't put it past Selkess to have the whole valley set on fire to smoke them out.

"They'll be safest where we can keep an eye on them," Eureka said.

"If they're going, then I should be able to go, too," the girl continued, glaring accusingly at Azzie. "*He's* barely old enough to be out of the nursery by himself. I know the city better than anyone, I'm fluent in common language, and none of the young warriors are better at tracking or stealth than I am."

"*No,*" Keida said sharply. "You will stay here and be ready to assist the warriors in their preparations."

"But *I* didn't get sick!" she protested. "Doesn't that count for anything?"

"You didn't get sick because you were, 'suspended for vandalizing school property,'" Keida countered, though he didn't sound too angry. Given the fact that the last part of his sentence sounded like he was parroting an official, Baltan doubted he knew or cared what the words meant.

"The locker room needed a fresh coat of paint," she shrugged.

"Naesa," Keida said. "I said *no,* and that's final."

Oh, he's her father, Baltan thought. Then he looked to Eureka, whose expression was nothing short of bewilderment. *Which means... he* could *be Azzie's, too.*

A woman slipped through the crowd and rested a hand on her shoulder. She could only be Naesa's mother; the resemblance in their faces—pointed chin, high cheekbones, sharp nose—was uncanny. Naesa wasn't placated, casting a forlorn look at Keida as she was guided back into the crowd.

"Does anyone have any questions?" Eureka asked.

"You haven't told us about the coward who did this yet," the warrior with the broken nose said.

Lleuwellyn curled his tail around himself.

"He's incredibly dangerous. That *cannot* be overstated," Baltan explained. "His name is Selkess. Some years ago, he murdered nearly all of Illdresil Gera's children, and he repeated his killing spree a year later in Marina Omega, which is when we caught him. If he isn't stopped soon, he and his followers *will* murder all of the children he kidnapped."

"How could he have gotten so close to their nursery?" a woman rounded on Lleuwellyn. "Doesn't your tribe *guard* their young?"

Following her lead, the rest of the gathered warriors turned their attention on him, and he shrank back from their intent gazes.

"He was their seer at the time," Eureka said, drawing the warriors' focus back to him.

He succeeded; all of them stared at him with wide eyes.

"You mean to tell me that you're sending our warriors into battle against a *seer* from *Illdresil Gera?*" an older woman snarled.

Baltan considered that for a moment. If it became necessary, would they hesitate to attack, or maybe even kill, a seer? She didn't sound as if she minded the idea of it. She sounded more like she didn't think it was possible.

"We'll factor it into our strategy and make it work. If our ancestors could defeat Illdresil Gera in the past, we can find a way to do it now," Keida soothed. "Are there any other questions?"

"How long is 'a few days?'" a man in the back asked.

Baltan closed his eyes for a moment, and tried to look more confident than he felt when he opened them again and answered, "Counting today, four."

There was a long pause. Some of the resolve in the warriors' expressions faltered for a moment. Even a few more days would have given them time to do more thorough reconnaissance, make sure they knew where Selkess was keeping the hostages, get a feel for what they were dealing with. At this rate they'd be lucky if they had a decent hunch before it was time to launch their offensive, and it would be all too easy for Selkess to fool them with a decoy. They didn't have enough time to be certain.

But, true to their reputation, none of them backed down.

Baltan looked to Azzie. He was concentrating hard on the meeting even though he didn't understand most of it. A lot probably went over his head due to age alone; he simply couldn't know what it was like to be unable to protect the people who mattered most.

Lleuwellyn didn't react to anything being said, making himself as small as possible. They wouldn't reveal his relationship with the killer, of course, but Baltan wondered if he was expecting it.

"We don't have a moment to waste. Everyone, get a light meal and meet in the training grounds. Taomin-Loloek will lead the sparring sessions," Keida said. "Eureka, find Beroan-Aroaen and train with him. Take Baltan with you; I want him to see how we fight. Lleuwellyn should help our medic gather more healing herbs and prepare salves. Azzie..." He paused in thought, "... will come with me."

XIX

The only word Azzie had for Kwoltan Gera was *alive*.

Old men and women sat together outside of one hut, gesturing wildly with their arms as they told stories. From the way they sliced the air with their claws, he guessed they were reliving old battles they'd won. A group of nimble warriors took fresh fish from a tiny hut supported by thick wooden poles and shared it with the elders so they could eat and listen to their tales.

Azzie caught a glimpse of Lleuwellyn's tail as he disappeared into a nearby hut. Eureka and Baltan were approached by an older man who smiled wide at Eureka and pulled him into a one-armed hug before nodding toward the sandy banks of the river. Azzie couldn't see them, but he could hear the growls and grunts of warriors practicing battle moves.

Keida didn't lead him as far as the training grounds, instead skirting around the warriors' hut to a smaller one next to it.

Despite being smaller, the inside still felt huge to Azzie. One section of the floor was lined with fur mats and soft-looking feathers, and the wall had multiple satchels hung up on hooks for clothes and other things, more than Azzie could number at a glance. There were more furs rolled up in the corner of the room. The rest of the space was left bare.

The girl who had spoken up at the meeting was the only other person in the hut. She was fussing over the satchels, but stopped what she was doing to narrow her eyes slightly at Keida.

"Have you come to tell me I can go on the mission after all?" she asked, and Azzie was relieved he knew what she was saying even if she sounded a little mean.

"No," Keida answered sternly. "But you can help. I want you to show Azzie some basic training."

"Why waste the time training him?" she scoffed and folded her arms, "I'm older, stronger, better trained, and I'm a good tracker." With a softer tone, she added, "If I go on this mission and survive, Egrieak-Kouran will make me a full warrior. He'll *have* to, no matter what he thinks of the school. Don't you want that, too?"

"*Warriors* listen to orders," Keida answered with no change in his tone. He nudged Azzie closer to her, "And *warriors* train apprentices."

She sighed, but she must have realized he wasn't going to change his mind. "Okay. Yeah. None of the other apprentices have gotten to lead a special one-on-one training like this, I guess."

Keida touched his forehead to hers briefly. "I have to check on things. Don't be too sharp with your cousin."

Then he was gone, and Azzie was left alone with the stranger.

She circled him once, sizing him up. He decided to do the same. He hadn't gotten a good look at her in the warriors' hut, but now he could see that she had ears like his own sticking out of her dark hair. She wore the same knee-length dress and over-the-shoulder sash that the other women did, but she also had bracelets and a choker that looked like they were from outside the tribe. Three horizontal scars marked her upper right arm.

He wasn't sure what to make of her, but she knew what she thought of him right away.

"Hm. You look weak. Most city kids are. But maybe we can work with your size…" She stood back, flicking her ears up. "I'm Naesa, by the way. Keida-Boitrat and Shaeda-Ashail are my parents."

"Azzie." She had said her parents' names with such pride that he felt awkward not adding anything else to his introduction.

She must have thought the same. "Weird," she said, but with a mischievous smile that made him think he was probably supposed to say something mean-but-not-really back. He couldn't think of anything and she rolled her eyes, then batted at his shoulders. "First things first, lighten up! You can't expect to be any good in a fight if you turn into a clam during training."

He curled his torso slightly at her jabs to protect himself. She responded by hooking a leg around the bend of his knees and sending him toppling to the ground. Before he could get up, she pounced, landing on him and grabbing his shoulders to roll him across the bare floor of the hut.

He tumbled away from her and got to his feet shakily. He really *was* weak, and she looked at him with alarm.

"What's wrong with you? Don't you know how to play?"

He shook his head. "Mm-mn."

Naesa's eyes widened. "Didn't Eureka play with you at all? Every cub in the nursery can playfight by the time they're three years old!"

"Mm-mn." Azzie tried to remember being three years old. All that came to mind was the inside of the cupboard and the fear that if Evanne really wanted to find him, she knew where to look.

Naesa touched her forehead to his the same way Keida had done with her. Azzie made himself stay still. He didn't want her to think he was rude by ducking away.

"That's terrible. I'm sorry. I couldn't imagine if..." She stood back and gave him a sympathetic smile. "Okay, so sparring isn't going to work. You're too new to fighting and you'll just get hurt." She smiled wider, but it didn't reach her eyes. "New approach! We're going to go watch the warriors train so you can get a sense for how it's supposed to be, then I'll do some moves and you can copy me."

The village center was calmer than when Azzie had left it, but there were still plenty of Azures talking and sharing food. Several of them nodded to Naesa, and both she and Azzie returned the gesture.

It was strange how they could still smile when their children were missing. Azzie couldn't help but think of the stark faces of the Illdresil Gera Azures. Would Kwoltan Gera share their fate?

Not if Baltan and Eureka win, Azzie thought, but he couldn't work determination into his steps. Anxiety trailed after him at the idea that something like that could happen to these people, and his choices might be all that stood in the way.

But what could *he* do? He wasn't a warrior or an investigator or a seer. He was just a kid.

In no time at all they reached the end of the village. The ground cut away, leaving a small drop to a sandy hollow. A sandbar extended further out into the river, carving out a calm pool between the training grounds and the hollow. Trees kept the grounds hidden from view and provided shade for the Azures who were resting on the almost-island to watch the sparring and their children playing in the shallow water.

Azzie hadn't expected to see children, but they were small, standing on wobbly legs and giggling shrilly as they splashed around. They were too young to be far from their parents, so Selkess hadn't gotten them.

Baltan was standing at the edge of the drop-off into the hollow, his fists clenching and unclenching as he watched the warriors below. Naesa was comfortable sitting on the grass and let her legs dangle over the side. Azzie stood somewhere between them so neither would hear his heart thumping in his chest.

The bubbling of the water was interrupted by the roar of battle, and Azzie couldn't believe what he was seeing wasn't a real fight. The warriors practiced much harder than Naesa had against him, slamming their bodies together and wrestling each other to the ground. Eureka only became visible when he threw a smaller warrior over his shoulder, winning a nod of approval from one of the older warriors before another rammed into his exposed side.

How could Naesa stand this?

He almost didn't notice when Lleuwellyn settled beside them, a bundle of freshly picked leaves and flowers in his hands. "It's a bit impressive, isn't it? There's not a scratch on any of them."

Azzie looked closer. He was right; despite their ferociousness, they weren't using their claws or teeth, and those that were knocked over landed harmlessly in the sand.

"Of course there's not! We'd never hurt one of our own tribemates on purpose." Naesa stood and gave Lleuwellyn the same once-over she'd given Azzie, but she looked much more satisfied with him. "Hello! Who is *this* mysterious stranger?"

The tip of Lleuwellyn's tail twitched and he looked away with an annoyed huff, but Azzie could see his cheeks darkening with blush from where he stood. "No one *useful*, since there's no need for medical attention here. Daelyn-Lleu sent me out to keep an eye on the training session, but I think he just wanted me out of his hut."

"Don't feel bad. Daelyn-Lleu is always like that," Naesa laughed. "It took him forever to take an apprentice. He should have had one a long, long time ago, but he really likes his privacy." Her cheerfulness wavered enough for Azzie to hear the concern and heartache beneath her brave front. "We're really going to be in trouble if we don't get Keldie back. I don't think Daelyn-Lleu will have enough time to train someone else."

A shiver ran up Azzie's spine, and he could swear he heard the river whispering to him. His stomach sank with a sense of foreboding and, like one of the children in the pool, he reached for Baltan's hand. It took a few tugs to get his attention, but the investigator bent his knees so they were eye-level.

"Hey, don't worry," Baltan said, as much to himself as to Azzie. "Eureka knows what he's doing and so do the other warriors. And they have a doctor in case anything goes wrong. It's okay."

Azzie frowned. The distinct feeling things would soon *not* be okay did not leave at Baltan's words. It didn't even let up, tension building in the air like static before a thunderstorm.

A shadow fell over him and he shuddered. The king arrived like a dark cloud to block out the sun. Azzie tried not to look at him or the woman next to him. Even if she did have the same eye color as Eureka and Keida, their harshness made them unrecognizable.

The two passed by without so much as a glance at him, but even when he was out of their shadows he still felt a chill in his bones. Lleuwellyn ducked out of their way and plucked petals from the flowers. Naesa returned her attention to the sparring warriors, staring uncomfortably.

Something horrible was about to happen. He *knew* it was.

"Hey!"

Eureka's voice broke through the growing darkness as he heaved himself out of the sandy hollow. The older man who greeted him earlier and a warrior with a crooked nose followed after him. Before he said anything else, Eureka touched his forehead to Azzie's and Baltan's in turn, nearly knocking Baltan over in the process.

"I'd like you to meet some people." He nudged the older man, whose deep wrinkles around his eyes and mouth reminded Azzie of Turnap. His kind features masked how old he was, but the dark braid that hung over his shoulder was beginning to fade with age. "This is Beroan-Aroaen. He was my mentor back when I was an apprentice!"

Beroan said something in Azure that must have been teasing because he broke out into a chuckle at the end. His laugh was deep and hearty, like Eureka's. It thawed some of the ice left in Azzie's frame.

Eureka went on as if he hadn't heard Beroan, shoving the warrior with the broken nose playfully. "And this is Patrioek-Totoag. We used to do everything together—especially if it involved getting up to trouble."

"Nice is to meet you!" Patrioek said, making up for his less-than-fluent common language by speaking louder than he needed to. He grabbed Baltan's hand and shook his whole arm, then bumped foreheads with Azzie. "I have a boy child about your year. Shame you don't meet him. You might be greatest friends, same as your father and me!"

The humor drained from Eureka's face. "Patrioek—"

"Oh, please," Naesa exaggerated rolling her eyes. "Gitean is the *worst!* He's always pulling pranks and making dumb jokes!"

"Same like Eureka and Patrioek," Beroan commented, the lines around his eyes more prominent as he grinned.

He should be king instead, Azzie thought. *I'd rather follow a nice person like him than that mean one. Maybe if he was king, Eureka wouldn't have left.*

"At least he's better than Beialk," Naesa groaned, then deepened her voice jokingly, "'I'm a whole year older than you, so you have to do what I say! I'm practically a warrior!'"

Their teasing didn't put Azzie at ease. Baltan was still stiff and Lleuwellyn kept sweeping his tail in a wide arc to make sure none of the warriors got too close to him. Eureka was pale, eyes distant, his mouth drawn into a tight line.

Naesa and Patrioek continued teasing each other with impressions of their friends and family, slipping back into Azure so Azzie couldn't understand them anymore. Beroan noticed Eureka's discomfort and put a hand on his shoulder again. "What is wrong, *tikuwo?*"

Eureka swallowed his uncertainty and answered in Azure. Whatever he said, it was serious enough to get Patrioek and Naesa's attention back in a heartbeat. Baltan turned away before Azzie could read his expression, and Lleuwellyn nearly dropped the plants.

The storm broke at last with a clap of thunder that sounded like, "*What?*"

At first Azzie thought it was in his head, but Keida was out of the training ground and standing in front of Eureka before Azzie realized he'd been in earshot. Naesa bared her teeth and pushed her way between Azzie and Eureka.

Azzie stumbled, only to be caught and led back a few steps by Lleuwellyn. His ears were ringing and he was suddenly aware of all the moving bodies in the hollow coming to a gradual stop.

"Are you suggesting that I've been unfaithful to my wife?" Keida snapped.

"With an *Eastern* woman?" Naesa added, not missing a beat.

Patrioek snorted and muttered, "*Any* woman?"

"No, I—well, now that you phrase it that way, I suppose I was—but I didn't mean to insult you. I don't know the details of your marriage, and if there was any possibility that Azzie could be your son, then I have to ask," Eureka stammered. "After all, if you could conceive Naesa, then there must be a chance..."

Son?

The word rang in Azzie's ears, distorting everything else into terrible noise that got louder and louder. He covered his ears, trying to block it out, but there was too much and most of it was coming from inside.

Son? Your son?

Keida is my father?

Azzie tried to remember what Evanne had told him about fathers. They were like mothers. They were supposed to care for their children, protect them, and... something else. But he didn't have a father. Evanne had told him that many times. He had no father, no mother, only her. If he did have a mother and father, they didn't want him.

Keida lifted his chin, and so did his daughter. His words broke through the haze. "Naesa is my only child."

"That's right," she spat, standing at his side, "Keida-Boitrat is a great warrior and father. He would never be anything less than loyal to his family or his tribe!"

"Neither would Eureka!" Baltan snapped, "You don't know anything about him!"

"And you don't know my dad!"

Naesa and Baltan were nearly nose-to-nose, and Keida's claws were tensed to draw blood. Lleuwellyn retreated, but his escape was blocked off by a wall of curious and concerned warriors.

Azzie felt sick.

Of course he doesn't want you! You're Bad, a voice that sounded a lot like Evanne's yelled in his head. *No one wants a useless, stupid son like you who can't even talk!*

"Hey, enough!" Patrioek dipped his head and forced his way between them with cautious movements. He stayed low, but his voice was firm. "Let's not sharpen our claws on each other."

"No. Naesa is right. I *don't* know you, Keida." Eureka fixed a glare on the king, who was watching with amusement a few meters away. "And we know who's responsible for that, don't we?"

Beroan shook his head and put an arm around Eureka. Despite that, his voice was full of disappointment. "Oh, Eureka..."

See how upset they are? the cruel voice continued. *See how Bad you are? How much trouble you cause?*

"A disgrace then, a disgrace now," the king sneered, darkening an already bleak sky. The woman at his side said nothing. Her cold stare was more than enough.

Keida rounded on him. "You have no place to shame him for fathering the boy!"

Run, a quieter voice whispered in Azzie's ear. His own voice, in sync with his racing heartbeat. *Run, run. Run, run.*

But there was nowhere to run to, and Azzie couldn't feel his legs.

The riverbank blurred and then tilted to reveal a clear sky overhead.

He heard Baltan's voice next, distant through the noise, "Azzie?"

Then Lleuwellyn's, "Azzie!"

Then, silence.

XX

In retrospect, their visit to Kwoltan Gera could have gone a lot worse. It also could have gone a lot better.

Baltan tried not to glare at all the people on the ferry staring at them. He couldn't blame them; they were already a motley group, and the fact that they had to carry Azzie onboard didn't make them any less conspicuous.

In a roundabout way, Azzie fainting was a stroke of good luck. It brought the all-out fight brewing between Eureka, Keida, Egrieak-Kouran, Naesa, and himself to an immediate halt so they could get him to the medic hut. And, thankfully, it wasn't serious; Lleuwellyn and Daelyn-Lleu confirmed he'd suffered a panic attack, but he would get better once he could rest somewhere quiet and safe.

The fact that he was still unresponsive was part of the panic attack and probably not something more severe. His breathing was even and his heartrate had gone back to normal, so the medic had given him a drawstring bag of mint and lavender to wear around his neck and sent him on his way—which sent the rest of them on their way to the ferry. Baltan didn't want to risk another heated argument breaking out.

He tried not to clench his teeth. They only had a handful of days left to come up with a solid plan to stop Selkess. They needed to work together, and they had managed to convince the warriors of that, but now he wasn't entirely sure they could count on their help.

He could only hope Keida's dedication to the rescue mission hadn't been completely broken by the argument. They still had the children to think about, and he must agree that working together with the outsiders was the best plan for getting them back.

Then there was the state of their own group to consider. Baltan still didn't fully trust Lleuwellyn, and Eureka had hardly spoken since they left the village. Azzie was in no condition for much of anything, let alone dealing with a murderous cult.

The timing couldn't be worse if Selkess planned it, Baltan thought. He was haunted by the creeping suspicion he *had* planned it somehow.

The ferry ride offered no chance to relax. Those who were used to seeing Azures in cities usually saw those with Kwoltan Gera heritage. Lleuwellyn was a rarity, and he'd already had to fend off no less than three people who wanted to touch his tail to see if it was real. With as jumpy as he was about being on the barge at all, it would be a miracle if they got to the other side without him kicking someone.

Azzie stirred, not for the first time. Baltan didn't have any doubt he had been awake for almost the entire ferry ride, but he kept his eyes closed and his body rigid, so he didn't try to interact.

He couldn't blame the kid, instead trying to imagine what was going on in his head. Watching the warriors spar was hard enough on him, and he had seen Eureka fight before. Azzie was absolutely terrified, and then Eureka had nearly been attacked for real for a second time that day.

Eureka's thoughts came to him easily. He was tearing himself up over not noticing Azzie was getting too upset, over quarreling with his brother when they needed his support, over missing out on so much time with his family, over not claiming Azzie as his son and being done with it. He got the feeling there was more to it than he knew, but that much was plain on Eureka's face when he looked at the helpless boy in his arms.

Baltan caught the tiny motions of his jaw and nudged him with his elbow. "Hey, stop chewing."

Eureka sighed, and for a brief moment Baltan saw the faintest stain of blue blood near his gums. "Sorry."

Vinez came into view just before dark, and by the time they departed and got their luggage, the sun had set completely. The streetlamps of the city blotted out most of the stars, leaving them with only a few twinkling lights in the sky.

The resort wasn't far enough to be worth paying bus fare on top of everything else, but after such a long day Baltan could have kicked himself for not opting in to the shuttle service.

They didn't walk for long before Filhi-Viriar, Erisolus-Ashail, and Teirik-Viriar emerged from the shadows between a bait and tackle shop and a fish market. Wet footprints marked their trail despite their dry, modern clothes as they approached and took the bags from Lleuwellyn and Baltan.

"We figured we would pose as hired help. No one here would think twice about that," Filhi-Viriar explained.

Baltan wondered if she was purposefully speaking in a higher octave to seem more girlish. He knew she was an adult, but she looked and sounded too young to be on a mission this dangerous.

Baltan let them take the bags. At least they were trying to be friendly, but he didn't miss the wary look in their eyes as they regarded him and Eureka. Erisolus had hidden the scar on his chin behind a bandage; he was less careful about hiding his contempt. Baltan was sure Keida had his reasons for choosing the young warrior, but he wasn't sure he could rely on him to follow orders if Baltan was the one giving them out.

In any case, they must still have Kwoltan Gera's support.

"We appreciate it. Thank you," Eureka answered a little too late. "Where's Keida?"

Teirik-Viriar—the only one of the three not easy to get a read on, if only because he seemed completely unwilling to make any kind of expression—responded, "Naesa disappeared not long after you left, so Keida-Boitrat and Shaeda-Ashail went to look for her. We have river pebbles to mark the way to wherever it is we're going, so I'm sure he'll catch up soon."

"It's not safe for her to be out by herself," Lleuwellyn hissed.

"I would not worry. Naesa can handle herself, and Shaeda-Ashail is our best hunter and tracker." Teirik-Viriar nodded to Azzie. "I'm more concerned about the little guy."

Eureka held him a little closer. "He's fine."

Teirik-Viriar shrugged and fell in behind them, like he was a normal Azure citizen doing his job. He seemed content to stay quiet. Baltan was surprised it was Erisolus-Ashail who struck up conversation, even if his voice held back a growl.

"I have a daughter. Thankfully she's too young to be enrolled at the school."

"There's one good thing that might come out of this," Filhi-Viriar said, the sarcasm making her voice sound more age-appropriate, "Maybe they'll shut down the school thanks to the scandal."

"Or reduce the enrollment age," Erisolus-Ashail added with a sneer Baltan chose to ignore.

Erisolus-Ashail was rather young to have a child already, but Baltan supposed that was how things were for the tribe Azures. Their numbers were dwindling at a rapid rate; marrying and having kids early was probably one of the only things they could do to sustain themselves.

How much worse must that have made being almost forty and childless for Eureka?

The Seashell Inn & Spa was visible long before they reached it—not because it was a large building, but because it was so flashy it wouldn't have looked out of place in one of the more affluent areas of Marina Delta. It helped that the surrounding buildings were already dull and obviously waiting on their paint jobs.

The exterior was meant to mimic an Eastern estate. A short set of stairs led them onto a wooden porch, where tall columns decorated with mosaics of sea life supported a gable emblazoned with an emerald seashell. The porch was wide enough to accommodate a number of guests and wait staff, but it was well past peak check-in time and only one of the several bay windows along the front of the building had any light behind it.

Just as Filhi-Viriar had predicted, they had no trouble getting into the room even though the reservation was for four, not seven. Baltan doubted anyone would come to check and make sure they were gone, but he hung the Do Not Disturb sign on the door handle anyway. This investigation was getting expensive enough without adding a penalty fine from the hotel onto their bill.

The warriors set the luggage down and Filhi-Viriar dumped the rest of the river rocks she had dropped every dozen or so steps out of the window. Baltan grabbed a lemon-lime soda out of his bag and downed it in record time.

Eureka set Azzie on one of the double beds and Lleuwellyn sat beside him, stroking his shoulder gently until he lifted his head. Baltan raised an eyebrow at that. What had happened between Lleuwellyn and Azzie when they ran off that allowed them to develop such a close bond so suddenly?

"Hey, we're here," Lleuwellyn said to Azzie, keeping his voice low until the kid was responsive. "Lucky you, you got to skip the whole thing. How are you feeling?"

Azzie rubbed his watery eyes. Eureka shifted as if he was going to take a step toward him, but stopped halfway.

That was enough.

"Eureka, would you mind taking a walk with me to secure the perimeter? I think Lleuwellyn and Azzie will be safe with three warriors guarding them," Baltan said.

"Of course," Eureka cleared his throat, "That sounds reasonable."

"We'll be right back, then."

Baltan walked out into the hall. There was a good amount of distance between each room, but he wanted to make sure they were well out of earshot. They circled the complex once before Baltan found a vacant bit of hallway suitable for a private conversation.

"I'm not going to pretend I know what you're going through or how you must feel," Baltan started, "But I do know you, and I know this isn't something you're going to be able to put aside until this case is over." He eased the concern out of his voice and tried to sound a little more positive. "Azzie is your son, and he couldn't have a better father. The sooner you get used to saying and hearing that, the better off you'll be."

"You also know it's not that easy," Eureka replied. "I knew there was a chance he might be mine. I even wanted it to be true. But now that we know it's true, it's... overwhelming." He paced across the hall, though it only took a few steps for him to make a full circle. "Things might be fine now, but what happens when he starts asking questions I can't answer? What happens when he wants to know what his mother was like, and I have to tell him I don't have any idea?"

Baltan hadn't considered that, and he didn't have any comforting words for it.

Eureka ran a hand through his hair, a few locks falling back down into his face. "And now I've done something stupid and hurt Azzie, and Keida, and my niece."

"You didn't mean to," Baltan pointed out. "You had to test all the options—"

"Keida was never really an option. I don't know how he and Shaeda had Naesa, but it's obvious Keida would never have an affair with a woman outside the village. He's too loyal."

Something in the way he said the word *loyal* made Baltan think there was a greater significance to it, and it was hard not to take it personally. Did Eureka regret being seen with him, an Easterner?

"And that's just like me, isn't it? What you said, I didn't *mean* to. Because I never mean to hurt anyone, but I do anyway." His shoulders slumped. "Egrieak-Kouran is right. I'm a disgrace."

"Ah, so that's what this is really about?" Baltan folded his arms and leaned his back against a wall. Watching Eureka pace was tiring him out.

"I don't know, maybe!" Eureka rubbed his forehead. "I know it was stupid, but I thought maybe, after all these years, maybe Egrieak-Kouran would regret sending me away. Maybe he'd want to see me, or see what I've done with my life and be proud of me, just a little bit. But he's exactly as I remember him." He sighed. "I can't stand the thought of Azzie looking at me like that—like I'm the biggest disappointment in his life."

Baltan laughed. "*You*? A disappointment? Please. Azzie looks at you like you're the sky and all its stars." When that failed to cheer Eureka up, he added, "Look, Azzie's a smart kid. He might not say much, but he sees and hears a lot. I'd be willing to bet that if you take the time to talk to him, he'll understand. Avoiding it and not saying anything is what's going to drive him away."

"When did you learn so much about being a parent?" Eureka asked, wiping his face until he started to look like his old self again.

"I might have done some cursory research at the library. Nothing major," Baltan shrugged with a small snicker. "I mean it, though. Talk to him."

"I will, the first chance I get," Eureka answered. "It's all so *much*. I've always dreamed about being a father, but the reality of it..." He shook his head. "I know it might not be what you wanted, but I'm glad you're here to help me figure it out."

Having met Eureka's father, his reluctance was starting to make more sense to Baltan.

"My uncle didn't know much about being a father either, as far as I could tell," Baltan offered, opening his arms. "But look how I turned out. I'm not too bad, right? I mean, I did run away from home, but... not too bad."

"You never told me you ran away." Eureka blinked. "Obviously I assumed you did, but you never *told* me."

"Yeah, well, you know, since we might be doing this parent thing, which I guess we are, then..." Baltan's face was flushing, he just knew it.

Eureka almost smiled, but it fell into a frown and he stared down the hallway.

Heartbeats later, Erisolus-Ashail came around the corner. "We've got trouble."

XXI

Keida hadn't bothered to change his clothes and was dripping all over the hotel room floor as he paced. He barely turned his head when Baltan and Eureka returned.

"You're sure she didn't run off somewhere to cool down?" Baltan asked, knowing the answer before he even asked.

"No. Naesa can be a little hot-blooded, but she's not inconsiderate. She wouldn't leave the village without telling someone at a time like this," Filhi-Viriar answered for Keida, who stopped walking in circles to stare anxiously out the window.

"She wanted to join the mission," Lleuwellyn offered. "Would she sneak out to follow us?"

"Maybe, but—"

"Shaeda and I found no trace of her on either side of the river." Keida's voice was low. "If she decided to follow us, she would be here before me." He turned from the window and addressed Azzie, "Did she say anything to you?" The kid didn't have a chance to try to respond before Keida barked, "Answer me!"

"*Don't* yell at him," Eureka warned.

Baltan caught Lleuwellyn start to take a small step back, then steady himself. The room was stifling enough with so many people in it, and the tension crackling between the brothers wasn't making it any more bearable.

"Shaeda-Ashail *will* find her," Teirik-Viriar said. "You probably missed something because it's dark out. Once daylight comes, she'll find Naesa."

Baltan uncapped a bottle of pomegranate soda, only to set it on the nightstand between the beds and let it sit. His stomach was turning in too many knots to keep anything down.

He had no clue what Naesa was like, and it was completely possible that a volatile teenager faced with the possible deaths of her friends had taken off for some time alone with her thoughts. However, given the reason *why* her friends' lives were in danger, he found that explanation far too optimistic.

He didn't dare suggest Naesa might be a traitor working with the cult in front of Keida, but there was no doubt in his mind that Selkess was involved. The only other option he could come up with was that Naesa tried to follow them and drowned. Baltan never thought he'd consider Selkess a kinder option, but if Naesa had gotten wrapped up with him somehow, there was at least a chance she might be rescued.

"What do we do now?" Lleuwellyn asked in a whisper.

Keida cleared his throat. "Stick to the plan. You— Baltan. You said you might know where the apprentices are?"

"I was able to put together some smart guesses," Baltan said, not meeting Keida's eyes. He couldn't face the disappointment of the warrior realizing he didn't have definitive answers. "There's a few warehouses near the riverfront; two vacant, one used for housing boats. Not too many people will be out boating in the cold, but it's still the least likely option since there are probably guards." He wasn't sure how much he wanted to discuss in the room, even if the odds of it being bugged were low. "The other two warehouses are new constructions, not in use yet." He swallowed. "And there's a slaughterhouse. Construction is complete and it has an owner, but it doesn't begin operation until after the solstice, so there's probably not anyone there. *Maybe* a guard or two, but since there's nothing there right now to steal... It's the closest to the school out of all the other options, anyway."

His words settled into an almost visible gloom. Teirik-Viriar didn't bother to make a hopeful comment.

"We'll split up and scout around each area," Keida said. "Erisolus-Ashail and Filhi-Viriar, you—"

The phone rang, once.

Baltan's stomach tightened with dread and anticipation, but the phone was quiet and unassuming on the nightstand next to the soda. If not for the others also staring at it and Azzie scrambling away from the noise, he would have thought he imagined it.

"Maybe they misdialed for another room?" Lleuwellyn asked, his voice shaking.

Baltan shook his head.

The call came when it did for a reason. They were on to something, and Selkess was reminding them they were being watched.

"I'm starving," Baltan said with a pointed look at Eureka. "Maybe you should take these guys to the fish market."

It took a moment for realization to erase the bewilderment from Eureka's face, but it stayed plastered on everyone else's. "Ah, yeah. Sounds good. What do you want me to get you?"

"You can decide when you're there."

"Okay." Eureka nodded to the warriors. "Let's go. We haven't got—"

The phone rang again.

And kept ringing.

After the ninth or tenth ring, it was clear it wasn't going to stop until someone answered.

Baltan's hands hovered over the receiver. He clenched them into fists and squeezed briefly to stop them from shaking, then carefully lifted the handset and pressed the speaker button at the same time, keeping his hand over the mouthpiece so the caller wouldn't hear their words echoing. It might be a ridiculous precaution since they were obviously being watched, but the old habit brought enough comfort to excuse any foolishness.

"It's late," he grumbled. If he could replace fear with anger, he might get through this without collapsing.

"It is, so let's be brief," Selkess answered without pretense, his voice dangerously quiet. "You have something I want, and I have something you want. I propose we keep things civil and make a fair exchange."

Baltan would have swallowed if his mouth hadn't gone completely dry. The warriors eased closer so they could hear better, and Baltan held the receiver closer to mask the sound of their movements before he replied, "You'll have to be specific." If he could get him to admit out loud that he had kidnapped children, they could—

"I requested we keep this brief," Selkess sighed, "So, please, don't dance around the issue. I'll leave you a signed confession of guilt if you want, but only if we can get on with this. Time is of the essence now more than ever."

The clatter of the phone hitting the floor shattered whatever hope Baltan had of remaining calm.

How could Selkess know what he was thinking?

How?

He wasn't shaking. He was utterly still. The only thing in front of him was a phone, but it terrified him as thoroughly as if Selkess was standing there, reading his every action and expression. How could he do that without looking at him?

Filhi-Viriar must have come to the same conclusion. She whipped her head toward the window and reached it in two steps, drawing the curtains closed with such ferocity that she nearly tore them from the rod.

"So, the exchange," Selkess went on, "Children really ought to be with their parents. I would gladly return the young warriors to their home... but that all depends on if you agree

to reunite me with my children. By that, I do mean Lleuwellyn *and* the other boy, since he's legally mine."

Azzie let out a feeble whimper and the color drained
from Lleuwellyn's face. Their pleading eyes sparked the tiny
ember of courage left in Baltan into a blaze. He fumbled for
the fallen handset and spat into the receiver, "Never."

"I hoped it wouldn't come to this." Another sigh.
"Break her legs."

Something whistled through the air. Then there was a
terrible THUD and a *SNAP!* and the piercing scream of a
teenage girl.

Baltan gripped the phone tighter, nearly throttling it
as he yelled, "What are you doing?!"

"It's called negotiating," Selkess retorted. "Think
again, and think fast. Give me my children and I'll give her
back, or resist and I will kill her right now while you listen. I
have plenty of sacrifices, so I don't need her, and I don't like
keeping around things I don't need. How I get rid of her is up
to you."

A scuffle broke out near the window as Filhi-Viriar
and Erisolus-Ashail fought to keep Keida from shoving it
open and charging out into the night. At first Baltan didn't
understand what he was doing, but a moment later the pieces
clicked together.

That scream was Naesa's.

"No—" Baltan gasped for breath.

"No?" Selkess sounded disappointed, but Baltan
could all too easily imagine his smirk. "I am being more than
generous, investigator. I offered to give you all of them back
for those two, and *you* turned me down. But you can still at
least save one."

Keida turned, eyes wide.

Eureka gathered Azzie and Lleuwellyn into his arms
and snarled a warning at his brother even as Lleuwellyn
struggled free.

"What about me? Just me?" Lleuwellyn blurted out.
"One child for another. That's fair. I know I'm the only one
you really want. Fine. You can have me! But leave Naesa and
Azzie out of it. They haven't done anything!"

"Very noble," Selkess commented, sounding legitimately proud. "But although it's true that you are more important to me, I want both of you, and I will get both of you one way or another. Those are my terms."

"We won't give you anyone!" Erisolus-Ashail snapped, shooting a glare at Lleuwellyn.

"If that's your final answer," Selkess replied, his voice even and cold, "This is mine."

The whistling sound came again.

Another THUD, another *SNAP*, another shriek of pain.

It didn't stop, and soon the snapping was joined by another sound—a sick, squelching sound, not unlike raw meat being pounded into shape.

Baltan stumbled back as Keida rushed forward and seized the phone. "*STOP!*"

There was silence on the other end of the line, but that was no mercy. Not when there should have been crying.

Filhi-Viriar raised her hands to her mouth and squeezed her eyes shut. Teirik-Viriar bit down on his lower lip and put an arm around her. Azzie, still in Eureka's tighter-than-ever hold, choked out a sob.

"This is your last chance," Selkess said. "She lives, but only just. Give them to me, or her blood is on your hands."

Baltan followed Keida's eyes to Eureka, who shielded Azzie from view, his own face stricken with horror. Behind them, Lleuwellyn shifted his weight from one foot to the other before finally settling onto the end of one of the beds with a resigned sigh.

"Eureka," Keida pleaded, "Brother, please. She's your niece, your family."

"But…" Eureka looked down at Azzie, holding his face in one hand and wiping a tear from his eye with his thumb. His voice was a ghost of a whisper. "But he's my *son…*"

Azzie held Eureka's head and pressed his cheek into his palm, holding it there for a few heartbeats. Then he pulled

Eureka's hand away and lifted his chin. His eyes still held a spark behind the mist of tears.

Determined to put himself in harm's way to help others, Baltan thought. *Like his father.*

Eureka and Azzie pressed their foreheads together, their eyes closed. The moment they pulled back, Eureka pulled him into a hug so fierce it was practically a threat against anyone who would try to pry them apart.

His voice still broke as he asked, just loud enough for it to be picked up by the receiver, "When?"

"Now," Selkess said, "Otherwise you won't get her to a hospital in time to stop her from dying permanently. A few members of my staff will meet you in the alley behind the hotel shortly. They will be watching for any sign of ambush, and have my instruction to kill her should there be any attempt to go back on our deal."

The line went dead.

"Hospital," Keida repeated, "Where's the nearest hospital?"

"There's an emergency clinic by the school. I can show you where," Erisolus-Ashail said.

"We need to keep our group small," Eureka pointed out. "Keida, Erisolus-Ashail, and I will go. Any more than that and they might think we've set a trap, or that we mean to take Naesa back by force."

"What about me?" Baltan asked. "I want... I *need* to be there." As much as he would hate admitting they lost, hate seeing Azzie taken away, someone had to be there to hold Eureka together.

"No." Eureka left no room for compromise. "You need to be here, working out exactly where they've been taken to."

Keida nodded in agreement and addressed Teirik-Viriar and Filhi-Viriar. "The moment you know, you two go back to Kwoltan Gera. I'll be there to form a new plan as soon as I can be. We need—"

"Don't!" Baltan snapped. "He's obviously got some way of knowing where we are. He might be able to record our private conversations, too. Don't say anything about any plan. Don't even think about it."

He must have sounded crazy, but Keida didn't speak another word. None of them did.

Not even when they left to hand Azzie and Lleuwellyn over to the cult.

Baltan left the two remaining warriors in the room as he crept down to the lobby and booted up the public-use computer. Looking up potential crime scene locations and downloading their blueprints wasn't all *that* different from searching local restaurants and clubs and printing bus tickets.

It took some doing, and more sheets of paper than he would have liked, but he managed to get the full layout of each of the four possible locations stapled together into a map.

He's always got the upper hand. Always one step ahead, always listening in... Baltan smiled grimly. *That's going to be his downfall this time.*

He laid the maps out on both beds, even though he had completely dismissed the boathouse already. There was no way a guard wouldn't have noticed Naesa's screams.

That left the two warehouses or the slaughterhouse.

The warehouses were empty. The noise would have echoed, which they didn't hear in the call. Even without that, one of the warehouses was bordered on either side by buildings that *were* occupied—an office complex and a storage facility. There probably weren't people in the office this late at night outside of, possibly, custodial staff. The storage facility, however, would have a night guard. They might not notice people coming and going in the empty warehouse next door, but they would notice noise coming from inside.

Selkess was arrogant, but he wasn't stupid. He wouldn't let Naesa make that much noise if he thought he would be caught and have to relocate his entire operation—so even if he *had* used that warehouse to torture her, he wouldn't stay there once he was done.

That left only one warehouse and the slaughterhouse.

The slaughterhouse was closest to the school. It was the only building out of the four that had any kind of soundproofing. And, with the taste of bile rising in his throat, Baltan saw it was the closest to their hotel. If Selkess meant to have Naesa delivered to them quickly, they would have to come from there.

Baltan waved Teirik-Viriar and Filhi-Viriar over to him.

He stabbed a finger onto the slaughterhouse's plans, where he'd written the address.

"The second warehouse," he said, "That's where they are. When you go back to Kwoltan Gera, make sure you tell them *this* location." Again, he pointed to the slaughterhouse address, even as he recited the address for the warehouse. "*This address.* Got it?"

Filhi-Viriar's eyes gleamed. "Yes, I think so." She folded up the slaughterhouse map and wrapped it in the plastic bag that lined the hotel wastebasket. "The vacant warehouse—it's so obvious."

She and Teirik-Viriar slipped out the window and disappeared around the corner, carefully avoiding the back alley as they made their way to the river.

Baltan's grin cut into his face.

We're coming for you, Selkess.

XXII

The alley was so cold, Azzie wondered if the sun ever reached the narrow crack between the hotel and the tall brick wall behind it. Two lanterns lit the space, but they did nothing against the chill.

Azzie pretended that was why he was shivering.

The only part of him that hadn't turned to ice was his left hand, held tight in Eureka's.

A tide of questions ebbed and flowed between them, and just when Azzie thought he could ask one, it rolled back out to sea.

Why did you say Keida was my father if you were?
Why didn't you tell me sooner?
Why did you leave me with Evanne?
Why didn't you ever visit me?
Did you know the whole time?

Did Selkess know?

Azzie felt confident answering the last question himself. Selkess must have known Eureka was Azzie's father from the beginning. That was why the Prophet sent him to find the man with eyes like the sea—like *his* eyes.

Eureka said nothing and kept his eyes fixed straight ahead, watching for movement in the dark. Keida and Erisolus-Ashail covered their back in case the cult members came from the other side. Lleuwellyn stood in the middle, so still Azzie would have thought he stopped breathing if not for the small clouds of fog that appeared in front of his face every few heartbeats.

Azzie caught the gleam of starlight in Lleuwellyn's eye. He turned his face skyward, but could only see darkness above them.

"They're here," Lleuwellyn said, standing at Eureka's shoulder.

Azzie squinted. He could barely make out a moving shape at the end of the alley. As it got closer, he saw four people. Two of them were holding a tarp that dripped dark blue liquid onto the cobblestones between them.

The cult members came a little closer, then set the tarp down and let it unfold.

The only sound in the alley was Keida's sharp gasp. He pushed his way to the front, blocking Azzie's view, but the stench of blood still pummeled his nose. Lleuwellyn gave a startled cry and stumbled over his own legs.

"Stay back!" one of the cult members shouted at Keida, and Azzie heard a dangerous *click*. Keida came to a stop and took a reluctant step away from Naesa.

Azzie saw her then.

Eureka knelt down and put his hands on Azzie's shoulders, turning him away, but it was too late.

Her skin was so pale, she was nearly white. Her chest heaved like a wounded animal as she struggled to draw shallow breaths. Her eyes were open, but Azzie doubted she saw them.

Her whole body was smeared with streaks of blood after being wrapped up in the tarp. At first Azzie thought she was cut up everywhere, but a heartbeat later he realized that wasn't true. The truth was no better.

From the knees down, her legs had been hacked off. Bits of bone and ragged flesh littered the tarp.

As far as Azzie knew, that was the first time he ever screamed.

"Hey!" Eureka held his face between his hands and put their foreheads together. Azzie could feel him shaking. "Listen to me, Azzie—listen to me. I won't let anything bad happen to you. I'm going to—Baltan and I—we'll get you out. We wouldn't let them have you if we didn't think, if we didn't *know* we can save you." With a glance over his shoulder, he added, "You *and* Lleuwellyn. Okay? So don't be afraid. Don't be scared. I'll come for you."

Azzie wished he could face the cult members bravely, but it was a lot easier to be brave in the hotel room. He could barely stay standing, let alone walk away with people who wanted to kill him.

No, he wanted to cry, but all that came out was a whimper.

"Send them over," a woman called, "Now!"

"No…" It was quiet enough for Azzie to hear Eureka's heart shatter into tiny pieces. They crashed together like the waves of a stormy sea and held each other close. Two fat raindrops hit Azzie's head and Eureka let out all the sadness in the world with a single shuddering breath.

"I'll come for you. I promise."

Azzie didn't want to let go, but he fell away from Eureka and let Lleuwellyn take his hand instead.

Close-up, Naesa was unrecognizable. The person lying there couldn't be the same girl Azzie had met in Kwoltan Gera. She was bright, warm, spirited. She couldn't be that cold body on the ground, barely clinging to life. She *couldn't* be.

The cultists surrounded them.

"The Prophet will be pleased," one of them smiled. Their hooded jacket made it hard to see much else.

They moved in formation, forcing Azzie and Lleuwellyn along.

When Azzie tried to look back, all he could see was the navy blue jacket of the cult member behind him.

Azzie thought they would be cuffed or restrained and led away to a dark, cold room without food or a window. That's what Evanne would have done, and she was a part of the cult. It made sense.

Instead, the cult members were almost unwilling to touch them, let alone try to tie them up or push them. Lleuwellyn's tail hadn't stopped moving, and the cultists purposefully avoided it. Once they were out of the alley, the cultists spread out to a more comfortable distance.

Azzie wondered if that might be more frightening. They weren't following because they *had* to. He and Lleuwellyn could make a run for it at any time and there wasn't much Selkess's followers could do to stop them.

But they were going along anyway, obediently, because they knew Selkess could do so much worse than a few coarse ropes or hard shoves. If they didn't cooperate, he might kill one of the kidnapped apprentices. He might kill Eureka or Baltan.

Azzie didn't dare imagine what it would be like to lose one of them forever. He would do whatever Selkess wanted as long as it meant keeping them alive and safe.

It was brave of Lleuwellyn to try to be the only one, Azzie thought. He wouldn't have been able to handle it alone.

They were led to the front of a large, square building. If not for the fact that it was the lair of an evil cult, Azzie probably wouldn't look twice at it. Maybe it was more interesting in the day, but in the dim light of the street lanterns it was blocky, gray, and ordinary.

The insides weren't much better. The speckled tile floor was so clean it reflected the lights above, making the whole place painfully bright. The dullness of the off-white walls was occasionally broken by a framed piece of art featuring colorful shapes.

"This place isn't operational yet, so you won't have to worry about disturbing the workers," one of the men explained, "Of course, that also means that we have full run of it for now. There isn't anyone here who will help you escape, so you should give up any ideas of trying to sneak away and alert the staff."

"Why would they want to?" a woman with a high voice asked in shock. "The Prophet has been *extremely* gracious in his treatment of our guests, and these two are being given the highest of accommodations."

Azzie didn't want to know what the cultist meant by 'accommodations.' If it was anything like what Evanne had done to him, or what Selkess had done to Naesa...

Their escorts didn't say anything else as they brought them to a room not far from the entrance. They showed them in, then closed the door behind them and locked it, leaving them with nothing but the words, "The Prophet will see you soon."

Those words could be a threat or a heartfelt farewell. For them, it might be both.

The room was made up like a bedroom, but it obviously wasn't supposed to be one and everything ended up out of place. A desk and chairs had been shoved to the side of the room, out of the way of an armchair. A small refrigerator and assortment of snacks was set up as a sort-of kitchen in the corner. A mattress piled with pillows and blankets lay on the other side of the couch.

Lleuwellyn inspected the room, though Azzie wasn't sure why. If Selkess wanted to kill them, he had plenty of chances to do it. He hardly needed to spy on them anymore now that they were in his trap.

Escape was hopeless. Even if they did get away, Selkess would probably find them again, or hurt people until they went back on their own.

Azzie frowned, recalling Eureka's tight hug. He wrapped his arms around himself to try to mimic the feeling. It didn't work very well.

He curled up in one of the blankets, letting it fall over his head to cocoon him. He screwed his eyes shut and tried to imagine where Eureka and Baltan were. Surely they were already on their way to rescue them. They would come bursting through the door any moment to take him back.

The mattress bounced as Lleuwellyn fell onto it, a heavy sigh escaping him. "I can't find a key anywhere, and there aren't air vents we can fit through."

Azzie wriggled free of the blanket enough to place a hand on his, and Lleuwellyn let his tail fall over him. "I'm sorry. This is my fault—if I'd given myself up sooner, maybe he wouldn't have taken you. But I am *not* going to let him hurt you or anyone else, no matter what I have to do."

Azzie tightened his grip, giving Lleuwellyn's hand a firm squeeze.

I'm not going to let anyone hurt you, either!

Lleuwellyn stared up at the ceiling. The grainy dots on the tiles almost looked like black stars against a white sky. "I guess we should try to prepare ourselves. Who knows what will happen tomorrow?"

Azzie wanted to boldly proclaim that he *knew* Baltan and Eureka were going to come to their rescue and save the apprentices too, but he couldn't talk, even to Lleuwellyn. And worse, he was afraid it would come out like a lie.

There was a knock at the door, followed by the jostling of a key being inserted into the lock. The handle twisted and Lleuwellyn was immediately on his feet and ready to fight, his tail arching over his shoulder to make himself look bigger.

Selkess half-dragged himself inside. The smell of his cologne was stronger than before, and even without looking at him Azzie felt the *wrongness* of his presence. He felt the same as the room, trying to be something he wasn't. But what he *was*, Azzie didn't know. Selkess was like the deepest, darkest part of the ocean, where monsters waited to feast on sunken ships, but he refused to associate Selkess with anything as good as the ocean. Even the worst part of the ocean was better than Selkess.

Azzie remembered his fear that Selkess might be able to read his mind, but he wasn't paying attention to Azzie anyway.

"Lleuwellyn," he breathed, his voice raspier than before. Azzie half-expected a snake to slither from his mouth whenever he spoke. He sounded like he had *something* in his mouth, though Azzie wasn't sure what.

Selkess took a step toward them, one trembling hand raised. "Let me see that eye…"

"Stay back!" Lleuwellyn snapped. He held his tail level behind him and dropped his weight onto one leg. "I'm warning you, I'll kick!"

"Where?" Selkess paused, a mocking smile on his lips. "My stomach, to burst my internal organs? My chest, to shatter my sternum and collapse my lungs? Can you go higher, cave my skull in? Or maybe you'll do to me what my followers did to the girl and break my legs…"

Azzie could see the beads of sweat forming on Lleuwellyn's brow, his tail lowering to the floor more and more with each venomous word out of Selkess's rotten mouth. "I could—" he coughed, "—I could snap your spine."

"You *could*, but you won't," Selkess chuckled. Still, he withdrew his hand. "Very well. I don't need to come closer. You're grown, you can get your bangs out of your face yourself."

Lleuwellyn shifted and stood up straight, his tail nearly tucked under his legs. He took a deep breath and tucked his hair behind his ear, revealing the dark, twisted skin beneath.

"Ah, good, the mark is still there. I was afraid I'd have to remake it."

Azzie gasped, but not because of Lleuwellyn's scars. He expected Lleuwellyn to say something back about not letting Selkess near him, or get angry about the fact that Selkess had hurt him before. But all he did was stand still, frozen in place as long as Selkess was looking at him.

In a few heartbeats, Selkess stomped out all of the fire in Lleuwellyn. He'd been ready to fight as he came into the room; now he was giving in without even trying to stand up to him.

I won't let him do that to me!

Azzie moved slowly. Selkess wasn't looking directly at him, and he probably couldn't see well out of his stitched eye. If he was stealthy, he might avoid drawing Selkess's attention long enough to pounce.

He could take him by surprise, knock him over, dig his claws in to his neck. The Prophet could barely stand, he wouldn't be hard to take down. Then once Lleuwellyn saw he wasn't an invincible monster, he could be hurt, he could be killed—

He looked down at his short nails, which barely dug into the mattress. He didn't have the sharp claws of warrior. Naesa had bowled him over with ease. And even if he *did* have the strength and the skill to kill Selkess, those terrible words lingered in his ears. Crushed skulls. Burst organs.

If he could do it, if he could dig his little nails into Selkess's throat, he'd be covered in a spray of blood. He'd have to watch Selkess gag and choke on it. The thought alone made him feel sick and a shudder rippled through his body.

Or maybe he felt sick because Selkess's stitched eye was on him now.

"I haven't forgotten *you* over there," Selkess said, "What did Eureka end up naming you? Azurite, wasn't it?" A thoughtful expression fell over his face. "That particular stone is said to heighten psychic abilities. I wonder if Eureka knew that, or if he named you for its color... Regardless, you've done very well. I'm proud of you."

Azzie curled his lip back to show his teeth and hissed.

"Oh, don't be that way," Selkess huffed, "All things considered, I've been rather generous. I made sure you got to see the ocean before the end of this world, which I did not have to do. And while I knew that using you was the best way to get Eureka and Baltan to cooperate with my plans, I also wanted to give you the chance to meet your biological father. As for Evanne..." He shook his head, "Leaving Evanne with the care of a child was a mistake, but she was the only one who your mother would trust. All I asked her to do was keep you hidden, not mistreat you the way she did. But she paid for that mistake already and it wouldn't do for me to speak ill of the dead."

His voice was calm, but his words stung as though he'd raked over Azzie's skin with needle-sharp nails. He wanted to curl up under the blanket to recover and protect himself from another attack.

Instead Azzie let the blanket fall away and stood beside Lleuwellyn. It wasn't fair to make him be the only one, and one look up at Lleuwellyn's face told him that was what the young seer needed.

"Why?" he demanded, crossing his arms in defiance. "You owe me an explanation. Why did you kill those children? And Turnap—why would you *ever* hurt Turnap? He believed there was good in you, and you killed him! Tell me why!"

"For you, of course."

"Me?" Lleuwellyn breathed. Those few words stomped the fire out again, and Azzie knew nothing he did would bring it back.

Selkess sank into the armchair, his head tilted back against it. "Who else? Now, I've had a long evening, so please don't pester me with any more questions for a while."

Lleuwellyn went quiet, and Azzie had no other option. For a long time they both stood exactly where they were, as still as they could, completely silent. There was nothing else they could do.

Azzie recalled a time a sea snake managed to slither into Evanne's home. He was looking at the pictures in one of her books on the floor while she ate her dinner. Then the black serpent appeared, sliding across the carpet. Evanne shrieked and stood up on the sofa, and Azzie froze where he was, watching the snake coil up in a corner of the room. They had stayed that way for ages, until finally Evanne fled to another room and the snake eventually moved on.

Selkess was like an entire room of sea snakes, and the place where Azzie and Lleuwellyn stood was the only spot where they might not get bitten.

When his unstitched eye began to drift shut, Lleuwellyn quietly asked, "You don't mean... you aren't going to stay *here* all night, are you?"

"I can't trust you to spend the night alone," Selkess answered coolly.

"We can't escape. We won't even try, we know it's pointless," Lleuwellyn said, panic rising in every word.

"There's no need for you to stay here, really. I'm sure you'd rather be somewhere else. Anywhere else."

Selkess turned his head toward him, a disapproving frown on his face. "There's more than one way to try to escape. I need to keep an eye on you, in case you try it. It would be an utter waste if you died *now*, when we're so close to achieving our goal."

Lleuwellyn tugged his sleeves down. "I don't know what you're—"

"Don't say that while you're trying to hide the scars on your wrists. It's insulting, and I expect better of you." He tilted his head back with a frustrated sigh, letting his eye close again. He murmured, "How do we treat cuts, Star?"

"Apply honeyleaf sap to close the wound, then an infusion of marigold to prevent infection." Lleuwellyn covered his mouth as soon as he finished answering.

"And did you remember to use the marigold infusion?"

Lleuwellyn didn't answer, keeping his hand over his mouth in case the words tried to escape.

Selkess rubbed his forehead with his thumb and forefinger. "All the better that we'll be holding the ritual tomorrow, then, since you cannot seem to manage the simple task of healing a cut. I taught you better than that."

"Ritual?" Azzie managed to force out when it became clear Lleuwellyn wouldn't ask.

"Yes, *ritual*," Selkess sat up briefly to snap at him, then winced and leaned back against the chair. "Forgive my temper, I have a headache—"

"Chamomile tea," Lleuwellyn stammered, "Taken with a mint leaf and a drop of violet. Or a feverfew infusion. Or sage."

"Stop muttering that nonsense! You'll only make my headache worse," Selkess snarled, rubbing his unstitched eye. With a jolt, Azzie realized there were faint traces of starlight in it. "It's so *blurry* lately…"

Azzie glanced up at Lleuwellyn to see if he noticed, but he was anxiously running his fingers through his hair.

Of course, Azzie should have expected that Selkess had special abilities. He was a former seer. He had once spoken to Lleu Gera, asked them for guidance and wisdom.

He followed an Eastern god now, but what if he never stopped getting messages from Lleu Gera? But the starlight was only in his unstitched eye. The other was dark, and only seemed darker by comparison. It didn't reflect any light at all, not even the light in the room.

Azzie's heart pounded painfully in his chest, and he knew he wasn't supposed to see that. There was something wrong with Selkess, something more wrong than he realized before, and he'd seen it, and it saw him.

Had the shadows in the room always been so dark, or were the lights dimmer than Azzie first noticed?

When Selkess opened his mouth again, Azzie didn't hear words. A stream of discordant screeching echoed in his ears, blinding him as he screwed his eyes shut and dropped to his knees in pain.

An icy feeling took hold of his gut when he realized Selkess was laughing. It was the *worst* sound he'd ever heard, like someone playing an album backwards on a broken record player. He wanted to cover his ears, but he couldn't move his arms, and he was afraid that if he did he'd find them bleeding.

"Azzie! What's wrong? What's happening?" Lleuwellyn's voice barely reached him. He felt a comforting hand on his shoulder and forced his eyes open again.

It wasn't Lleuwellyn's hand on his shoulder.

Azzie jerked back, his claws lashing out in a wild strike that connected with Selkess's arm.

The skin peeled away easily, catching under his nails and coating his fingertips in a thick, black substance.

Selkess only chuckled as he examined the rapidly vanishing scratch, but the stitched-open eye was still on Azzie.

Azzie flattened his ears. That dark eye was looking right through him, straight into his soul, to see all his fears. When Selkess smiled at him, he knew he'd seen a way to make them real.

"What have you…" Lleuwellyn's whole body shook, "What have you *done*?"

"Nothing you won't get used to." Selkess grabbed Azzie's arm and nearly pulled it out of its socket with one swift jerk to bring him to his side. "But I see now that you can't stay here. There's too much warrior blood in you. You'll have to go with the others."

Azzie thought his heart might stop altogether.

Using Azzie for support, Selkess managed to hobble toward the door faster than he could on his own. He was nearly there when Lleuwellyn managed to move again. "No! Wait!"

"I'll be back later."

In one fluid motion Selkess opened the door, shoved Azzie through, and locked it behind him. Azzie picked himself up from off the floor, scrambling against the opposite wall. He knew he wasn't far from the entrance, but the stabbing pain in his ears made it hard to see straight. Which way was out?

"Prophet!"

Two cult members hurried down the hallway toward them. One was an Eastern woman, and the other was an Azure man. Despite his animalistic ears and tail, he didn't look like the Azures from Illdresil Gera or Kwoltan Gera at all. He must have been from some other tribe Azzie didn't know about.

There's so much I don't know, Azzie thought, and with it came a more desperate thought. *I don't want to die yet!*

"There you are, Prophet," the woman said, bowing low. "We wanted to—" She gasped. "Is that blood?" Her face was suddenly centimeters from Azzie's. "What did you do, scum?"

"Peace, Revah. It's nothing permanent," Selkess said, hand resting on her shoulder until she stepped back. He nodded to the man. "Perel, please take him to the others until tomorrow."

Selkess's voice was distant, preoccupied. His good eye still glinted with starlight that, Azzie realized with a jolt, *never* stopped.

Perel took Azzie's hand, smearing his palm with Selkess's blood. He seemed pleased at that, and Azzie didn't struggle for fear of what he might do once his Prophet wasn't looking. "Come, now. Let's try to make things less stressful for the Prophet. He hasn't been feeling well lately."

Azzie looked around, his head starting to feel better as soon as he was away from Selkess. But even if he managed to fight Perel off and ran, if he did escape, what then? Could he find his way back to Eureka and Baltan? Or should he stay where they knew he was, and wait for them?

It was better to go along for now. They'd come. He *knew* they would.

Besides, Perel was going to lead him to the kidnapped apprentices. If he knew where they were and somehow managed to get free later, he might be able to help Eureka and Baltan save them.

The hallway got colder and colder the further they walked. Their steps echoed louder and louder. Azzie was sure they were in a different room now, but it was too dark to see anything in it.

The cultist stopped at a thick, metal door, only visible thanks to the glow of the keypad next to it. He pushed a few buttons and the door clicked open.

The chill wasn't the only thing that froze Azzie to the spot.

Hooks hung down from the ceiling, and looked like they were piercing the apprentices' hands to hold them up. He tried to scream, but his voice stayed hidden in his throat and refused to come out.

Thankfully the hooks were only holding up the chains of their handcuffs, but his stomach didn't stop twisting at the sight. All of them—more than he could count with both his hands—were in bad shape, and they must have been that way for days. They weren't even shivering anymore, and if not for their shallow breathing he would have thought they froze to death.

"We're out of hooks, so you'll have to be a good boy," Perel said, gesturing to a corner. "You can be good, can't you? It would be better for everyone if you were." The fake sweetness in his voice soured with every word. "Sit down and go to sleep, and we'll come and get you when it's time. Okay?"

He shoved Azzie further into the room and closed the door, making sure it was locked with a loud *click*.

Azzie took deep breaths, trying to stop the panic he felt rising in his chest. He couldn't faint. If he fainted, it was all over.

Lleu Gera had told him his choices mattered. His choices could really change the world.

And now was the time to choose courage.

He took a few more deep, steadying breaths. He felt his heart beat, and even though it was fast, he let the fact that it was still beating comfort him until he was calm. Then he looked at the hooks with defiance.

Yes, I can be good.

XXIII

The silence made the room colder. Azzie felt almost like a light blinking out, flickering, and he didn't know how long he would last until it went dark. He had to act fast, before he was too weak to do anything.

Once he was sure no one was coming, Azzie stood up on tip-toe to get a better look at the hooks. They were too far above his head for him to have any hope of sliding the chains off, but maybe if he could lift up one of the others, they would be able to slip free.

Their arms might be too strained to do much, but it was worth a try.

He approached a muscular girl with hair trimmed short on one side but long and dyed silver on the other. He circled her once, trying to find a good point to support her from.

He crouched in front of her and wrapped his arms around her legs, hoping he could hold her up high enough to get the chain over the pointed end of the hook.

The moment he touched her he was knocked back, kneed square in the chest while she hissed, "Touch me again, if you dare! See what happens!"

The rest of the apprentices stirred, most of them snapping awake in a heartbeat. Maybe they'd never been asleep at all.

"What's happening now?"

"Who's that?"

"Torva, you okay?"

"I'm fine," the silver-haired girl snarled. "Just some kid being rude—not one of *them*, thankfully. Not the worst thing that's happened to me lately."

I was trying to help, Azzie wanted to explain, but he couldn't speak in a room with this many people, even if a lot of them were probably not much older than him.

"Maybe he knows what's going on. He must have just gotten here, after all," another girl said. She was much bigger than Torva, closer to Eureka in size, and a darker blue than most of them. She was the only one who wasn't straining on tip-toe to touch the floor; instead a weighted ball and chain was clasped to her ankle to prevent her from going anywhere. She looked at him with gentle eyes. "Hello, there. I'm Toua. What's your name?"

Azzie flicked his ears and felt his face heat up despite the frigid temperature.

"That's fine, you don't need to talk. You must be scared," Toua went on instead of waiting for him to answer. "You can nod or shake your head. Do you know if anyone is looking for us?"

Nod.

"Are they Azures?"

Nod. He didn't think they would mind if one of their rescuers was an Easterner.

"Are they from our tribe? Kwoltan Gera?"

Nod.

The entire room sighed in relief.

"Well, that's it, then. We're as good as rescued!" a boy with long ears laughed. "I wonder what took them so long? Traffic?"

"We aren't saved yet," another girl with her hair brushed over one shoulder said, her voice stern and commanding. "Do any of the people looking for us know where we are?"

Azzie shrugged. Baltan and Eureka must have an idea, and he was sure they would figure it out, but he couldn't say they knew for certain.

The stern girl sighed. "Then it's back to coming up with escape plans."

"I guess it would be pretty lame to have to be rescued this late in my apprenticeship," the long-eared boy said, trying to sound light but unable to cover the heavy gloom beneath his words.

Azzie flicked his ears at the serious one and tried to explain his idea about the hooks to her with gestures. She hardly paid attention at first, clearly deep in thought, but when he repeated his actions a few times she tilted her ears toward him.

"If I'm understanding you correctly, that might work," she said. She nodded toward her left, where a small, lighter blue boy with curled hair was struggling to stand. Next to him was a darker girl with a short haircut. They looked like they were his age. "Start with Lumin and Erieta; they're not as heavy, so they'll be easier."

Azzie made sure they understood what he was going to do before he tried it. His arms protested, but he pushed through by imagining how terrible they must feel, stuck in that uncomfortable position for so long. Mustering every ounce of strength and resolve he had, Azzie somehow managed to get them off their hooks.

They crumpled once they were free, resting on the floor and letting their arms fall to their sides.

"Thank you," whispered the girl. Azzie assumed she was Erieta. Lumin tried to curl up but didn't have the strength for it.

If *they* were the least heavy of all the kidnapping victims, Azzie had no idea how he was supposed to help the others. He'd never manage it on his own and both Erieta and Lumin were exhausted. And the longer he waited, the less strength he had. His mouth was painfully dry, his head ached, and his stomach protested against any movement. How was he going to get them all free?

"The guards will come again in the morning to give us food and let us use the bathroom," the stern girl said. "Once they let us down, we'll create a diversion. The three of you should be able to escape in the confusion if you rest well tonight."

Azzie lowered his ears. She hadn't believed he could save them. She only wanted him to help Erieta and Lumin because she knew he wasn't strong enough to get anyone else down. And she was right.

What would Eureka and Baltan do?

He was pretty sure running away and leaving them to a horrible fate was the last thing they would ever consider.

Azzie looked around for the next smallest victim and he decided on a boy whose hair was long on one side like Torva's, but not dyed. He couldn't have been much older than Erieta and Lumin.

Rousing him took a little more effort. He was right under a vent, and colder than the rest.

"Who's there?" he asked groggily. When he saw Azzie, he tried to smile. "Oh, hi. Are you new? I'm Toluoi."

Azzie nodded in response, wrapped his arms around Toluoi, and heaved with all his might. He managed to lift him a little bit, but not nearly enough. He tried again, and instead of getting the chain off the hook, he accidentally caught the center of one of the links on the tip. It slid down and got stuck on the thicker middle of the hook.

"That's an improvement," Toluoi said, forcing a smile. "Look, my feet are flat on the ground now."

"Moving up in the world. Or, down, I guess," the long-eared boy said. Azzie considered trying to free him next, but despite having energy to make jokes, he looked awful. His eyes were dim and had dark bags under them. He wouldn't have the strength to help Azzie lift and he was far too big for Azzie to do it on his own, thin and wiry though he was.

He tried Toluoi again, but his arms felt like they didn't have any bones in them and the chain was caught fast on the hook. He couldn't make it budge no matter how hard he tried, and he was losing strength every moment.

"That's enough," the stern girl said. Azzie wondered if he should ask what her name was, if he could. "Go rest with Erieta and Lumin. If it's possible for us to free ourselves, we'll find a way."

Azzie made slow steps over to the only two he'd helped. They managed to drag themselves closer to each other, and when he sank down beside them they made room for him. "It'll be warmer if we're close together," Erieta said.

Azzie tucked his nose underneath his arm and curled in close to them. It might be a little warmer, but he was too numb to notice.

At least we aren't alone, he thought. His mind turned to Lleuwellyn, who would be lucky if he was alone and not trapped in a room with Selkess overnight.

He closed his eyes and concentrated instead on what the others were saying. They were speaking the same language the tribe Azures did, but he tried anyway. Maybe, just maybe, Lleu Gera would help him understand.

The longer he kept his eyes closed, the more the icy room disappeared around him, until he was floating. He knew Erieta and Lumin were still beside him, but he wasn't touching them anymore. The warm glow of starlight replaced the chill, working life back into his bones.

Their voices mixed with the notes of a clear night, and he listened—*really* listened—to what they were saying. Maybe their words were the same; maybe they weren't. But he knew what was in their hearts all the same.

"We can try overpowering them when they take us out of here," Torva suggested, a storm in every word.

"It's hopeless," the long-eared boy countered in the tone of dead leaves drifting in a breeze.

"It's still worth another try!"

Toluoi's voice was tight with concern for a girl so pale she nearly blended into the ice on the walls. "Sergie doesn't look good. What can I do to help her, Keldie?"

"I'm not sure there's much any of us can do but let her rest." The voice of a healer, of flowers and herbs that hid thorns of pain and helplessness. "She's very ill, and if we spend much more time in here like this, we'll probably all get sick. I can't do anything."

"Will she be able to walk out of here if we get down?" That was the stern girl, but more than stern—caring, loyal, ready to put her tribe above all. She would be either the last to leave or the first to die.

"I don't know. I can't get a good look at her."

I can check on her, Azzie thought, but his muscles wouldn't respond when he told them to get up and go over to her.

One by one the others' voices became less distinct, overtaken by the crashing of violent waves against an unprepared shore. The starlight faded, the cold drifted back in, and he was all alone in the dark.

Azzie was having a bad dream. He was familiar enough with them to know that immediately, but it didn't make it any less scary.

He was running away from something on the beach. He didn't want to look back to see what, and although his view shifted to show him anyway, he never actually saw what it was. If he did, he surely would have gone mad, unable to ever wake from the nightmare.

Even in a dream, he couldn't run forever. His legs sank into the sand, deeper and deeper the more he struggled.

The awful, horrible noise that made his ears bleed whenever Selkess spoke echoed from every seashell, every grain of sand, every drop of water. Seagulls dove down to peck at his ears, his eyes, until he was too far beneath the sand for their beaks to reach him anymore.

He was engulfed in that miserable sound, and only then did it ring clearly in his mind.

How are you enjoying Lleu Gera's gift, *boy?*

Azzie woke to find it wasn't sand trapping him, but the softer forms of Erieta and Lumin. They were shifting in their sleep, too, which helped them keep a little warmer on the freezing floor. Azzie could hear Lumin's labored breath and

Erieta's too-fast heartbeat. They were cold, but still warmer than he thought they should be.

He felt sick, but not like when he had woken up in Baltan and Eureka's home. He could go on. He had to help the others.

The older apprentices might have found a way out while they'd been asleep. He wished he could ask—all of them looked exhausted and unconscious from what he could see, but they might be pretending again.

Erieta shook and groaned as she woke, blinking until the fog of sleep left her eyes. She looked hopeful for a moment, then deeply disappointed when she realized she was still in the meat freezer. She reached across Azzie and nudged Lumin until he woke up, too.

"We should stand by the door, so when they open it, we can sneak out easier," Erieta said.

Azzie looked at the others who were still hanging up on the hooks and flicked his ears. Shouldn't they try to get more of them down? Now that there were three of them, they could probably manage at least one or two. And there was a healer among them—Keldie, if he remembered right. She could help the others if they got her down.

Erieta and Lumin didn't notice his gesture, instead struggling to their feet and moving to the sides of the door. Azzie recalled it opened out, so they wouldn't be able to hide behind the door itself when it opened. They could only hope the cult member who came in kept their eyes forward and didn't notice them. They looked so small and weak they might not be seen against the cold steel walls.

Azzie's ears pricked up. He could hear movement beyond the door.

This is it!

A few high-pitched beeps signaled the door unlocking. Azzie, Erieta, and Lumin crouched, ready to move. Azzie tried to remember the route the cultist had taken the previous night to get him there. Should he try to retrace his steps back to Lleuwellyn, or focus on escaping and finding Eureka and Baltan?

The door swung open, revealing a mass of cult members. The three darted forward, trying to squeeze between them, but it was no use. Erieta almost made it past them, but they grabbed her and threw her back into the freezer with Azzie and Lumin.

So much for that plan.

The cultists filed into the room until they stood shoulder-to-shoulder from one end to the other. Then, as if on cue, they took the apprentices down from their hooks.

"No breakfast today," one of them said.

Breakfast, Azzie thought with longing. His stomach might lurch at the mention of food, but he'd give anything to be back home with Eureka serving cake, piled high with strawberries and blueberries and smothered in cream...

"We don't want your awful food anyway," Torva snapped, trying to kick the cultist, but she could barely lift her leg. Her skin was paler than before, and frozen sweat made her bangs stick to her forehead. How would she have any strength to fight in that condition, especially if she didn't eat anything?

The cultists ignored her, looked between the three who tried to escape, and pulled Azzie out of the freezer. "The Prophet wants to see you."

As glad as he was to be out of the cold, Azzie almost tried to go back in. He'd rather suffer that alongside the others than face Selkess alone.

But I'm not alone, he remembered.

Lleuwellyn came forward alongside the Prophet. Heavy shadows hung under his eye. He must not have slept a wink with Selkess in the room. His tail wouldn't stop twitching and his jaw was set stiffly.

Selkess beckoned Azzie over to them, and he thought better than to leave the cult leader waiting. He made himself stand still when Selkess put an arm around his shoulder, but he couldn't fight the shiver that went up his spine.

"There we are, now. All safe. All happy," he said. "For now, at least—and maybe longer. That depends on what you both decide."

Decide?

Was this the chance he'd been waiting for to change the world?

"It appears that we are at a *crossroads*," Selkess went on. "Can anyone tell me what a crossroads is? Anyone?"

"It's a split path!" one of the cultists shouted.

"Correct, Yerebah. Very good, very good," The cultist beamed from ear to ear at Selkess's praise. "Yes, a crossroads is where *roads cross*, meaning there are many paths that can be taken. And while I can see many of these paths, I cannot always distinguish which one will be traveled. It's at times like this I need a little extra guidance." He smiled like a snake that had cornered its prey at Lleuwellyn. "This is where you make your decision."

Lleuwellyn shook his head. "Whatever you want me to do, I won't do it."

"You will. I *have* seen that far, and I *know* you do." Selkess spoke with confidence and the cult members leaned in eagerly to listen. "Use your gift and tell me what the warriors in Kwoltan Gera are doing right now, so I can better follow the paths of the future and find out what *we* should do."

Azzie's eyes widened. Could Lleuwellyn really do that? He knew he could talk to the dead, but that was completely different from knowing what living people were doing from so far away.

"How did you know about that?" Lleuwellyn asked, his tail bristling.

"Because I saw it in your future, obviously," Selkess replied evenly. "It's unfortunate I never had time to train you in using your gift to its fullest potential, but that path dead-ended ages ago. Though, I do have to wonder how much my instruction could have helped you, when you don't seem to have retained much else..."

Hurt flashed in Lleuwellyn's eye before it was overtaken by shame.

"Of course, I mastered my power ages ago. There wasn't much to do in that miserable prison cell. I've kept an eye on your entire life, and Eureka and Baltan's as well. I mapped out your futures and made sure they intersected where I needed them to, with some help from my followers."

At this Selkess gave Azzie's shoulder a small clap, and his gut twisted worse than ever. "But none of that matters right now. What matters is *your* gift, weak as it might be."

"No." Lleuwellyn swallowed, coughed, and swallowed again. "No. I won't help you. I'll prove your vision wrong."

"I knew you were going to say that." Selkess motioned to the gathered cult members, and without a word they opened the freezer door once more. Moments later they dragged a girl with long, wavy hair out by her chain while she struggled feebly against them. Azzie heard the stern girl calling out, "Keldie! *Keldie!*" until her voice was hoarse.

The cultists stood her up, and she wobbled on her exhausted feet.

"This is Keldie, the future medic and seer of Kwoltan Gera," Selkess lifted her chin. "Daelyn-Lleu is old and frail. He will be dead within a year. Even if he took a new apprentice this very moment, he would never have time to train them, and a tribe without a seer cannot survive. She is the last hope Kwoltan Gera has for a future." Laughter rippled through the cult's ranks. "Perel?"

The man who had taken Azzie to the freezer looked even more malicious in the light. He pulled a knife from his pocket, held it to her throat, and smiled with anticipation.

Lleuwellyn shifted his weight. "Kwoltan Gera doesn't matter to me."

"Oh, yes, it does," Selkess said. "*She* doesn't matter to you. The warriors don't matter to you. But Kwoltan Gera itself very much does, because it's a chance to prove you can do something right. To be recognized as good. And you want that, desperately."

Lleuwellyn started to argue, but Selkess held up a hand for silence. "If you tell me their plans, yes, some of them will die. They're prepared for that. But... I'll let *her* live. I'll send her back to the village, and in time, they will heal."

"I'm still not convinced," Lleuwellyn said, trying to sound disinterested. Azzie wondered if everyone could hear how worried he was, or if it was just him. "Tell me, how do you know I agree to this? If you can see the future and all, what argument sways me to help you?"

"You do it because you're my son, and you can never escape that," Selkess smirked. "You've tried so hard to prove you're nothing like me to people who hate you for it. Did you never stop and question why?"

"You killed my friends!" Lleuwellyn snapped. "You tried to kill me!"

"I tried to *save* you," Selkess shot back, "I'm still trying to save you, and I'm not going to fail again."

"The ritual—what's it for? What are you trying to do?" Lleuwellyn demanded. Although he still sounded angry, Azzie could hear real curiosity in his voice, and he was less defiant with each passing moment.

Selkess smiled wide, and the horrid screeching returned when he opened his mouth again. Wincing, Azzie forced himself to listen.

"The summoning ritual will make you a demigod, like me. Beyond death. Beyond pain. No one will ever be able to hurt you again." His laugh nearly deafened Azzie. "Kreor has been very generous with me! What are the lives of a few dozen children, when I can make my own *immortal*?"

Selkess's voice softened.

"You see now, how everything I've done has been for your own good? How I've cared for you, when no one else does? How I've sacrificed for you? Everyone else scorned you, hated you. Eureka and Baltan will never trust you. You can try to please them all you like, but you will never have a home out there." He held out a hand. "You belong with me, Lleuwellyn."

Lleuwellyn lowered his head, his tail twitching from side to side. He stayed that way for a while, and Keldie breathed in so sharply Azzie thought Perel had cut her with the knife.

"You can't," she whispered, "You can't seriously be thinking of *joining* him!"

Azzie didn't want to believe Lleuwellyn would betray them. Although they hadn't known each other long, they were friends! But he had also been stuck with Selkess for a whole night. There was no telling what awful lies he'd been told, again and again, until he believed them.

When Lleuwellyn looked up again, his expression was as smooth and cold as the stone of the Together Place. His eye was dark, except for the specks of starlight that flitted across its surface.

No!

Azzie pulled back, but Selkess tightened his grip on his shoulder.

"They're putting together their strongest and most resilient warriors for battle. Keida-Boitrat is leading. He's more determined than ever after what you did to Naesa. They're planning... they're planning a full-scale assault on the back entrance. They assume it will be the least guarded and easiest point of access. Once they get it open, two dozen warriors will attack, with an additional dozen serving as a second wave once those are all in. The second wave's goal is to get in, get the apprentices, and get back to the village. They won't be with Eureka and Baltan. Their trust in them is too shaken." He let out a deep breath, rubbing his eye until it was back to normal. "That's all I saw."

"No! How could you? *How could you?*" It was Keldie who screamed, but her words echoed in Azzie's heart as he wrinkled his nose to keep the tears in.

"Very good," Selkess nodded. "I've seen this possibility in the future, but it's good to know for certain. Which leads me to you, little one." Selkess leaned down and hissed in Azzie's ear, "Is he lying?"

Azzie studied Lleuwellyn's face through blurred sight. He was rigid, not looking at any of them, staring straight ahead.

Except for one impossibly tiny moment.

For just a heartbeat, Lleuwellyn lowered his gaze to Azzie's and showed the tiniest hint of emotion.

Azzie squeezed his eyes shut. "N-no," he forced out, less because his voice was strong and more because he was afraid of what Selkess would do to get it out of him.

"Thank you." Selkess smirked. To Perel, he ordered, "Take her to the office. We'll let her out once the ritual is complete."

He took the knife away from Keldie's throat, his disappointment at the lack of bloodshed clear.

She tried to lunge at Lleuwellyn with shouts of, "Coward! Traitor! You've killed them all!" but she was still weak from being in the cold storage room, and two cult members were easily able to overpower her and drag her down the hall.

Selkess reached for Lleuwellyn again, but he turned away with a flick of his tail. "I'd like to go back to my room now, please."

"Of course. I'll tell you more about the ritual there."

Azzie glared at their backs as Perel pulled him back into the freezer and snapped silver handcuffs around his wrists.

His smile was all sharp teeth. "We've got a free hook now."

As if it was no effort at all, he slung Azzie onto his shoulder and looped the chain over the hook so he could hang like the rest of them. His shoulders strained and popped as his feet scrambled to find solid ground, and despite the cold his stomach was on fire from being stretched.

The cultists slammed the door when they left.

Azzie was afraid his tears would freeze on his face.

XXIV

The setting sun was timed to the frantic beating of Baltan's heart.

The winter solstice had at last arrived.

He took a deep breath to calm his nerves as the night sky overtook the horizon. Now was not the time to panic.

He'd felt these jitters more times than he could count in the past, but this time they were so much worse.

Baltan spent the whole night studying the blueprints to figure out the best approach. He couldn't get any sleep with Eureka's shaking shoulders and shuddered breath reminding him of their failure.

There were three entrances into the slaughterhouse: the front door for employees and visitors, the side door for garbage removal, and the loading dock in the back. The children were likely being held in either the employee rest area or in the meat lockers. Given the number of them and the cult's penchant for inhumane cruelty, Baltan was staking his and Eureka's lives on them being in the freezers by the back entrance.

If Baltan was wrong, they were as good as dead.

How and if Kwoltan Gera used the blueprints was entirely their decision. Baltan wasn't going to tell Keida how to lead his warriors after he'd failed to come up with a way to rescue Naesa. And the less they said, the better, in case Selkess was listening somehow.

They still didn't know if Naesa would live or not. She was young and strong, and if they got her to the hospital in time, she stood a good chance of survival—assuming the hospital was equipped for Azure patients, and the staff cared enough about an injured Azure girl to take action, and she wasn't left waiting in emergency care all night while she bled out, and infection didn't set in, and a million other things that could go wrong.

Baltan tried to steady his shaking hands. He was too out of practice at being calm and keeping his distance from the case. But how could he? This was Eureka's family. Eureka's *son.*

And all they had up their sleeve was a half-baked *idea* of a plan.

He and Eureka would create a distraction at the front entrance in order to draw the cult away from the back. A few guards were sure to stay behind, but if they could get *most* of Selkess's followers away from the loading dock, they might have a fighting chance at defeating the cult.

If the reinforcement from Kwoltan Gera attacked from the loading dock.

If their diversion lured enough of the cultists away.

If the kids were in the meat locker and not somewhere else.

If they even had the right place.

Baltan hoped that not planning every detail of the siege out loud might throw Selkess off. They could maintain some element of surprise by not explicitly stating where or if Kwoltan Gera would join the rescue effort, and that might let them steal back the upper hand.

Still, going off without absolute confirmation of when, where, or even *if* reinforcements were coming put Baltan on edge.

Eureka had gone on ahead of him for that reason. Splitting up, as difficult as it was, might throw off anyone who was watching them.

It was desperate. It was stupid. Rushing in with brute force and wishing for the best was never a good idea.

But when dealing with an enemy like Selkess, who had everything else planned for, who could probably turn any plan back on them, it was the only way they were going to get anywhere. They could go back and forth until the sun came up on what Selkess was expecting them to do, and they had.

Baltan closed his eyes.

I can't believe I'm doing this, but if you're up there, Lleu Gera or Khalpi or Ahezia or whatever... please let this work.

Maybe not the most earnest or humble prayer, but it was all he had in him.

The sun finished its descent, leaving a line of red in the sky. The stars that formed the Dread Serpent began to appear, but not all of them were visible yet.

It was time to move out.

Baltan took a deep breath and checked his supplies. Both of his pistols were holstered at his sides with extra magazines loaded into the straps. Twenty bullets ready, thirty more to refill. Hopefully he wouldn't need all his ammo, but he wasn't taking that chance.

Forward.

He didn't run despite the silent command coursing through his veins. It wouldn't do any good to show up out of breath. At least it was easier than the trek up the hills to Illdresil Gera.

Baltan picked up his pace a little, not jogging, but not far from it. He told himself it was to fight the new winter chill in the air.

He didn't like the idea of Selkess and Lleuwellyn being together, and he couldn't figure out if it was concern for Lleuwellyn or fear they might have been working together all along. He pushed that thought away; there was no chance Lleuwellyn could have communicated anything about their plans to Selkess without him or Eureka knowing.

It was possible Azzie was a member of the cult and had only been following instructions from Selkess the whole time. Selkess had implied as much on the phone. But Baltan didn't buy that; Azzie's interactions with them might not have always been what he expected, but they were too genuine to be acting.

Lleuwellyn, on the other hand...

Right turn.

There was a good chance Baltan would die. Did he have any regrets or last wishes he could clear up before he went headfirst into this insanity? No, none he could think of. Maybe one last soda would have been nice, but he'd run out the previous night.

Maybe he could have stopped Eureka when he showed up at the door with Azzie. He could have carried on filling up the empty space in his life with booze and bedmates that never lasted long enough for him to miss them when they were gone.

It was too late for any of that now.

Left turn.

A steady relationship could have been nice, but it would be selfish, leaving a lover waiting at home to receive the call that he'd died. The leftover money wouldn't be much of a comfort. Then again, as prickly as he was, who could stand being in a relationship with him, especially when his heart would always belong to someone else?

Round the corner.

Eureka was there, as planned. Relief flooded Baltan's senses and washed away most of the doubt.

It would have been the perfect time to go through the plan again, or exchange what might be their final words.

One look into Eureka's eyes eliminated any need to speak.

There was nothing Baltan would change about his life. Every heartbeat that led him to that moment was one worth living.

The front door to the slaughterhouse wasn't locked.

Eureka took the first step in, before Baltan could stop him, as always. The plain lobby—nothing more than a couch, table, and receptionists' desk—didn't offer many places for enemies to hide. Baltan held his pistols at the ready anyway.

"Clear," Eureka announced once he finished scoping out the lobby.

"Let's start making some noise." Baltan stomped his way across the room even though it went against every instinct he had to be inconspicuous during a takedown.

The route was etched into Baltan's mind from tracing the blueprints with his eyes and fingers. He was determined not to let fear or anxiety erase it.

Through the lobby, into the hallway. They slowed their movements to check if anyone had detected them yet. The building was dead as far as he could see or hear.

There was no doubt Selkess knew they were already inside. Why wasn't he sending someone to intercept them? They should have encountered some kind of obstacle by now.

Baltan fought to keep calm. This *had* to be the right place. And if it was, the fact that there weren't any guards coming after them meant they were probably all with Selkess and the ritual had begun, or they were guarding the kids.

So much for causing a distraction.

A few doors broke up the hallway. On the right, offices; on the left, the employee break room. No guards meant the kids probably weren't there now, but they couldn't leave them unchecked.

Baltan jerked his head to one of the break room entrances and Eureka slipped down the hall to the other. On the count of three, they threw the doors open and ducked behind them. The volley of shots that usually followed didn't come, leaving them in a still, silent hallway.

Inside was a mattress on the floor that looked like it was used recently, and a few stale chip bags littered the table. Eureka inhaled deeply, then leaned down to pick up a strand of long, dark hair from the pillow. "Lleuwellyn was here. Azzie, too, but his scent isn't as fresh. They must have been separated some time last night."

"I'm amazed you can still pick it up over that cheap cologne." Baltan tried to get a closer look, but nearly stepped in a small puddle of something black. "What the *fuck* is that?"

Eureka rubbed his nose. "It smells like iron, but it's... not right."

Baltan tasted the bile rising in his throat as his mind came up with a dozen horrible explanations. "There's no one here now. Let's go."

A loud shriek of, "Keep out, or else!" echoed through the hall as soon as Baltan's hand touched the handle of the first office door.

Baltan readied his gun and tested the handle. "Locked."

"Let me see." Eureka ran a claw around the keyhole, assessed whether he could successfully pick the lock, then braced himself against the door and tore the handle out with a swift jerk.

They stood aside, ready for gunfire, but were met with only a startled scream.

Eureka pushed the door open. With a fierce cry, an Azure girl threw herself at him, pounding her fists weakly against his midsection.

"Hey, hey!" he shouted in alarm, grabbing her wrists to stop her feeble assault.

She looked up at him for only a moment before breaking out of his hold and pressing against his side. "Keida, I'm so glad to see you!" She sniffed. "The others will be okay after all... It was awful, I thought you were all going to... but you're *here*..."

Eureka put his arms around her, rubbing her shoulders. While he comforted her, Baltan's eyes scanned the office for traps or surveillance devices.

The office wasn't anything unexpected, just a desk, a chair, and a row of filing cabinets. It would have been only too easy to overlook the neatly stapled pile of papers sitting on the desk if it wasn't turned to face the door.

Baltan picked it up, skimming the first few pages with wide eyes.

"It's... it's the cult's plan," he gaped. He briefly thumbed through the stack. "Those idiots! There's information about Evanne and Turnap's murders!" He mustered some genuine enthusiasm and beamed at Eureka. "It's not quite a confession, but it'll hold up in court. They've handed us all the proof we need!"

His voice broke the girl out of her bubble. She gasped when she pulled back to look at Eureka again and saw what her bloodshot eyes missed the first time. When she finally noticed Baltan, she bared her teeth. "Who are you?"

"I'm Eureka—Keida's brother," Eureka answered. "This is Baltan. We're here to help you. Where are the others?"

"They were in a freezer when I was with them," she said, her face twisting with grief, "But, if *you're* here, then are the others going to the back?"

"Probably," Baltan replied.

"No, it's a trap!" she wailed, "He knows! He *knows* they'll go that way! That other Illdresil Gera Azure told him what they were planning!"

Baltan was sure his blood stopped running in his veins.

Had Lleuwellyn been a spy all along?

The evidence in his hand wasn't a slip-up or a mistake. It was a deliberate statement, assurance that the cult couldn't afford to let any of them walk out alive.

"Then we need to get there first." Eureka's voice was calm, commanding, and just what Baltan and the girl needed to stop panicking. "And you need to get to safety. Do you think you can run?"

"If I have to," she said.

"Take these," Baltan handed her the stack of papers despite her hesitation to accept anything from him. "Do you know where the nearest emergency response center is?"

"I... yes, I think so. There's one near the hospital my brother works at."

"Good. Take these there, tell them Marina Delta's Investigative Department requires backup at the Riverside Abattoir, and wait for someone to come get you. I promise, someone *will* come get you."

Every part of her radiated fear, from her trembling ears to her quavering lips to her unsteady hold on the papers. But she bit down on her lower lip, nodded, and left the office with them. They stayed there long enough to listen for the lobby door, then headed further into the hallway once they were sure she had gotten out. They couldn't afford to wait another moment.

The work area where livestock was killed, skinned, and disemboweled lied in wait beyond the next door.

Baltan shoved his growing dread aside and examined the lock. Key-card activated, and there weren't any spares in the break room from what he could recall.

"Stand back." Eureka steadied himself and rammed the door with his shoulder, making a sizable dent and a lot of noise, but it didn't budge from its hinges. Eureka pulled back with a wince.

"You okay?" Baltan asked.

"I'll manage."

One more slam knocked the door loose from its hinges. It swayed for a moment before falling inward. They only had one breath to prepare for what was on the other side, and they took it.

The massive work room encompassed most of the building, but Baltan saw everything he needed to within heartbeats of stepping inside.

A line of cultists armed with hunting rifles stood at the loading dock doors in the back, ready to open fire on any intruders. Baltan's gaze swept the ground at their feet, but it was free of the dark blue Azure blood he'd feared might already be there.

He didn't want to see the captives. He'd spent too many nights wondering what, exactly, Selkess had done to those thirty kids fifteen years ago, and he would rather keep wondering than know for sure. But that wasn't the hand he'd been dealt.

Baltan looked up.

The sight punched him in the gut, leaving him struggling to breathe while his stomach tried to escape his body.

The victims hung by ankle chains, face-down and blindfolded, from the conveyor belt that took the carcasses through processing.

They were in terrible shape. Their chests heaved. Their skin was pale, stretched too tight over their bones. Their limp arms dangled, useless, above the floor.

The heart-stopping agony in his chest when he saw Azzie was nothing compared to the waves of fury rolling off Eureka.

The few cult members who weren't guarding the back entrance stood beside the kids with knives, ready to slit their throats when Selkess gave the word.

Selkess stood in front of the line, clutching one of Lleuwellyn's arms. Silver handcuffs restrained Lleuwellyn at his wrists and ankles, with so little chain that even one step would be difficult.

His lifted a curved knife to Lleuwellyn's throat.

If Eureka or Baltan made any quick moves, he could kill Lleuwellyn right then and there.

"This may be a tad overdramatic," Selkess said, his tone entirely too casual, "but I thought it would be the most considerate to the people who own the facility. This isn't the designated bleeding area, but there is a trough here that's meant to collect any extra fluids that might spill out while the organs are removed."

Baltan couldn't think of anything more intelligent to say than, "Let them go!"

He raised his pistols, but Selkess tapped Lleuwellyn's neck with the flat side of the blade in response.

Baltan hesitated. His fingers itched to pull the trigger and rid the world of this monster, but he couldn't risk hitting Lleuwellyn, or Selkess slicing his throat before the bullet struck.

The risk might be worth it to put an end to all of this, especially if Lleuwellyn had joined his father, but he didn't know if Selkess might have ordered his followers to kill the others if anything happened to him. They were too vastly outnumbered to have any hope of saving them all.

Gritting his teeth, he lowered his guns. He heard a growl rising in Eureka's throat.

Selkess barely spoke above a whisper, but his voice was clear. "So, this is how it ends." His smug tone was a slap in the face. "I must say, I feel I owe you my gratitude. You played along with my plans so perfectly. Though, of course, that is to be expected."

"Prophet, should we begin?"

"No. Kreor will need nourishment for the ritual, and any sacrifice made before the constellation is in full view will not be received. Wait for my signal."

They all stood in complete silence.

As time scraped by, each grim moment feeling longer and longer, Baltan urged his brain to churn out some miraculous idea, some unseen option that would let them save the day and stop the massacre.

There *had* to be a way. The massacre could *not* happen.

Not while Baltan was watching.

Not when Azzie was going to be a victim.

Then, so quietly that at first Baltan wasn't sure he'd really heard it, Eureka asked, "Are you sure?"

"Of course. I've seen it, and Lleuwellyn confirmed my vision," Selkess answered, "The two of you are unable to take action. The warriors arrive at the back entrance and are picked off by my followers before they can reach their children. The ritual is completed successfully, and then... then... I don't know." His lips drew back into a snarl. He let go of Lleuwellyn's arm, pressing a hand over his stitched-open eye. "How can it be so fuzzy now? It was all clear last night!"

"Prophet!" a few of the cultists abandoned their posts on the kill line to assist him.

"I'm fine! Get back to—"

The side door burst open with the force of a tidal wave and unleashed a flood of furious warriors.

The cultists who had so carefully watched the back entrance scrambled over themselves to turn and get a clear shot. They fumbled like amateurs, and the first to fire was knocked back by the butt of his own rifle as the bullet flew way off course into the rafters.

Keida led the charge, clearing the distance between the side entrance before most of the cultists had a chance to react.

A few of the cult members dropped their guns and ran when the roaring of victory in battle surrounded them in a ferocious echo. They didn't get far before the warriors crashed into Selkess's forces.

Baltan considered himself the luckiest man on the planet to not have to face the might of Kwoltan Gera. He tried to line up a shot, but there was too much movement. In the blink of an eye the warriors divided the cultists' ranks.

Some of the cultists positioned closer to the loading dock had the chance to back up and steady themselves. Gunshot split the air like thunderclaps as they fired in a panic, not caring if they hit one of the warriors or one of their own.

Those closest to the warriors disappeared in sprays of blood. Some were struck from behind, holes blown through their chests and shoulders from stray rifle bullets. Azure claws shredded others, tearing them open as easily as wet newspaper and casting their bodies aside in the same blow.

"Which one of you did it?" a woman's fierce voice rose over the din, "*Which one of you bastards hurt my daughter?*"

It wasn't long before the triumphant war cries and furious howls transformed into shrieks of pain. The worst of them were cut off too soon, the last sounds some of the warriors would ever make.

The element of surprise had served them well, but it could only last so long.

Injured warriors and cultists dragged each other down, determined to never let their opponent rise from the floor. One warrior grabbed the barrel of a rifle and jammed it back into its owner's jaw, only for them to pull the trigger at the last moment and decimate the warrior's neck and shoulder. Both collapsed in a heap as the battle raged on around them.

Eyes wide, Baltan realized there weren't enough warriors to keep the assault going. What had initially looked like a huge surge was, in fact, only about a dozen or so against at least twice as many cult members. And not all of the cultists were amateurs with their guns.

The smell of blood permeated the air so thickly it choked Baltan's senses, paralyzed him.

It didn't matter. They'd gotten Kwoltan Gera's help, and it didn't matter. They'd only succeeded in adding more bodies to the pile.

How did it all go so wrong?

Then the back entrance opened.

Patrioek-Totoag stormed in, hardly recognizable from the good-natured man Baltan met in Kwoltan Gera. Another dozen warriors fanned out behind him, bringing fresh blood to the battle and reinvigorating the warriors still standing.

Selkess's followers never stood a chance.

A high-pitched scream drew Baltan's attention from the bloodbath.

One of the cultists started to cut into a captured girl's neck, no longer waiting for Selkess's signal. The Prophet was still reeling from the asinine revelation that he could be *wrong*.

They were there to save the kids. That's what he needed to focus on, and they could *not* afford another lapse in attention.

Baltan raised a pistol and fired, leaving a neat, steaming hole in the cultist's chest.

A trickle of blood darkened the girls' neck, but it wasn't a deep cut. She'd survive if they got her down soon.

One shot was all it took for the other cultists to step back. A few dropped their knives.

"I'll get the kids. You take care of Selkess," Eureka barked. "Erisolus, Kariet, Shaeda! With me!" The warriors responded in an instant, abandoning the rear guard and refocusing on the cultists trying to kill their children.

Baltan narrowed his eyes and squared his shoulders, every bit of fear and anxiety and doubt in him replaced with seething, untempered rage. Selkess would pay for every moment of pain and fear he'd ever inflicted on any child.

Lleuwellyn tore himself away from Selkess as soon as his grip weakened, but the chains stopped him from walking. Instead he crawled across the floor as quickly as possible toward the broken door.

Selkess drew his hand away from his stitched eye, saw Lleuwellyn was gone, and made an unsteady dash for him.

Baltan was ready to pull the trigger to stop him, but Lleuwellyn was faster. He rolled onto his side and kicked as hard as he could once Selkess was close enough, his foot connecting with a sickening *crack*.

Selkess toppled to the ground, some bone definitely broken, but he was barely fazed by it. Without missing a beat, he grabbed a fistful of Lleuwellyn's hair and yanked it, forcing his head back and exposing his neck.

"You lied to me," Selkess hissed, bringing the knife to Lleuwellyn's throat. "You betrayed your own father!"

"You aren't my father anymore," Lleuwellyn forced out through gritted teeth.

Baltan couldn't aim well enough to take Selkess out. If he fired, he could hit them both—or he might hit only Lleuwellyn.

He holstered his guns and ran.

They weren't far away, but every step seemed to stretch on and on. Why couldn't he move his legs faster?

He wasn't going to make it.

Lleuwellyn was going to die right in front of him, then Azzie, then Eureka...

Baltan willed himself across the room, fueled by adrenaline and fury.

He didn't know what he was going to do when he got to them, but it wasn't going to be pretty. Shooting Selkess in the face at point blank range sounded ideal, if he could *get there in time!*

Lleuwellyn elbowed Selkess hard in the ribs, but he didn't flinch. Instead of loosening his grip, he tugged harder, drawing Lleuwellyn closer so he could cut deeper.

Baltan grabbed Selkess's shoulders and heaved him off Lleuwellyn, who narrowly avoided having his neck sliced as the knife was jerked back. Baltan pivoted, using momentum to shove Selkess hard against one of the support beams for the conveyor belt, and pulled a gun from its holster.

Got him!

It would feel so good to unload the clip into him. It might even be necessary. They had no reason to think Selkess would come quietly, not after leaving all that evidence lying out for them to find.

His trigger finger twitched, but the air was not split by triumphant gunshot.

A shout of anguish loud enough to bring down the building tore from Eureka's throat.

Baltan knew that thundering sound too well. His heart stopped, and it wouldn't start again until he knew Eureka was okay.

Blood poured from a gaping injury in Eureka's shoulder, seeping through his clothes and flowing between his fingers as he tried to keep pressure on the exit wound. More blood dripped from his lips.

Was there an internal injury? Had buckshot created deeper damage, pierced a lung?

Was Eureka too old to recover? Had he pushed his limits too many times?

Who shot him?

He couldn't see. He couldn't hear.

"Eu—"

Couldn't speak, couldn't *think.*

"*Eureka!*"

Something moved in the corner of his eye.

Selkess lunged at Baltan. Both of them fell to the floor in a flurry of limbs. Baltan barely registered his back hitting the ground before he pushed up, tackling Selkess and rolling them both away from the conveyor belt.

The guns, thrown from Baltan's hand during the scuffle, clattered to a stop across the concrete floor. Baltan paid them no mind. All that mattered was hurting Selkess however he could, but he shrugged off every kick and punch like it was nothing.

Selkess pinned Baltan with one hand on his chest, the other still holding the knife. He pushed down with all his might, fingertips pressed into Baltan's sternum hard enough to bruise as he slid them up toward his neck.

Baltan was a rookie again, on a case no other investigator would take, not yet able to trust his partner, facing the most dangerous criminal he would ever come across and hopelessly in over his head. He struggled futilely against Selkess, trying and failing to push him off. He didn't look strong, but even willowy Azures like him were stronger than most Easterners.

Spots began to dance at the edge of Baltan's vision as breathing became harder and harder, and he wasn't sure if it was because of the pressure Selkess was putting on his chest or the sheer, simple terror.

"My, but doesn't this feel familiar?" Selkess's words dripped with venom and his stitched eye somehow widened further. "You're not as fresh as you used to be, but—" He glanced at Lleuwellyn with a smirk as he watched on in horror, "—I always catch my prey in the end."

Baltan punched him with as much force as he could muster. The iris in that wretched eye broke, the pupil distorted as dark fluid leaked out into the sclera.

Selkess still didn't flinch, but his sneer transformed into a snarl.

He leaned heavily onto Baltan, cutting off more of his air supply.

The steel of the knife gleamed in the fluorescent light. Baltan struggled against Selkess's weight, but his vision was beginning to blur. He couldn't pry Selkess's fingers loose, couldn't push him off.

His head fell back onto the cold concrete. Lleuwellyn's terrified face was going to be the last thing he ever saw, and he couldn't even see it clearly.

The pressure on his neck loosened slightly and Selkess grinned wide in anticipation. "Your final words, investigator?"

"You lose," Baltan choked out. "We win. *You lose.*"

The weight on his chest doubled as Selkess pushed against him, lifted himself up, raised his arm, and then—

"No!" Lleuwellyn shouted.

—Selkess brought the knife down in a sweeping arc.

XXV

Azzie's ears rang.

He couldn't tell if it was from the howls of the living or the wails of the dead. It didn't matter. Fear and pain washed over him from all sides.

Closing his eyes didn't help. It only made the shouts and cries more deafening, the stench of blood more sickening.

He didn't know what to do. There was nothing he *could* do but hang there, useless, and watch while Lleuwellyn struggled to escape from Selkess and Baltan ran to his defense.

His mind fled into a dream where he joined the battle after being freed from his chains and fought with the bravery and skill of a trained warrior. But he'd watched the apprentices go limp after the warriors got them down from the hooks. He wasn't in any better shape than they were. He'd be lucky if he could walk on his own once he was unchained.

One voice rose over the dreadful ringing, and for a moment his dream became real.

"Azzie!"

The warriors working down the line of kidnapped children came to him at last. A few of them bled from knife wounds, but they were all mostly in one piece. A bit of Patrioek's left ear was missing, though it might have been that way before.

Eureka reached for him and Azzie imagined finding the strength to raise his arms and give him the biggest hug.

"I've got you," Eureka said, smiling in spite of everything.

Azzie sobbed once, his tears flowing up and over his forehead. He was confused for a heartbeat—he had only cried when he was sad or scared before—but it was swept away with relief and joy. He almost felt silly for being so scared. Of course everything was going to be okay. Eureka and Baltan and even Lleuwellyn had all made promises, in their own way, that they wouldn't let him get hurt.

Eureka's claws were almost on the chain when he jerked back with a shout. The smell of blood hit Azzie's nose with more force than ever as Eureka pressed his hand to the wound.

No!

Kariet-Loloa leapt at the cult member who had shot him and slashed his arm to ribbons, but it didn't make Eureka stop hurting. He stumbled as more and more blood soaked into his shirt.

No! No!!

Azzie turned away. The snarls and screams and bloodshed were too much to handle already. He couldn't close his eyes, but he couldn't stand seeing Eureka in pain either.

Baltan looked way from Selkess to see what was wrong. Horror spread over his face like a mask, blinding him to anything but Eureka.

Selkess didn't hesitate. He leapt at Baltan.

"B-Bal... Bal...!"

His voice was too hoarse to be heard over the fighting. Baltan was caught off-guard and he and Selkess tumbled to the ground. They rolled, but Selkess gained the upper hand, pinned Baltan down. Baltan fought back, but he couldn't get free.

Azzie could only watch as Selkess raised the knife.

"No!" Lleuwellyn struggled toward them and threw himself against Selkess, but he was too late. Both of them lay sprawled on top of Baltan's motionless, red-covered body.

Azzie must have screamed, because Eureka and the warriors looked at him with shock, but he didn't hear it. He didn't want to hear anything. What if the next words in his ears would be Baltan's last before his spirit left for Lleu Gera, or wherever Easterners went?

But he still saw, no matter how he wished to look away. The sight of Baltan's blood paralyzed Eureka. The limp arm hanging at his side, the battle, the whole world was forgotten as his eyes clouded with dismay.

Lleuwellyn jerked away from Selkess like he'd been burned, searching frantically for something. He kicked against the ground and forced himself forward, twisting so he could grab one of Baltan's discarded pistols. He sat up, his shaking hands steadied on his knees. His fingers twitched and fumbled against the trigger.

Selkess stood, one side of his hip jutting out awkwardly and making his stride even more unbalanced than usual as he walked toward Lleuwellyn, knife in hand, pausing only to wipe Baltan's blood onto the leg of his pants.

"Put the gun down."

The order did not come from Selkess.

Eureka stalked toward them, and his voice turned Azzie's blood to ice. "Put the gun down, Lleuwellyn. He's not for you."

Selkess was slow to turn away from Lleuwellyn. He steadied the knife in his hand and regarded Eureka like a coiled snake judging the distance between itself and its target before it struck.

Eureka looked at him with the same predatory menace. Azzie was reminded of a large cat, waiting to pounce on its prey and kill it with a swift bite.

It all came down to which moved first.

Selkess drew back a step, glancing past Eureka and at the scattered remnants of his cult. From what Azzie could hear, there weren't many left. Most of them had run off. A few were moaning in pain. The rest were either dead or disarmed, but they were quiet. Half of the warriors were gone, too—some injured, dead, or dying, but others had carried their children out of the slaughterhouse, to safety and freedom.

"So," Selkess repeated, "this is how it ends. Back to jail, then? Another fifteen years?" He put his wrists together and offered them, palms-up, in mock surrender.

"No." Eureka moved forward, and Selkess took another step back. Then another. Eureka continued his advance. "You got fifteen years because you only killed Azure kids. Because Easterners don't care too much about Azures killing Azures. We usually come back, anyway." Each word was edged with the glint of a bared fang. "But do you know what you just did? You attacked an Easterner. And there's a zero tolerance policy against Azures attacking Easterners."

The knife slipped out of Selkess's hand. "But you wouldn't," he said, his voice strained. "Not you. Baltan, yes— if you hadn't been hurt, he would have shot me between the eyes. But not you. You would never... You're too good for that." He laughed, but there was a nervous hesitance to it. "You're not a killer, Eureka. You're not cruel."

"I killed you once."

Selkess touched the scar on his neck. "Not... not *permanently*, not when I'm willing to comply." He stumbled back another step, nearly tripping over Lleuwellyn. "Killing me now would be in cold blood. That isn't what you do."

"Cold blood?" Eureka roared, "Baltan's blood is still warm! The blood of my people is still warm! *Get out of the way, Lleuwellyn.*"

The gun clattered to the floor as Lleuwellyn scrambled away, dragging himself toward Baltan and keeping his back to what Eureka was about to do.

Azzie's chain shook. A woman whose face was a lot like Naesa's gripped it tightly so he wouldn't fall on his head, then jerked the links apart. She was going to lift him over her shoulder, but he squirmed until she set him down with a sigh.

He wobbled, every part of him exhausted and screaming for rest. He would have fallen down if the warrior hadn't kept an arm around him. She brushed his hair with her fingers and nudged him toward the side entrance. A few of the other apprentices were heading that way, guarded by a small band of warriors.

Azzie was tempted to lean into her and let her take him. It would be easy. It might even be what Eureka and Baltan wanted.

He forced himself away from her and did his best to walk on his own. His feet were heavy and his legs were light. He fell a few times, but he managed.

Selkess didn't stir from where he lay, twisted, on the ground. A pool of thick, dark liquid poured from his throat and mouth. His stitched eye had filled with it, giving it the appearance of an empty socket.

Azzie's ears twitched. He could hear something he was sure none of the others did, like he had with Turnap and far too many other people that day. The final words of the dying.

He almost tried not to hear it when he realized it was coming from Selkess. His throat was filled with sludge, but Azzie still heard the words trying to come out. His unstitched eye was starting to lose focus and turn glassy, but it was doing its best to stay trained on Lleuwellyn.

Look at me!

Then, with a shuddering breath, he was gone.

The last apprentice was freed and led away. A few warriors stayed behind, surrounding a group of cultists who could only hold up their empty hands and beg for mercy. In the distance, Azzie could hear an odd wailing sound.

The battle was over. The day was won.

"Oh, Baltan..." Eureka cradled his body as best he could. "I told you there wasn't any need for you to put yourself in harm's way, but I—I wasn't—if I'd just..."

Azzie leaned against Eureka's good arm. Lleuwellyn joined them on his other side, his tail curling around them both as the wailing got louder and closer with each passing moment.

Epilogue

The clouds of a stormy gray sky were breaking apart. The sun was coming through, shining brighter than ever. But even when the sky was clear, the rain wouldn't stop falling.

It seemed so strange that, after everything they'd been through, the sun still rose every morning, set every night, and people went about their business in between. They still got hungry, still ate when the hunger got bad enough, still took showers and went to sleep. The world carried on.

That was the miracle they had all sacrificed for.

Azzie watched the people around them as he walked. They all had their own lives that he was completely unaware of, and they were completely unaware of his. They would never know what he'd been through.

It had been a rough Capricorn, especially for Eureka.

He led the way through town with his head held high and shoulders back. No one who saw him would know how he'd been hurt. But the pain was there, showing only in how much time he spent cooking. He rarely ate anything, but the radio couldn't play more than five or six songs before he wandered back into the kitchen.

Azzie tried to help him with whatever he was making, and sometimes Lleuwellyn pitched in when he could be pulled away from his library books. They had conversations and Eureka tried to help Azzie learn to read with the recipes, when he used a recipe at all. They made all kinds of things, and Lleuwellyn brought Eureka back a new cookbook every time he went to the library. But even as the delicious aromas of fresh-baked pies and sautéed squash and roasted lizards filled the house, they all knew they wouldn't actually eat much of it, if any. They usually ended up taking it to the neighbors or the strays.

Flower sellers called out to them as they passed, trying to sell off the last blooms before the true chill of winter set in and killed them. Eureka stopped briefly to purchase a bouquet of yellow roses, then set off again at a brisk pace.

Lleuwellyn's long legs could easily match, but Azzie had to make an effort to keep up.

"Hold on to me. Don't want you getting lost," Lleuwellyn said, offering a hand to him. Azzie looked at it, then at Eureka, who kept his gaze fixed firmly ahead. He didn't need to hold Lleuwellyn's hand. He knew where they were going.

All the same, he hopped forward a few steps and linked his hand with Lleuwellyn's. At once, Lleuwellyn's tail quit twitching irritably against the crowd, and Azzie was able to walk at Eureka's pace without as much of a struggle.

The last constellation had brought Lleuwellyn and Azzie closer than ever. Though Lleuwellyn insisted he would find a job and move out soon, Eureka had managed to find a stacking bed for a reasonable price and brought it into their home.

"There's no use in you sleeping on the couch every night," he'd told Lleuwellyn.

Azzie was certain getting rid of Baltan's old bed was harder for Eureka than he wanted to admit. He'd barely come out of his room that evening, leaving Azzie and Lleuwellyn to settle who would sleep on which bunk.

The top bunk went to Azzie, since it was too close to the ceiling for Lleuwellyn's liking. He couldn't stand tight spaces, and he said the way the blankets draped from the top bunk made the lower one feel a bit like the medicine hut. He found a string of decorative lights at a secondhand shop and strung them up from the support beams of the top bunk to mimic the firefly lanterns in Illdresil Gera.

He did snore a bit, and sometimes mumbled in his sleep, but Azzie didn't mind. Having Lleuwellyn so close made Baltan's absence easier for him to bear.

Though the hospital tried to look friendly with its colorful art pieces and fresh flowers, there was no masking the clinical atmosphere of IV drips, waiting rooms, and the smell of cleansing chemicals.

The three crowded into an elevator and Eureka pressed the button for the third floor, where long-term rehabilitation patients stayed. Lleuwellyn and Azzie followed Eureka down the left corridor until they reached the right room, though they all knew the way by heart already.

Eureka knocked on the door three times, waited, then added a fourth knock.

Behind it, an unenthusiastic voice called, "Come in."

Azzie frowned, and Eureka released an expected sigh before saying, "Wait here a moment. I'll be right back."

Baltan tried to imagine what the hospital room looked like. Charts and health posters on the walls changed subjects every time he pictured them. The wallpaper would be ridiculously tacky. Two windows on either side of the cot would let sunlight in, but the view outside would be a stark, depressing cityscape.

There would definitely be a few dents in the walls from where he'd thrown a chair. Now all his guests had to stand.

"I smell flowers," he said. That wasn't unusual. He'd received more flowers in the last few weeks than he ever had in his life. A few iris bouquets had arrived from anonymous senders who Baltan assumed were the happily reunited families in Kwoltan Gera. Captain Stotsan had sent his customary bundle of white daisies, which Baltan ordered the nurse to throw away. He wasn't an investigator injured while on duty; he had no right to those flowers anymore.

"Yellow roses. Your favorite." Eureka's voice both soothed and saddened him.

Baltan grabbed them after a few tries and moved the flowers closer to give them a good sniff, only to end up smacking his forehead with them. He lowered them to his nose with a grunt.

"Thanks. They're great."

Silence.

Baltan was sick of silence. He knew what Eureka wanted to say. He'd said it before. They'd had every version of this argument over the last week, and still Eureka kept coming back to have it all over again.

"You're allowed to come home today," Eureka said softly.

"No, thanks. The hospital has an assisted living program."

"Why?" Eureka was as exhausted with this fight as Baltan, and it was apparent in every syllable. Yet he still came by almost every day to have it.

"I think it would be better, now that I have a permanent condition," Baltan huffed, leaning against the pillow he'd propped up. "I've gotten all the details. It's affordable. I can have visitors as often as I like, from midday to sundown, excluding certain holidays when the facility is closed to the public. And there are planned group activities. It sounds like a great time."

"You hate group activities," Eureka pointed out with a hint of a laugh.

"There's always the radio."

He could hear the squeak of Eureka's shoes against the polished floor as he looked for somewhere to sit and realized there was no more chair.

"There's no need for that. Baltan, you know I don't mind helping to take care of you, and I'm more than qualified. And you still haven't answered me. *Why*? Why a facility? Why not come home and let me—"

"*That's* why!" Baltan snapped, "I don't want you to take care of me!" His fist collided with the mattress with an unsatisfactory *thumpf*. He could feel his face screwing up, his lower lip trembling, but there were no tears. He didn't have tear ducts anymore. "I haven't fought by your side, risked my *life* for you, to have you treat me like one of your stray kittens! I'm *not* helpless, and I'm *not* a child!" He gritted his teeth. "And don't forget, you have one of those to take care of now."

The slightest note of indignation crept into Eureka's voice. "What do you mean, I have a child to take care of now? What does that have to do with you going to a facility? If anything, it's all the more reason for you to come home!" He let his anger go in a heavy breath. "I know you aren't helpless. I haven't forgotten all that we've been through together, and I promise I won't forget what you can still do."

Eureka touched their foreheads together. "I still need you. I always will. And I'm not the only one anymore." For a moment, Baltan dared to think Eureka might press more than their foreheads together. "I can respect that you don't want to be taken care of. But that doesn't mean you aren't cared *for*."

As if on cue, there was a knock at the door. Baltan bit his bottom lip to keep it still when the handle turned and Lleuwellyn called in a whisper, "Can we come in now?"

Silence again. They were waiting for his answer.

"Sure, why not?" Baltan shrugged. Despite still imagining Lleuwellyn with Selkess's face half the time, Baltan found his presence far more tolerable now that it was just his voice, which barely resembled Selkess at all. And besides, it was hard to completely dislike someone who saved his life. Baltan would sorely miss his sight, but it was better to lose that than have his throat slashed open.

"Now that everyone's here, how about we get those bandages off? Or would you rather wait for the nurse?" Eureka suggested. His upbeat tone failed to cover up the lingering tension in the room.

"Might as well do it now, since you're so qualified."

Eureka's touch was light as he carefully peeled away the layers of cloth from Baltan's face. Were Azzie and Lleuwellyn leaning forward to get a good look at him? Or did they stay back in anticipation of the worst?

The bandage fell aside and Baltan hesitantly opened his eyes. It made no difference. It wasn't dark, necessarily. It was nothing. He was told it would be this way, but he still expected to see something—blurred silhouettes, bits of familiar color, *something*. He closed his eyes and opened them again. Nothing changed, and Eureka felt far away even though his breath tickled Baltan's ear.

His right eye was made of glass, an exact copy of the other. Thanks to Lleuwellyn, Selkess hadn't cut Baltan's throat, but he had destroyed one eye and grazed the other badly enough to blind him. The line where Selkess had drawn his knife was permanently marked on his face, starting at his left temple and taking a notch out of his nose.

He ran a finger along the bridge of his nose, tapping near the top where the surgeons had replaced the missing bit. There was a scab, but nothing that wouldn't heal in time. "Well? How is it?" he asked.

"It's kind of nice, actually," Lleuwellyn offered. "Up close, your eyes are more gray. The pupil is a little less defined. But from further away, no one would notice a difference."

Baltan tried looking around. His remaining eye responded as well as ever, and his muscles tried to move the glass eye, but he could feel it lag. "I want an eyepatch."

"You want—what?" Eureka asked.

"It's creepy. It doesn't move the same as my other eye. Plus, eye patches are cool. And..." he searched for the right words. If this moment got any sappier, he'd start crying, and that was the last thing he wanted. "And if any of you have touched my soda I'll beat you over the head with my walking stick, which I will be getting."

"Then you'll come home?" Eureka didn't miss a beat.

"You won't last another constellation without me."

Something warm and soft slammed into him, knocking the breath from his lungs. Baltan's arms flailed for a moment before the feathery touch of a feline ear brushed against his cheek.

He returned Azzie's hug, and sniffed despite himself when Eureka put their foreheads together again and he felt Lleuwellyn's long hair drape over his face as he rested his chin on top of Baltan's head. It was the exact kind of sappiness he'd been trying to avoid, but he wouldn't trade it for the world.

The walk home was blissfully uneventful.

Baltan listened to the sound of their footsteps on the cobblestone street, trying to match each pair to their owner. The sharp click of heels striking the ground was undoubtedly Lleuwellyn. Eureka was given away by the pebbles and loose bits of rock dislodged by his steps. Azzie's quiet gait all but disappeared between Baltan and Eureka's, but Baltan didn't need sound to locate him. The kid was holding his hand, and gave it an enthusiastic swing out of sheer delight every few steps.

Still, after being in the hospital for so long, the walk winded Baltan. He felt for the wall and headed upstairs for a rest on his own, his heart jolting when his foot fell through the air at the top. He'd have to count the steps on his way down so he wasn't caught off-guard like that again.

The bedsheets were rumpled, and it was obvious that Eureka hadn't been bothering to make the bed in the morning. Baltan reached for the edge of the covers and tugged them up, then let himself fall on top. He sighed out every terrible thought, every moment of anxiety, every fear he'd suffered over the last few weeks.

He was home.

Baltan was drifting off to sleep when Eureka crept up to the bedroom, probably to talk privately about something not for the others' ears. He closed the door behind him, and Baltan noticed the squeak of the hinges. Had it always done that?

Eureka took a moment to speak, and Baltan could clearly picture him fiddling with his nails and looking awkwardly to the side. "Sorry to bother you, but, it's about Selkess."

Baltan rolled his eyes—still bothered at how the fake one didn't respond as quickly—and sat up. "Please tell me he's dead."

"Yes. He's dead, never mind how." Baltan could only assume the less Eureka had to talk about that, the better. "The papers we found were enough to get Azzie cleared of all charges, and the cultists gave enough testimony for their plea bargains to pardon the Kwoltan Gera warriors found at the scene. A few members of the cult got away, but without Selkess to lead them, they'll likely be picked up for minor crimes before too long. But... he left a will."

"Is that so?" Baltan hadn't thought someone as assured of his victory as Selkess would bother with a will.

"Apparently he wrote it up and signed it last year," Eureka said. "Baltan, he left us nearly everything."

The hair on the back of Baltan's neck stood up. "What's 'everything?'"

"For starters, custody of Lleuwellyn and 'any other child legally entrusted to him.' There was a large sum of money, too. Not sure where he got it, probably donations from his cult. But, in his own words, it's 'ours to use as we wish,' as long as we help Lleuwellyn get settled." Eureka swallowed. "And he had... he had references to things that Turnap left him in *his* will. He gave Turnap's house and farm to Illdresil Gera. Everything else was left to some Eastern general."

Baltan shuddered and found himself without a smart remark.

"Listening to it being read was unsettling, to say the least. Lleuwellyn was there, too, but he doesn't want to talk about it any more than he has already. I don't blame him."

"Great." Baltan tried to sound unbothered even though his heart was pounding. "Have you found a way to get rid of the money yet? Because if there's nothing you want, I suggest we find a nice charity or a good tide to throw it into."

Eureka snorted. "Did I bring the right man home? I must have gotten mixed up. There's no way the Baltan I know would turn down this much money."

He chuckled at his own joke until Baltan punched him lightly on the arm.

"But to answer your question, yes, I have," Eureka continued. "I was thinking, now that it's not just the two of us... with Azzie, I mean, and Lleuwellyn not having the easiest time finding a job or an apartment anywhere..." Baltan heard his claws brush the hair at the back of his neck. "I was thinking, maybe we could afford a bigger place? Not too far away, and not too big, but somewhere with enough room for Azzie to grow. And maybe a cat or two."

Baltan's first instinct was to say, "No." They had lived in their tiny two-bedroom since they retired. Even if it wasn't the best place, he had always thought they would stay there forever, measuring out their fortune to suit their needs as the years came and went.

He knew that wasn't possible anymore. There was Azzie to think about, and his hospital bills would have cost them quite a bit already.

It would be foolish not to take the money from the will, even if it was from Selkess.

"I guess he does owe us," Baltan conceded.

"I hope the stars were there to greet him. I wouldn't want his restless spirit wandering around," Eureka muttered. "It's like he knew the whole time. He set it all up. Everything. Me finding Azzie, bringing Lleuwellyn to Marina Delta—all by design. Makes you wonder if he planned on dying in that slaughterhouse, too, and why he bothered with it all in the first place." He sighed. "In his will, he called us the 'noblest and truest friends he could have had in life,' despite everything."

Baltan sniffed. "I think that's the craziest thing to come out of him yet. Was there anything else?"

"From him, no. A few losses in Kwoltan Gera's ranks." Eureka's frown was tangible. "Egrieak-Kouran won't be happy to see us if we ever go back. According to him, the apprentices were rescued by Kwoltan Gera Azures alone, and all the glory is theirs. Naesa's doing okay in the hospital, at least. We paid for her treatment."

"Of course." There was no sarcasm or passive-aggressiveness. Though Selkess had been the one to mangle her, Baltan couldn't help wanting to take responsibility and do everything he could to help her recover. With that on his mind, he asked, "Are Azzie and Lleuwellyn in therapy?"

"Not yet. I want to spend a little more time working on Azzie's communication skills before I enroll him. He's getting better. He can say certain phrases daily, and he's growing from there. And Lleuwellyn is going to take some convincing. He's still punishing himself and doesn't think he deserves help."

Baltan shook his head. So much happened while he was in the hospital. He should have tried to keep up with them more, made more phone calls. It was probably safe to use the phone now.

The mattress bounced as Eureka sat down next to him. "And what about you, Baltan? Do you want to go to therapy? You've been through a lot too, and I know it's going to take longer to heal than you'll let yourself have."

"I'll think about it."

At the very least he might find help in learning how to adjust to being blind. The hospital had offered a few resources, like a cane or enrolling in the seeing-eye animal program. He'd gotten the cane, but he didn't want to have to use it in his own home. And it wouldn't help him read.

"That's all I had to say, except for..." Eureka took a deep breath. "About what I said at the hospital—I meant every word of it, but I don't think I said enough." He paused. Coughed. Paused again.

"Look, it's fine. You don't have to say anything," Baltan said.

"No, I do." Baltan knew Eureka was looking at him. He tried to remember the exact shade of his eyes. "I thought I lost you, and it was the worst moment of my life. Worse than any other time I've been hurt. I don't know what I would have done without you." His voice wavered, and Baltan placed a hand on where he thought Eureka's would be, landing on his forearm instead.

"Hey, I'm still here," Baltan soothed.

Eureka pulled him close. "I know how you feel about me, and I'm sorry I can't give you the kind of relationship you want. You mean so much to me, and I never say it because I don't want hurt you by giving you the wrong idea. But I *care* Baltan, I care about you *so much*. So don't... don't..."

Baltan let Eureka hold him for a while. The bittersweet clenching in his heart that usually accompanied these moments was absent as they shared the silence and the warmth of each other's simple presence.

He placed a hand over Eureka's heart, wanting to feel its beat under his fingers, but he was instead met with scratchy wool.

He pulled back as far as Eureka's arms would allow, his lips twitching into a smirk. "Oh, wow. Here I thought one advantage to being blind would be escaping from these dreadful things, but I can *feel* how ugly this sweater is. It is hideous to every single sense."

Eureka burst into laughter, and Baltan smiled wider than he had in constellations, until he was laughing, too.

"I'm going to buy you the brightest shirts I can find," Eureka threatened.

"No."

"I am."

"*No.*"

Eureka stood, the mattress bouncing. "*The Night Train* should be coming on soon."

"I think we've left the kids on their own long enough," Baltan nodded.

They headed downstairs, and Baltan counted twelve steps.

Even though he couldn't see his way around the stacks of books and bottles anymore, his heart knew the way to the couch, and he settled in his place while Eureka turned on the radio. Azzie curled up in his blanket beside him, letting his ear flick against Baltan's shoulder in greeting, and he tousled the kid's hair with affection. Lleuwellyn took the edge of the couch, not sitting yet, but leaning against the arm.

The strings were just striking up when Eureka took his place, and Baltan felt content to ever-so-slightly lean his head against his shoulder. Eureka didn't move, humming along to the theme music.

"Tonight, the intriguing tale of an eccentric millionaire, his mistress, and an unusual dinner party at a notoriously haunted house. Who will walk away with a fortune—and, indeed, who will walk away at all? Keep your wits about you as you board... *The Night Train!*"

The Story will Continue in:

DARK
LIGHTNING

Book Two in the *Stellar Eclipse* Series

Check www.roselinproductions.com
for more information!

ABOUT THE AUTHOR

Roselin Productions is a team comprised of Avalon Roselin, R. Hamlin, J. Rudolph, and J. Smith. Roselin Productions is committed to producing independent, original fiction.

Other books from Roselin Productions:

ALiCE

Like Falling Stars

See more of our work and our full mission statement at our website:

www.roselinproductions.com

CPSIA information can be obtained
at www.ICGtesting.com
Printed in the USA
FSHW012138230519
58416FS